THE INFERNO SERIES

YOLANDA OLSON

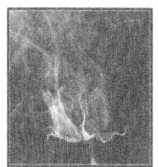

Copyright © 2017 Yolanda Olson
All rights reserved. No part of this publication may be reproduced,
distributed, or transmitted in any form, or by any means, including
photocopying, recording, or other electronic or mechanical methods, without
the prior written permission from the author, except in the case of brief
quotations embodied in critical reviews and certain other noncommercial
uses permitted by copyright law. This book is a work of fiction. Names,
characters, places and incidents are products of the author's imagination or
are used fictitiously. Any resemblance to actual events, locales, or persons
living or dead, is entirely coincidental.

ORIGINAL SERIES BY YOLANDA OLSON

Inferno
Cinere
Sparks
Embers

INFERNO WORLD NOVELLAS

Verboten by Abigail Davies
Malignus by Dani René
Iniquity by Emery LeeAnn
Burned by Jennifer Bene
Obloquy by Murphy Wallace

ABOUT THE AUTHOR

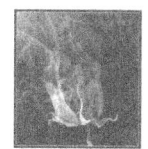

Yolanda Olson is an award-winning and international bestselling author. Born and raised in Bridgeport, CT where she currently resides, she usually spends her time watching her favorite channel, Investigation Discovery. Occasionally, she takes a break to write books and test the limits of her mind. Also an avid horror movie fan, she likes to incorporate dark elements into the majority of her books.

You can keep in touch with her on Facebook, Twitter, and Instagram.

SPARKS

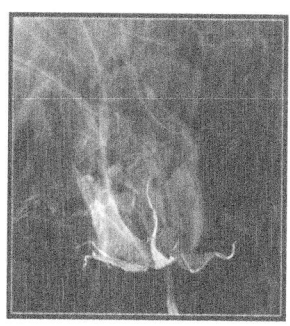

ACKNOWLEDGMENTS

My funny ladies that kept telling me just do it and don't give up on it no matter how hard it is. Lis, Linda, and Dawn —I'm pretty sure you guys are crazier than me sometimes!

Abigail Davies of Pink Elephant Designs. I'm such a huge fan of your covers and I can't thank you enough for continuing this series for me!

Dez of Pretty in Ink Creations for editing this and giving it that Inferno series formatting. Always coming through in the clutch and saving the day. Thank you for stepping in when I need you the most!

To the Twisted Rabbits. I know how much of a distaste you guys have for this family, so I appreciate you sitting through this chaos. We're almost done!

UNTITLED

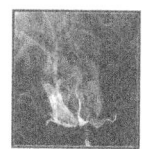

To my readers. You asked me one day, "What's his Mom like?" Get ready to find out. This one is for you guys.

PROLOGUE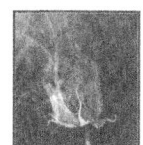

My God, what have I done?

What's become of me that in my need for feeling the touch of another, I've looked to my own son? Why is he so ready to love me in ways that he shouldn't and why am I so eager to allow it?

I'm not a sick woman, but it feels like an illness has taken over me, making me crave him in ways that I never did his father. He's so willing to learn—so keen on making his mother happy, and it's like a drug. A pill that I shouldn't swallow, a tonic that should never cross my lips, and an ambrosia that was only meant for the gods.

And yet it's here.

In my own home, under my roof, waiting for me on nights when I need it the most and can't control my hunger for it any longer. I indulge in the euphoria of his moans and the way his hands feel when they explore my body.

I'm not worthy of this bliss and I'm not immune to the fact that what we're doing is forbidden, but we love each other—even if in ways that a mother and son never should, and that has to mean something. The universe can see what we've become, and it has yet to strike us dead, and until that happens, I'll do my best to savor every drop that I was never meant to taste.

As I sit on the edge of my bed, watching the sunset on another day that should never have been, I wonder if Luke understands this as I do. That we should never have been together, and that we're not meant to live like this.

I wonder if he cares, but I know the boy. I knew him before he came into this world,when he was still growing inside of me. I felt his malcontent for humanity then and I can see it in his eyes when he watches people from the perch of his bedroom window walking down the street.

He cares for no one except for me. Not his father, his siblings, or any strangers that pass by his line of sight. I only hope that one day his love will grow—blossom into something that it should, and that he'll be able to learn to love a stranger and give her his heart as he's done to me.

Until that moment comes, he's mine and even though I know in my heart it's wrong, I'll keep him close by when I need to feel the gentle caress of true love.

CHAPTER 1

A TEAR ROLLS down my cheek as I hold the veil of my old habit in my hands. It seems like a lifetime ago that I was a nun, and even though I have a good life now, there are days when I find myself longing for the simplicity of poverty and chastity again.

The man that changed my life came to me for guidance one night in the wake of a terrible argument with his then-wife. It wasn't my place to be his spiritual leader that night, but Father Moore had already gone to the rectory for the evening and he was so distraught that I didn't have it in my heart to turn him away.

I listened to his confession and I absolved him as much as I could. We became friends after that. He knew that I didn't have the authority to forgive him, but my willingness to try and ease the anguish in his soul was enough to make him a frequent visitor to the church after hours.

The last time he came to me as someone seeking counsel, he brought his wife with him in a last-ditch effort to repair what little hope there was left in the marriage.

I sat in the dimly lit chapel and listened to them for

hours, wondering how it is that I let this charade go on as far as I had. If Father Moore ever found out about what I had been doing—the counseling of the broken, he would have had me excommunicated from the Church.

He never got the chance, though.

The man returned two nights after his wife left him, after I failed them, and I felt the sting of shame when he revealed it to me. He promised me it was for the best and assured me that my friendship was valued.

It wasn't until a month after that visit that I saw him again. He attended services one Sunday morning, then when the congregation was emptying, he asked me to accompany him for brunch. I tried desperately to decline because there was something about the way he made me feel, but he managed to convince me that it was just a meal shared between two friends.

Father Moore gave me permission and strict instructions on how to handle myself for the day in the company of a man not of the cloth, and I did as he told me to.

I tried so much to remember my teachings, the instructions from my parish priest, and even the vows I made, but when he smiled at me and placed his hand on top of mine to cool my nerves, the woman inside of me came to the surface and I lost sight of who I had become.

All it took was as simple touch to render me useless.

Nothing happened that day between us, yet when I got back to the convent, I dropped to my knees and begged for forgiveness because I had lost myself in the moment of feeling his skin against mine. I cried myself to sleep that night and did not attend services the next day.

I didn't think I was worthy enough to show my face in such a place of Holiness, and yet when he came calling again seven days after our first brunch, I slipped out of the convent without letting my sisters or Father Moore know where I was going.

It happened that way every seven days for two months until he finally broke down and confessed to me.

He told me he thought of me in ways that he shouldn't, that he wanted to know what it was like to feel my hands on his body, and how he longed for the gentle heat of my lips against his.

When I told him that it's something that could never be, he looked at me with shattered eyes, but agreed to take me home.

I just didn't know that he meant his home and not the convent.

I grip the cloth tighter in my hand, balling up the material as the memories continue to flood back to me. Another tear falls and as I wipe it away angrily, I let my thoughts continue as they were.

He pulled up in front of a two-story, split-level ranch style home and turned his car off. At first, he kept his hands on the steering wheel before finally running a hand back through his hair and giving me a hopeful glance.

"Just once—no one will ever have to know," he had begged me. "You've made me feel so much more like a man than that bitch ever did and I just want to repay the favor."

"I'll pray with you, but nothing more," I had replied, my voice trembled with the possibilities of what could happen behind the doors of his home.

I sigh and let the habit fall from my hands as I close my eyes. It's so hard to remember all of it, but it's even harder to try and suppress it.

I did get on my knees and he next to me, and we did pray, but that only lasted for so long before I felt his hands on my body.

"I won't force you," he had whispered into my ear, "but I can't not at least touch you."

My body felt like it caught fire when he moved behind me and wrapped his arms around my waist. I felt like I was burning in the heat of his passion when his lips grazed my neck, but when he used his hands to begin lifting the hem of my dress, I felt my desire as a woman becoming much stronger than my vows of chastity.

"Just a little taste," he said, his breath hot against my neck.

I leaned my head back against him as he lifted the hem even higher, exposing my thighs and trembling legs. A small chuckle escaped from somewhere deep inside of him and as he reached up and removed the veil from my head, I knew that I would be lost to the Church forever.

I didn't stop him.

I wanted his touch, the feel of his strong body pressed against mine as our bodies writhed in sweat and pleasure. I wanted to know what it felt like for just once in my life to be in the arms of a man who had such a need for me as a woman and not as someone to help them through a spiritual crisis.

And my God, did I ever find out.

He was so gentle with me. The way he pressed his lips so softly over parts of my body that I had never exposed before. The slow pressure I felt when he pushed into me for the first and last time, wearing the blood of my virtue on his glorious cock like he had been marked by eyes unseen.

He taught me that night how to move on top of him, how to please him the way he needed to be, how to understand that what we were doing was a natural act, and not a sin.

And when we were done, he took me back to the

convent, promising me that it would always be our secret, and no one would ever find out.

He had been right for the most part. No one did find out—at least, not until I started to show. What he didn't know was that one night we spent together in each other's arms, a seed had been planted.

When that seed had grown to a point where it was no longer possible for me to hide it any longer, I confessed to Father Moore and laid my habit at his feet before leaving St. Thomas and never turning back.

Sometimes, I find myself wondering how he's doing these days. If what we shared that one night was enough to help him feel like the man he so desperately wanted to be again and if he wondered about me to.

If he does, I'll never know because until recently, I never did make an effort to find him again. I had pushed him to the back of my mind and was content to keep him buried there until I was asked about him.

"Mom?"

I turn and glance over my shoulder, wiping away any left-over tears, and smile at the young man standing in the doorway of my bedroom, watching me curiously.

"Hey," I say to him, as I get to my feet.

"You okay?" he asks.

"Yeah, just some bad memories came flooding back again is all," I reply brightly, sitting on the edge of my bed. "What's up?"

He looks so much like him.

Tall, dark hair, five o' clock shadow on his youthful face, and eyes that can see so far inside of you, that you wonder what kind of void it is that he's peering into.

"Nothing," he finally says, narrowing his eyes slightly. "I

thought I heard you crying so I wanted to make sure you were alright."

"I'm fine, honey. Thank you for checking up on me."

He nods, a small grin spreading across his face as he runs a hand back through his hair and glances around the room once, before turning and walking back out.

He's so much like his father that it will consume me one day.

CHAPTER 2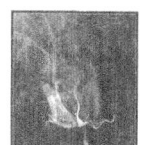

When I finally find the strength to leave my room again, I'm pleasantly surprised to find that Luke has already made dinner. He's sitting in the living room with the television off, quietly eating his barbecue chicken wings and potato wedges.

As soon as he feels me watching him from the doorway, he reaches for his napkin to clean his mouth, before glancing up at me with a smile.

"I thought you might be hungry, so I made us something simple."

"Thank you," I say to him softly. His smile spreads across his face and I can almost swear I saw him proudly puff his chest out. The smallest amount of praise and Luke feels like he's done a world of good. He's an amazing boy and I let him feel like the wonderful young man that he is because he's worthy of the praise.

He deserves so much more than I can give him, but he seems content to stay inside of these walls with me instead of going out to make any friends.

I fix myself a plate, grab a fork and a couple of napkins before I head back to the living room.

"Mind if I join you?" I ask Luke who nods without glancing in my direction. While I know that I don't have to ask his permission to do anything in my own home, I like to treat him as an equal.

"It looks nice outside today," I begin conversationally once I've sat down, "wanna go for a walk later?"

"Nah."

"Honey, you have to learn to take walks every now and then. Go outside, breathe in the fresh air, maybe make some friends?"

He scoffs, "The only friend I need is sitting right across from me. If I want fresh air, I can open a window, and there's no point in walking anywhere when it all leads back to the same place."

"And what place is that?" I ask, stabbing a potato wedge with my fork.

"Home."

I manage a tight smile, not that he's even looking at me, before I pop the potato wedge into my mouth and begin to chew thoughtfully. There has to be a way to get him out of this house—I don't want him to turn into a hermit.

"What if I go with you? I can afford to stretch my legs a little bit," I offer brightly.

Luke slowly raises his eyes from his plate and stares deep into mine. The look he gives me tells me he thinks it's a trick of some kind, but I'm fresh out of tricks to get him outside of these doors.

"I'm serious," I reply with a light laugh. "We can go outside and see what the world looks like. Just once, I promise that if you don't like it, I won't make you do it again."

He tears his eyes away from me and cranes his neck to look out of the living room window before he finally sighs and drops his eyes back to his plate again.

"Okay. But only if you go with me." "Then it's settled! Once we've finished

dinner, I'll go freshen up and we can go for a little night-time stroll."

He nods as he begins to pick at his chicken with his fork and I can't help but

wonder what's going on inside of his head. Luke seems to be really preoccupied these days, but he's fiercely private and doesn't share much with me—no matter how hard I try to get him to tell me things.

We finish our dinner in silence, with a few stolen glances and small smiles at each other. I don't mind the silence for the most part, it was something I had become used to in the convent, but since no longer being a part of the Church, I long for conversation and noise—something my son isn't fond of.

It makes me wonder if that's something he got from his father, because I know in my soul that those traits haven't come from me.

Once we're both done and have sat around for a few moments, Luke picks up his plate as well as mine, and disappears into the kitchen. When I hear the sink turn on, I sigh and walk back toward my room to find something comfortable to wear. If this is the one time I can get him outside of these doors, then I'm going to make him walk for as long and as far as I can.

I settle on a pair of loose, black sweatpants, a crimson colored tank top, and

1. brand-new pair of running sneakers that

I've kept at the bottom of my closet. I saved them specifically for this occasion and I hope my feet don't blister too soon into our walk. I walk over to my vanity and find a hair tie, then loop my long, blonde hair back into a loose ponytail and give myself a glance in the mirror before I turn off the light and walk out.

"Are you ready, honey?" I call out as I walk down the hall.

"Yeah," comes the glum reply. I find my son standing at the other end of the hallway by the front door, arms crossed over his chest, and an unhappy look on his face. "Let's get this over with," he says, pulling the door open and stepping aside to let me through.

It's a lovely, brisk night in Sandpoint and I almost immediately regret wearing a tank top, but I know that if I go inside to change, Luke will say that we went outside and that our trip is over, so I bite my lower lip as I loop an arm through his and begin to lead him away from our home.

"Do you wanna go to the Byway?" I ask him cheerfully. "I'm sure if we hang out there long enough we might be able to see the Northern Lights."

He shrugs but doesn't veto my idea. Unfortunately, because I don't want to push him too hard right now, I drop the subject and continue to walk with him in silence.

After about twenty minutes we've reached the town center and I walk over to one of the welcome center maps to see where we can go next.

"Can I ask you something?"

I jump. His presence, while strong, is often forgettable due to his overwhelming need for silence.

I giggle nervously as I try to hide the fact that I forgot

my own son was with me, and nod at him.

"What's a good age to have kids?" "What?" I ask him in confusion. Luke is

only fifteen years old, so that's not something I would expect him to be wondering so soon in his life.

"Well, how old were you when you had me?" he asks, shifting on his feet.

"I was about twenty," I reply, raising an eyebrow. "Why?"

He shoves his hands into his jean pockets and glances away from me. "And how old was he?"

I wrinkle my nose in confusion. I don't understand what kind of information he's looking for and he's damn good when it comes to beating around the bush—too good for my liking sometimes.

"He, who?" I ask, raising an eyebrow curiously.

"My dad."

"Oh. Um, thirty-five, I think."

He nods and takes a deep breath before he walks over to me and stares at the map.

"Where to now, Magellan?" he asks, a small smile on his face.

"Wherever we want to go. See anything that looks good?" I reply, resting my head on his shoulder. Luke is a tall boy, much like his father, and he dwarfed me when he turned about twelve. Puberty shot him up the rest of the way and it astounds me that he's not done growing just yet.

He puts an arm around me as he leans closer to the map and runs a finger down the list of places closest to where we're standing.

"Nah. This all looks kind of boring. We can go to the beach, though. The sun is almost gone so there shouldn't be too many people there."

"Sounds good to me," I reply softly, as I pull away from him and we loop our arms together again. Luke seems to be slightly less apprehensive about being outside, and I'll let him lead me anywhere he wants to go right now if it'll make him happy.

I just want my boy to know that he's loved—I want him to feel it as much as he feels the obvious desolation of only having one parent and not knowing much about the other. This isn't the first time he's asked me about his father, and while his question took me off guard, I have a feeling it holds some kind of personal relevance to him.

Maybe one day, he'll tell me what it is.

CHAPTER 3

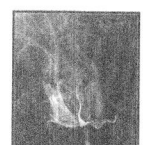

On the boardwalk near the beach there are some small bars, a few outdoor diners, and multiple paths that lead to the sand. Luke seems a bit overwhelmed because he expected a ghost town of sorts, and to be honest, so did I.

We settle on one of the smaller diners with outdoor seating because it seems to be the least populated of all of the buildings surrounding us. Since I'm not very hungry, I order a small bowl of ice cream and he orders a club sandwich. Our server moves quickly and seems to be completely frazzled by the amount of people out tonight, which makes me smile.

She can't be much older than Luke— maybe two or three years, and she seems to have a good head on her shoulders. I find myself wondering if my son would be interested in getting a job at a place like this, but the way he's picking at his sandwich tells me otherwise.

I also wonder if he notices our young server stealing glances in his direction. She's mostly frazzled because of the crowd, but I can tell that part of her nervousness comes from his presence. I know it because it's how I would act when his father would come to visit with me.

"She is pretty, isn't she?" I ask him once she's out of earshot again.

"Huh?" he turns his eyes up toward me as he finally takes a bite out of his sandwich.

"The girl serving us, silly," I reply with a laugh before I lick my spoon and dip it back into the bowl.

Luke shrugs as he leans back in his chair, "I don't know. I haven't seen her yet." I shake my head at him and lift another spoonful of ice cream into my mouth. The world could come tumbling down on his head and he would still be trapped somewhere in his own thoughts without even noticing the destruction around him.

"I have seen that guy over there that keeps staring at you, though," he adds quietly.

Now it's my turn to roll my eyes internally. When I was a young girl and first told my mother that I wanted to join the convent, she told me that I was too pretty to waste my life on my knees praising anyone except a man that would return the favor. She wasn't being cruel, she just wanted me to make sure I knew that I was equal to anyone that walked the face of the Earth and she wanted me to know my worth. She wanted grandchildren and since my brother had cancer when he was a teenager, the radiation treatments left him sterile. It was up to me to fulfill her dream and I wonder if she would be proud of me now—even if the way I went about becoming a mother was completely unconventional.

"Take a look," he says, nodding almost imperceptibly in the direction of my admirer.

I sigh and lean back. I reach up and pull my ponytail tighter, glancing over to where Luke motioned toward and almost fall back out of my chair.

"We have to go," I say to him once I regain my bearings.

Luke nods as he folds his arms across the tabletop. "Yeah, I thought he looked familiar." I get to my feet quickly, almost knocking the chair down, and reach down for my son's wrist.

"We need to leave. *Now*."

"I'm not done with my sandwich yet," he says, pulling out of my grip. "And I may want to take a look at the waitress now that you've mentioned how pretty she is."

I want to walk away and leave him, but I don't know if he would be able to find his way home. I don't want to abandon him here because I see an old ghost, but I don't want to face my past right now either.

"We'll come back tomorrow night. Let's go," I say, putting my hands on my hips.

Luke looks up at me and a strange smile plays across his lips. "You look so adorable when you're angry. I try not to laugh, but sometimes I wonder if you'd be capable of making me do what you want me to do."

"Please," I hiss at him. "We'll take the fucking sandwich with us, but I want to pay this bill and go before …"

"Before?" he asks, glancing over in the direction of my ghost again. "Oh, here he comes."

I'm horrified—wishing the Earth would open up and swallow me whole, but I know that's not how things work. A wish is nothing more than a hopeful sentiment that rarely ever travels where it should.

"Hello, Taylee," my ghost says in a frosty tone.

I jump, not realizing how close he had gotten already, before I turn to face him, a huge smile forced onto my face.

"Father Moore! It's been years since I've seen you," I exclaim. I clear my throat to remove the sudden falsetto tone it's taken on and sit back down in my chair. "Would you like to join us?"

He glances down his nose at Luke who's now sitting back in his chair, arms crossed over his chest, eyeing him dangerously.

Father Moore holds Luke's glare with an even stare of his own before he slowly shakes his head.

"No thank you. I just thought I would come over and say hello since it's been so long," he explains with a tight smile.

I begin to wring my hands nervously as Father Moore looks me up and down with an un-approval I haven't seen since I first told him about Luke's father.

The loud scrape of a chair brings me back to the moment and when my son drops an arm around my shoulder and pulls me protectively close to him, I let out a small breath of relief.

"Mom, is this the priest? The one from your old church?" he asks in a mischievous tone.

"It is. Luke, this is Father Moore. Father Moore, this is my son, Luke."

Father Moore extends a hand toward my son who shakes his head and waves him off.

"There's no need to pretend we like each other, mister," Luke says evenly. "Actually, I'd be much obliged if you got the hell away from my mother and maybe shove that nose up your God's ass where it belongs."

"*Luke*," I hiss at him, giving his leg a swat. He smirks at me, tightens his grip, and turns his attention back to the shell-shocked priest. I'm sure he's heard quite a few things in his day, but I don't think anyone has ever been quite as harsh during their first talk with him.

"I should have known that anything that fell out of your womb would be as rotten as the man that put it in there," Father Moore says, before he turns on his heel and stalks away from us.

"Come on, I'm bored with this place," Luke says, walking back to his plate and taking one last bite of his sandwich before he heads to the register.

"How did you recognize him? The priest, I mean?" I ask Luke on our walk back home.

"From the pictures in that box at the bottom of your closet," he replies, scratching his chin.

"Wait a minute," I say, pulling him to a halt. "What are you doing snooping around in my room?"

I'm angry that he's admitted to being a snoop, but not angry enough to punish him over it. He's just a curious child and always has been, though I will have to set some rules for him now apparently.

Luke shrugs and looks down at me. "Sometimes when you're gone, I miss you and I go into your room because it smells so much like you. I'll take a nap in your bed or I'll just look around and see if maybe I can figure out what you were like before you had me. I know it sounds weird, and I'm sorry for poking around in your shit, Mom, but it just makes me feel better until you finally come home."

I'm taken aback by his explanation. I've never known him to have a warm bone in his body for the fifteen years he's walked on this damn planet, but he always manages to say the sweetest things when it comes to me. It's almost as if he knows that I need the kind words to keep me going day in and day out.

"Don't go in my room anymore without my permission, okay?" I say to him, looping my arm back through his.

"Sure thing," he replies, pulling his arm out from my grip and wrapping it around my shoulder. "You know, I'm not scared of much in this world, but I think the only thing that would do me in is not having you around. I know I don't say it a lot, but I love you, Mom."

"Oh honey," I sigh. "I love you too. You've always been the perfect son, in your own way, and I know that we'll be okay. No matter what happens between us—we'll be okay."

The rest of the walk home is silent, and it doesn't seem to bother him anymore than it does me. Luke will make some woman really happy someday and I can only hope that she'll treat him the way he deserves.

CHAPTER 4

I DIDN'T REALIZE I had left the bedroom window open and my room is chillier than the weather outside. I wrap my arms around myself and with a shiver, walk over to that side of the room and lower it until only a small sliver of the breeze can come in.

A heavy sigh escapes me as I turn around and look at my closet. I wonder what Luke was really looking for in there, but it wouldn't surprise me if it had been some kind of neatly stowed away memory of his father.

It makes me sad to think I don't have anything I can give to him that would be a token of the man because he seems to becoming more and more interested in as the days go on —even if he doesn't ask me about him, things like poking around in my room tell me as much.

I decide to not think about it right now, although I make a mental note to try and see if maybe I can find him online tomorrow somehow.

A son should get to know his father and I only hope they both feel the same way.

Tomorrow, I'll make this right. I don't care what I have to do, but Luke will know who his dad is and maybe I can convince them to meet up.

I pull my tank top over my head and toss it onto the floor, the sweatpants following shortly thereafter. I have the same feeling washing over me that always does when I think of his father and I don't have the will to fight the urge tonight.

I walk over to where I left my veil earlier and for the first time in a few months, I place it on my head, pushing my hair beneath the thin fabric. I walk over to the mirror and look at myself.

A woman still lost in the hopes of a young girl's dreams that were shattered when I broke my sacred vows. But the one thing that will make me feel better is already at the forefront of my thoughts.

I turn to the side and look at my body. Slender, short, and taught—the same way I've always been. Mom once told me that if I had long legs, I could have easily been a model, yet as I turn my body back toward the mirror and stare into my cold, blue eyes, I keep telling myself that I've done the right thing with my life.

I did what I wanted to do—I joined a convent, I did my best, and some pre-designed plan decided that I was destined to become a mother instead. I have a beautiful, caring son who loves me and would never abandon me like his father did, and I couldn't ask for anything else.

I let my eyes wander down my reflection as I reach back and unclasp my bra and shrug out of it. Even at my age now, my breasts are still perky and full which makes me smile. It's one less thing about getting old that I won't have to worry about right now.

My eyes are giving me an accusing stare as I wallow in the pride of my body and I have to look away. Pride is one of the sins that Father Moore always preached vehemently against, and in the quiet moments when I'm pretending to still be a chaste nun, I always manage to fall headlong into that damnable emotion.

It doesn't matter.

This is about me right now. It's about how I feel and what I want to do to remember the man that gave me the precious gift that's more than likely perched in his bedroom window watching the moon slowly drift across the night sky.

I force myself to face my own accusing stare as I reach a hand down and open the top drawer of my vanity. Inside, hidden away in a black felt pouch is one of the only things that really holds meaning to me from my days in the church. I look down as I pull the pouch out and give the drawstring a tug, revealing a set of beads inside.

I pull out the necklace and drop the pouch back into the drawer, slowly pushing it closed as I turn and walk back toward my bed. This was the rosary that Father Moore gave me when I made my vows and just holding it makes things seem as simple as they used to be. I miss those days for the most part, but I wouldn't trade my son for them if that were the only choice I would be given, and I know it is.

I lay down on my bed and set the rosary on the pillow next to me. For what I've done, I already know that my soul is condemned for all eternity, but for what I am about to do, I welcome the Hellfire.

Closing my eyes, I think back to that moment so many years ago when I was in his arms. I think of how his hands gently caressed my skin and how he hungrily reached for my panties, pushing them aside and how he began to rub me.

I suck in a shaky breath as my hands do the same. I allow myself to be swallowed by the memory from time to time, and I play out what happened between us because it's one of the few things that makes me feel alive anymore.

My body is shaking as I begin to gently circle the tip of my finger around my bud over my underwear and arch my back slightly off the bed. I remember the way his fingers moved, and I move mine the same way, bringing a pool of desire against my cotton panties.

Even though his fingers touched my skin, even though they moved with purpose and skill, I've never been able to find the will to touch myself the way he did, so I always leave my panties on.

The feeling, however, is tantamount to what I felt when he circled his finger faster and faster, kissing my bare neck and whispering what he wanted to do to me. How he wanted to taste me completely and lick away the juices before shoving his dick into me.

My breath is coming in heaving gasps now as I continue to rub myself. I want nothing more than to experience the hands of a man on my body again, but until that moment happens, my own will have to do.

I squeeze one of my breasts tightly in my hands as the heat of my finger starts to bring forth the euphoric release I've been searching for.

My mound is engorged, and the heat of my core is becoming almost too much to bear. Just when I think I can't take anymore, my body becomes rigid and I can feel the orgasm take control over me. I bite my lip as hard as I can as to not cry out or make any noise. And when it's over, when it's finally done, and I open my eyes again to look at my rosary and beg for a silent forgiveness, I see the figure hiding behind the cracked doorway.

Luke apparently watched the entire thing.

CHAPTER 5

AFTER I'VE CLEANED myself up, I turn the light off in the bathroom and linger in the doorway for a moment. I'm not entirely sure if this is something he's willing to talk about, but I know it has to be done. I'm not too worried about what his reaction will be honestly, I'm more embarrassed than anything else.

I take a deep breath and decide to just talk to him. I don't know what to say, but I'm sure the words will come when I need them too.

Walking down the hallway, I stop when I reach his door and gently knock.

"Honey?" I call out. "Can I come in?"

I hear some rustling inside, he tells me to give him a minute, before he finally opens the door and peers down at me curiously.

"What's up?"

"Can I talk to you for a sec?" I ask, wringing my hands. Luke sighs and crosses his arms over his chest. He's eyeing me critically because he knows what I want to talk about, but finally he grunts, nods, and steps aside.

I walk into the dimly lit room and sit on the corner of his bed while he lingers by the door. He's looking for an easy way out in case this becomes too uncomfortable of a conversation for him to have, and I don't blame him. I think I would have died if I had caught my mother fingering herself.

"Are you okay?" I ask him softly.

"Peachy. Is that it?" he responds.

"You know it's not," I reply with a little force behind my tone. "I want to make sure that you're okay with what you saw. I mean, not okay with it, but that you're okay. Up here," I say, tapping the side of my head.

"Mom, it's not like I haven't watched porn before. I jerk off every now and then too, I just don't dress up and make a show out of it," he replies with a heavy sigh.

Interestingly enough, I think this talk is making me much more uncomfortable than it is him.

"Well, okay," I say getting to my feet. "I just wanted to see how you were doing and I'm sorry you had to see that."

He shrugs and tilts his head to the side. "It didn't bother me. Is that weird?"

I raise an eyebrow as I stop in front of him. "A little bit, yeah."

"Guess I'm just different then."

"I'll see you in the morning. Good night, sweetheart," I say leaning over to kiss him on the cheek, but he pulls his face away from me and turns his gaze toward the carpet.

"Have a good one, Taylee."

I slept like shit last night. I think what bothered me the most was that Luke called me by my name when I left his room instead of by my title and that's something I'll have to correct when he joins me this morning in the kitchen.

He usually likes to sleep in late and because it's a weekend and not a weekday, I'll allow it. Come tomorrow morning though, we'll get back to our school work and he'll remember that I'm the adult in this house— no matter how he thinks he can speak to me.

I turn on the coffee machine and drop a single-serve cup into the appropriate compartment and wait for the magic to happen. I won't be very nice to him until I've had some caffeine in my system and I don't like to be unkind to Luke when it's something that's beyond his control.

The wait for the coffee is my doing—the calling me by my name is *his* fuck up, soon to be addressed.

Seconds turn into minutes and minutes turn into hours before he finally walks into the kitchen. His hair is a mess, his eyes are still showing signs of sleep, but he smiles when he sees me, and I nod in return.

"Good morning," he says, as he walks over to me and kisses my cheek.

"Morning," I reply curtly. I turn my back to him so I can reach into the cupboard for his favorite mug. It's simple— dark green—his favorite color and has a small cobblestone, well design in the middle of either side.

"Thanks," he says with a wide yawn once I've set his mug in front of him. I take the seat across from him and clasp my hands together on the island top and wait for him to take a few sips.

"Luke?"

"Yeah?" he asks, sucking his teeth. "You can't call me

Taylee. My name—to you, is Mom. Do you understand me?" I ask him quietly.

His eyes linger on the caramel colored brew in the mug and he chuckles.

"Sure thing."

"I'm serious. You're the son and I'm the mother and no matter what you saw, you have to remember that," I insist firmly.

"Got it," he says, blowing out his breath and looking at me with amusement dancing in his still tired eyes. "Anything else? *Mom?*"

I sit back in my chair and stare at him. He seems to hear what I'm saying, but I don't think he's taking it too seriously.

"You're not too old to spank. I don't care how much bigger you are than me, I'll bend you over my knee if I have to get some respect out of you," I warn him.

A small smile curves the edges of his lips, but when my eyes turn stern, it fades away as quickly as it began to appear.

I get to my feet and am ready to go clean up the counter and turn the coffee pot off when Luke speaks up.

"I just have one question for you," he says conversationally.

"What?" I ask much louder than I mean to. I clear my throat and give him a sheepish glance to which the smile begins to appear again.

"Are you gonna dress up before you spank me?"

CHAPTER 6

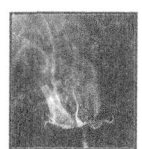

I SENT Luke to his room for the remainder of the day, but that still didn't feel like enough distance between us, so I decided to go out for a walk.

Maybe this will keep me from wanting to throttle him, I think as I make my way back down toward the beach.

I'm not looking to do anything in particular, I just want to get my mind off of how defiant he's suddenly become. Good children aren't defiant; they listen to their mother and they do as their told, yet he feels that because he caught me in a moment of weakness—of self-pleasure, that he no longer has to see me as his mother.

Bullshit; I'll beat him before he treats me any differently than he did when I was still some kind of sanctimonious idol in his eyes.

I decide to go back to the diner we had went to the previous night. If I can find our waitress, maybe I can talk her into going out on a date with him. Hopefully that'll shake some sense into him, but knowing Luke, this is a dead horse before it's even been beat.

I walk up the small wooden walkway and wait patiently

by the front booth for someone to notice me. The hostess is the same one from last night and she smiles brightly when she sees me.

"Just one?" she asks cheerfully.

"One is more than enough right now," I reply with a chuckle. She gives me a nod and tells me to follow her, sitting me at a table in the middle of the restaurant. Once she's sat the menu down in front of me, she walks away after telling me that my server will be with me soon.

I decide on a Coke and maybe a small salad since I'm not too hungry right now. I sigh heavily as I lean back in my chair and glance around the place. There are only two other families in here and just me.

It makes me feel like shit to see happy parents and their children. I always wonder how much differently he could have turned out had his father maybe showed up once in a while to take him out to do some male bonding. Instead he's stuck with me—a whore that can't keep her hands off of herself and apparently forgets to lock her fucking door when she gets the urge.

I wish I had someone in my life that could take care of my impulses as they come, but most of all, I wish I had someone in my life that could be a father figure for Luke. He deserves it—no matter how angry he made me last night, he's a good boy and I know even though he didn't want to show it, what he saw bothered him.

The server isn't the same one as the night before. She's not as pretty as her either, but I think I'll still see if she wants to meet my boy when I'm done and maybe take his mind off of things.

I smile up at her as she places my drink and salad down, shaking my head when she asks me if I need anything else at the moment. I pull the straw out of the paper wrapping and stick in into the carbonated drink before picking up my fork and stabbing a few leaves of lettuce, some tomato slices, and cheese strips.

"I can't believe it."

I almost choke on my food.

I didn't know that anyone had approached me and the sudden sound of someone standing so close startles me. With a laugh, I reach for my napkin to wipe my face before I glance up at the person that scared me almost shitless then feel my mouth run dry.

"Oh my God. It *is* you," he says, taking in a breath.

My lower lip begins to tremble slightly, and I have to turn my eyes away from him.

"How have you been?" he asks in disbelief as he pulls out the chair next to me and sits down.

It's almost as if I'm looking into a mirror of my son. True the years are much higher in this reflection, but they look enough alike to assure anyone who his father is.

"Hi," I reply quietly, dropping the napkin next to my plate. A wave of nausea takes over me, followed by guilt. Had I not grounded my son he would be here with me and he would finally know the man that gave him half of his life.

Selfish cow.

The edges of his eyes crinkle kindly when he finally smiles at me. "I think we're past 'hellos', don't you?"

I clear my throat and glance around the establishment again. Is he here with his family too? Or is he just another absentee parent like me trying to get away from an impending sense of doom?

"Are you alone?" I ask him, my voice cracking slightly.

"Yeah. The wife and kids are at home," he says, running his hand back through his hair.

Just like Luke.

"Congrats," I reply bitterly, rolling my eyes and picking up my fork again.

"I ... I never stopped thinking about you, you know?" he says softly.

I glance at him and raise an eyebrow. "You should probably have spent your time thinking about the son you left behind instead. Excuse me. I just lost my appetite." I get to my feet and push my chair in, but before I have a chance to walk away, he grabs me by the wrist and pulls me back toward the table.

"Sit down, Taylee. Let's talk. I want to know about him. I've always felt so fucking bad for never going to visit him. Tell me about him? Please?"

The sheer look of hopelessness in his eyes hits me in my core and I feel myself faltering. I should just walk away, maybe run back home and get Luke. He might still be here by the time we get back, but what if he's not?

With a heavy sigh, I pull my chair out and sit back down.

"He looks exactly like you. He's tall too, very quiet and reserved. Doesn't have much to say—even when you try to have a conversation with him. It's usually short sentences or one-word answers."

Trenton chuckles, his eyes showing signs of tears threatening to spill as he lets go of my arm. "He definitely didn't get that from me."

"Right."

I cross my arms over my chest and give him my most defiant stare realizing in this moment that maybe Luke is more like me than I've noticed.

Trenton reaches for a napkin and begins to nervously rip pieces from the corners of it. "Um ... is he ... um ... here?"

"No."

"Fuck," he says tossing the torn napkin with a sigh. "I would have loved to meet him, you know?"

"I'd rather not upset him," I reply, jutting my chin out.

Trenton sighs again and looks away for a moment. "Maybe we can have dinner tonight? The three of us?"

"Maybe. Listen, I have to go," I say getting to my feet again. This time I'm walking out of here no matter what he has to say.

"Okay. Um, I'll come back here later then. Say around eight?" he asks, looking into my eyes with so much hope that I could almost swear he's about to burst from it.

"I'll talk to him and see what he wants to do," I promise softly.

Trenton nods as he gets to his feet, the smile still on his face, and uses a knuckle to wipe away a stray tear.

"If I don't see you guys later, I ... Goddamn, Taylee. It was good to see you again," he says as he shakes his head thoughtfully.

I clasp my hands in front of me and look down at my feet. If what he says is true, if he really thought about me all of these years, then why the hell did he get married again?

Why didn't he look us up?

But the young girl in me that fell for the tall, dark, mysterious, semi-stranger is starting to come to the surface again. I lean over and give him a quick peck on the cheek before I turn around and run out of the restaurant.

And I don't stop running until I get home again.

CHAPTER 7

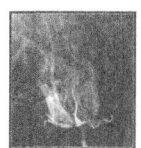

"It's about time you got home."

I raise an eyebrow at Luke who's laying on the living room couch. I'm trying to catch my breath from my sprint and doing my best not to blurt out what just happened, but I'm honestly more disappointed in him for not being in his room where I sent him earlier.

"What are you doing out here?" I snap at him.

Luke chuckles as he swings his long legs off the couch, sits up, and runs a hand back through his hair.

Just like Trenton.

"I got bored in my room and I came out to see if you wanted to watch some T.V. and you were gone. *That's* what I'm doing out here."

I sigh and rub my face tiredly. I don't want to argue with him now. Hell, I don't even want to tell him who I just ran into, but it wouldn't be fair to leave the choice out of his hands.

"You look wrecked, Mom," he comments with a curious tone. "Want the couch? I can move over to the love seat."

As he gets to his feet, I shake my head and walk over to

take the empty spot next to him. Luke keeps his curious gaze on me because he can tell there's something I need to say to him and once I've told him what I have to say, he'll either laugh and walk away like he does with normal things, or he'll go to his room and slam the door.

It's always one of the two with him. Luke hates serious conversations almost as much as I hate to have them with him, however this is important.

For both of us

"I went back to the diner," I begin slowly. "Mom, I'm not interested in that waitress, so I really hope you didn't try something stupid," he says, vehemently

shaking his head.

"I ran into your dad," I blurt out softly. Luke blinks rapidly a few times before he

slowly turns his gaze away from me, and moves further down the couch, trying to put a little more distance between us.

"Honey, he wants to meet you tonight," I say, moving closer to him.

Luke gets to his feet and scoffs. He walks over to the living room window and pushes the blinds aside, gazing out into the mid-day sun. I can't tell what he's thinking, but I can feel his anger. It radiates from him like a nuclear shock and in a weird way, I can feel myself becoming angry for him too.

"We don't have to go. I didn't agree to it. I told him that I would talk to you and he said he would wait for us to show up. He can rot there for all I care," I say, getting to my feet and walking over to him. I put my hands on his shoulders and rest my cheek against his bare back and sigh. I won't force my child to do anything he doesn't want to do because that's not the kind of parent I am.

"I wanna go," he finally says.

"Are you sure, Luke? I'm just fine with us having a night in," I assure him.

He pulls away from me, then turns to face me. "It's okay, Mom. I want to meet him at least once."

There's something in his eyes that's telling me I should more than likely send him back to his room, but I can't deny him this opportunity.

"Alright," I reply. "He said he would be there at eight, so we can get there before or after—whatever you're most comfortable with."

"Guess I should go chill in my room for a while before it's time to go then," he says with a distant look in his eye. "Thanks for not hiding this from me. I know you could have, and I wouldn't have hated you for it, but now I won't have to wonder anymore."

Around seven-thirty Luke comes out of his room. His hair is neatly combed, he's wearing a brand-new black t-shirt, and a pair of slacks. He's got on his best shoes and he even smells slightly of aftershave even though his face shows no signs of having recently being shaved.

He's trying to impress his father, I think, but in a way so am I. I'm wearing a blue and yellow sundress, beige colored wedge sandals, and have my hair pulled back in a loose French twist.

"Well damn, Mom," he says with a sly grin and a nod. "You look really pretty."

"Thanks, baby. You look exceptionally handsome tonight," I reply, reaching for his now extended arm. I'm just under his chin now with the extra added height and I can tell he's amused by it.

He reaches into his pocket for a moment then nods. I heard the jingle of his house keys, so I knew he was making sure that we'd have our way back in.

Here goes nothing, I think nervously as we step outside.

We walk in silence all the way to the town center, and Luke's grip tightens on my arm once the diner begins to come into view. He's trembling slightly, and I can't tell if he's nervous for himself or for me. Nothing seems to ever bother him, but just the prospect of knowing that his father might be waiting for us seems to have stirred something in him.

"I'll go first," he offers quietly as he gently pushes me behind him on our way up the walkway. After all of these years, he's still trying to protect me from possibly getting hurt again.

Once we're inside, Luke puts a hand on the booth and waits for the hostess to finish her phone call.

"Two tonight?" she asks, barely glancing at us.

"No. We're here to meet ... um," his voice trails off as he cuts his eyes toward me and I step in without missing a beat.

"Trenton Miller."

She nods as she looks over the small dry erase board sitting on the pedestal and then checks off a box with a red pen.

"Your party is already here. Follow me." We wait patiently while she reaches down for two menus then leads us toward one of the booths in the back of the diner. I can see him nervously sitting in his chair, hands gripping his drink tightly, and glancing at the time on his watch.

Luke stops short of the table and turns around to face me, blocking Trenton's view as he grips my arms tightly.

"Are you sure you want to do this, Mom? I couldn't care less, but I have a feeling this is helping you more than it would me," he says, searching my eyes.

"Oh honey. I'm doing this for *you,* not me. Trenton doesn't mean anything to me anymore. I just wanted to give you this chance so you wouldn't always wonder, you know?" I reply as I reach up and gently lay a hand on the side of his face.

Luke lets out a deep breath and nods. He reaches down and grabs my free hand before turning around and leading me the rest of the way to the booth.

Trenton is on his feet now and the hostess is standing by him, waiting for us to take our seats. The closer we get, the more his eyes widen, never taking them off of his son. When we finally get to him, he extends a hand to Luke who stares at it for a moment before he scoots me into the booth, then sits down.

"Mr. Miller," he greets him with a nod. Trenton bites his lower lip nervously before he looks over at me and gives me a forced smile.

"You look nice tonight, Taylee," he compliments in a kind tone.

"Thanks," I reply, shooting a nervous glance at Luke. He feels my eyes on him and leans back in his seat, giving me a quick eye roll before turning his attention to the menu.

"What did you have earlier when you were here?" he asks me conversationally.

"Salad," Trenton and I say together. Luke glances up at him and chuckles,

shaking his head. "Thanks for answering, *Mom.*"

I lean under the table and give his thigh a firm pinch. It's my "cut the shit" move when I'm in a position where I'm unable to verbally chastise him.

"Um, what are you thinking of having, um ..." Now it's Trenton's turn to fail at the name of his own blood, but my son doesn't seem bothered by it.

"Don't know yet, Mr. Miller," he replies pointedly. "Still looking."

"You don't have to call me that. You can call me Trenton, if you want."

Luke rolls his eyes at his menu before he replies.

"Sure thing."

CHAPTER 8

Dinner is quiet for the most part. Luke seems to have already become completely oblivious to the fact that his father is at the table with us and I've been spending my few spoken words attempting to spark a conversation between them.

By the time picking a dessert comes rolling around, I'm completely over how they're being with each other, so I do the only thing I can think of.

"Sweetheart, when she comes back, can you order me a slice of Key Lime pie? I'll be right back," I say to Luke.

"Where are you going?" he asks, grabbing my wrist and looking at me with earnest eyes.

"I'm just going to the bathroom," I reply with a light laugh as I wrench my arm out of his grip.

He grunts as I begin to walk away. I catch Trenton's eyes before I leave, and mouth *talk to him* before I disappear from sight.

I walk through a small maze of chairs and tables until I finally see a sign for the restrooms and when I walk in, I let out a heavy sigh. I don't really have to use the bathroom, but it's the only thing I could think of that would force the two of them to communicate.

Heading over to the sink, I place a hand on either side of the cool ceramic and look at myself in the mirror. For some reason, my eyes are red and half open, but I don't pay my reflection any mind.

It's always been something of a liar when it comes to the real me. I know what Taylee Greene really looks like and it's not the woman in the mirror.

I decide not to look at her anymore because she's starting to taunt me with her wicked smile and darkening eyes. There's something brewing in her mind and I'm afraid of what she'll make me do if I hold her stare any longer.

Turning on the faucet, I splash some cool water onto my face to try and get rid some of the red in my eyes. I reach blindly for the paper towel dispenser and rip off a piece to dry my face with, balling it up and tossing it into the garbage receptacle as I walk out of the restroom.

I've been gone long enough to give them sometime to at least introduce themselves to each other, I think, and I'm hoping that my little ruse worked.

When I approach the booth again, and see them huddled in deep conversation, a small victorious smile spreads across my face.

Looks like it worked.

The moment Luke sees me, he coughs loudly, then leans back in his seat. I sit back down next to him and he smiles at me, slipping a protective arm around my shoulders and I lean my head against him.

"Sorry that took so long," I say to him.

He shrugs and gives me a squeeze.

The waitress returns with our desserts and I pick up my fork to dig into my pie when I notice that Trenton is watching me with serious eyes now. He looks like he's debating on saying something and I raise an eyebrow.

"Are you okay?" I ask him, the fork hovering in front of my mouth.

He steals a glance at Luke who gives my back a quick rub, then nods.

"Yeah. I'm fine," he finally says, clearing his throat and glancing down at his small bowl of ice cream.

"Vanilla?" I ask with a grin.

"Old habits die hard," he replies quietly, digging his spoon in. Luke seems to have taken after his father in the ice cream department, but I can see some chunks of chocolate something or other in his scoops.

"Want some?" he asks, when he notices me inspecting his bowl.

"No thank you, sweetheart," I reply before I finally put a piece of pie into my mouth. I sigh happily and lean back. "This is *so* good. Here; try it," I say cutting off another small piece and holding it out to my son.

He smiles, leans forward, and takes the piece I offered him, then nods in appreciation. "Yeah, maybe we should order another slice to take home."

"Sounds good to me!" I reply happily. I cut another piece of my pie when I suddenly realize that Trenton is staring at me again.

"What's wrong?" I ask, raising an eyebrow at him again.

He clears his throat and pushes his ice cream around with his spoon, stealing another glance at Luke, before looking up at me with that damn serious expression he had when I sat down.

"How are you doing these days, Taylee? *Really* doing?" he asks quietly.

"Fine," I reply evenly. "Why? Have you been told something different?" I ask, turning in my seat to stare at my son who's pushing his ice cream around in his bowl.

Just like his dad.

"What do you do for a living?" Trenton asks, leaning forward. "Like, how do you afford your bills and the place you guys live in?"

"I don't have a job. I get assistance," I reply, my eyes still on my son who's doing his damnedest not to meet my stern gaze. "And because I'm able to stay home, I keep Luke home too. I teach him from a curriculum certified by the school board. Did he tell you *that*?"

"He mentioned it," Trenton replies evenly with a nod. "What else do the two of you do?"

"That's none of your goddamn business," I hiss at him, slamming my hand on the table.

The people at the booths and tables around us turn to look at the three of us and Luke chuckles.

"Leave her alone, Trenton," he says quietly.

"What lies have you been telling him?" I shout at him angrily, giving him a shove.

"I haven't told him anything!" Luke says, holding up his hands to defend himself.

"Taylee, keep your hands off that boy or so help me God, you'll never see him again," Trenton warns, leaning across the table and pulling me away from Luke.

"Is everything okay here?"

I sit back down and glance up to see our server along with some middle-aged man who's wearing a "manager" tag pinned to his shirt, watching us carefully.

"My fault. Totally. We're okay," Luke offers with a smile.

"Alright then," she says with a curious nod, before they turn and walk away. I can see where they've positioned themselves at the end of the bar so they can keep watch over us to make sure that I don't raise a hand to my son again and it's making me angry.

"Well this was a great fucking idea," I say sarcastically, shoving my plate away.

"You're pouting," Luke quietly points out.

"I think you've apparently said enough tonight, don't you?" I shoot back at him, in a low tone.

Trenton clears his throat loudly again before he takes out his wallet and drops a hundred-dollar bill on the table.

"I'll see you guys around. I should probably go before my wife starts wondering where I am, anyway. Remember what I told you, son," he says, glancing at Luke who nods nervously.

And just like that, Trenton Miller walks out of my life again when I need him the most.

CHAPTER 9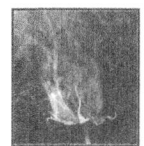

By the time we get back home, the silence between us is so deafening that I can tell Luke is absolutely uncomfortable with my demeanor. He's brought this upon himself though by saying things to his father that he had no business telling. And even though I'm not entirely sure what the extent of their conversation was, I have every intent of finding out before he has a chance to go lock himself away in his room.

As soon as we step into the house, I slam the door behind me, then shove Luke against it.

"What did you tell him?" I shout at him angrily.

"Nothing, Mom! I swear! I didn't tell him anything!" he replies, holding his hands up to protect himself.

"Liar!" I scream, swatting his left arm. "After all I've done for you, this is how you treat me? Would you rather live with *him* and his family? Because you're more than welcomed to get the fuck out of my house if you can't appreciate me the way I deserve to be!"

Tears begin to roll down his cheeks and instead of

seeing the confident young man I'm used to, I'm presented with a scared boy that I have no time for.

I reach up and grab him by the back of the neck and shove him toward the hallway.

"You can go to your room and you can stay there until you are man enough to tell me what bullshit you spewed to that piece of shit, do you understand me? I don't want to see your face again until you're ready to step up and own your fucking words," I scream at him.

The tenor of my voice scares me because the pitch is not quite me, and the look of abject terror on his face tells me that he knows what will happen soon if he doesn't disappear from sight.

Luke scrambles to his feet and barrels down the hallway to his room. He slams the door, and seconds later I can hear the unmistakable sound of furniture being move. He's so afraid of me when I'm like this that he tends to barricade himself for a day or two until he's sure I've gotten over whatever rage has taken hold of me. Even then, he's very careful with peeking too far out of his room without permission because I'm liable to snap at him erratically.

I drop down onto the floor and put my face in my hands. I don't like to be this way with him—he loves me unconditionally and I'll only push him away from me with my moods, but I refuse to poison myself to make things better and he seems to be doing okay with it.

As okay as he can be, anyway.

The more time passes that I'm alone on the cold floor, the more hopeless I feel. I want my son to hold me and tell me that everything will be okay, but I've already done enough damage to our relationship for the evening which means I'll just have to deal with the feeling of emptiness.

I get to my feet and walk quietly down the hallway, my

arms wrapped tightly around myself as I stop in front of his door. I place my ear against the wood and sigh. I can't hear anything inside—not the panting sighs of exertion, not the soft whimpers of fear. I hear nothing which tells me that he's more than likely climbed out of the window as he tends to do sometimes and left me alone again.

"I'm sorry," I whisper softly as I pull away from the door and turn to walk to my room.

Once inside, I collapse on the bed and bring my knees up to my chest and begin to sob quietly. I've never meant to hurt my boy—physically or emotionally, but sometimes things get too much for me to handle alone and this monster comes out of me, lashing at the only thing that it can reach.

I'm always afraid he'll grow up to hate me because of the things that happen behind these walls, and I would never fault him for that.

I've done unspeakable things to my son and nothing ever seems to drive him away from me except for when I speak bitter words to him.

That's when he hides.

That's when he shows me he's still very much a boy and not the man I often mistake him for.

I hope that when the time comes for him to leave me, he doesn't hate me too much for all of the pain I've caused him.

CHAPTER 10

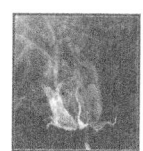

WHEN I WAKE up the next morning, I have a splitting headache. So much so, that the small sliver of sunlight that's peeking in through the blinds causes me to grimace and shrink under my blanket, but the material doesn't move because it's not just my arm weighing it down.

"What?" I grumble to no one in particular.

"Go back to sleep, Mom," the tired voice replies, pulling me tightly back against him.

It's obviously Luke, which surprises me considering how I left our relationship dangling by a thread last night.

I don't have the heart to argue with him, to tell him that he shouldn't be pressed so tightly against me, instead, I close my eyes again and hope that he gets tired of having to coddle me soon.

After another half hour passes and I can tell he's fallen asleep against me again, I take a deep breath and do my best to slip away from his arms without waking him up. As I get to my feet and turn to face him, I run my hands up my arms, my body shivering.

I never knew I would be able to make something as

beautiful as my son, and yet here he is. Fifteen years of age and as much of a man as any other I cross on the streets.

It's no wonder that I have to indulge myself from time to time.

And it's no wonder that he lets me. He's always told me since he could talk

that I was the most beautiful mommy in the world and his touch proves it time and time again.

I turn my back to him and try as quietly as I can to walk out of the room when a pillow lands squarely on my back. I gasp in initial shock as I turn to face my son who's sitting up on his elbows grinning at me with a tired expression dancing in his eyes.

"I'm sorry. I didn't mean to wake you up," I tell him softly, pushing a strand of hair behind my ear.

He looks so fucking innocent when he's lying in my bed and it's in these moments that I desperately want to touch him the most.

I bite my lower lip and take a step closer to the bed, when Luke raises his eyebrows at me. He knows what I want, but will he be willing to give it to me again so soon?

"Do you love me?" I ask him in tone soft enough that I know it will harden his cock. It's a little trick I use when I want to love him with more than just my touch.

"Aw, mom. You know I do," he replies, leaning back against the pillows and crossing his arms loosely over his chest.

"Then show me," I say simply.

Luke runs a hand over his face as he darts his eyes toward the bedroom window. It wouldn't be the first time he's tried to jump, but it will be the last time if he sees fit to defy me again.

"Ow," I say, putting my hands to the sides of my head.

"Are you okay?" he asks curiously. I have to hide the smile that slips across my lips when I hear the bed creak. While it's true I do suffer from headaches that render me useless every now and again, this isn't one of those times.

I just want to feel his cock inside of me again, and the only way to do this will be to take him off guard.

Luke comes over and takes me by the forearms, pulling my hands away from my face, and leaning down to look into my eyes.

"Mom?" he asks timidly.

When he sees the devious smile on my face, he takes a staggering step back, but I'm faster. I rush forward and push him onto his back, our bodies bouncing on the bed as I straddle him and grin.

"Show Mommy how much you love her, little boy," I whisper as I reach down and pull my shirt over my head.

Luke pushes me away, but I pull him closer. I'm much stronger than he is when it comes to moments like this, even if I don't look it.

He knows he won't be able to resist me once I slide my hand into his boxers, but this sweet boy—he's constantly torn between pleasing his mother and saving his own soul from the monster I've become.

"Mom, please?" he begs, pushing me away again. "I don't want to do this anymore." I raise an eyebrow and drop my hands to my sides. He should know better than to deny me the one thing I want most from him, and he knows that defiance isn't something I handle well.

Show him that he'll always need you.

I smack him across the face as hard as I can, the sound echoing off the walls in my bedroom and he takes a step back in shock. I'm fighting a war inside of my head right now to be Taylee, the mother and not Sister

Taylee, the whore that let his father fuck me like the worthless soul I had become.

But it's no use.

Not when I see his shoulders drop and the determination now gleaming in his eyes. He knows that he has to love me because no one else will.

Nor will they love him—not like I do.

Not ever like I do.

I just have to be gentle with him and ease him back into the bed instead of knocking him over like a rabid animal sick with disease and he'll do what I want.

He always does, because he's such a good boy.

CHAPTER 11

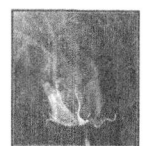

I LET OUT a moan as Luke pushes deep inside of me. He struggled a bit at first but after a few slaps to the face, a stern reprimand, and a warning that I'd never suck his dick again, he finally folded.

I've only ever had two men inside of me like this, the other being his father, but his cock is so much more than just that. I can feel his love for me as he reaches down and pulls my hair, arching my body back toward his. I feel like an actual woman for what feels like the first time again when I feel his breath hot against my neck. The way he reaches around and squeezes my throat, like he knows that I need to be punished for what we're doing, only strengthens my resolve for our moments together.

"More," I command him through grit teeth as he continues to fuck me. He's thrusting into me with conviction, fucking me harder than he ever has, his hand tightening just a little more as I let out a gasp of ecstasy.

Luke lets out a loud moan and I can feel him spill his seed inside of me, but he knows better than to stop until I'm done too. I've nicked his balls with a knife before for thinking it was okay to just finish and let me fend for myself.

Luke rests his head against my back for a moment before he pulls out of me, slapping his dick against my ass, then turns me onto my back.

A delicious grin spreads across his face as he leans down and gently bites one of my nipples while he slides himself back into me.

The way our flesh sounds as he rams his dick into me is enough to make anyone jealous, but he's mine—all mine and no one else will ever have him.

"You about ready there?" he asks me, leaning down to kiss my neck.

I nod and reach my hands up, gripping his shoulders tightly.

Luke nods, the grin still on his face as he leans his body down against mine, wrapping a hand around my throat again.

My boy is so good to me and he loves me and that's why I'm very proud of our relationship.

No one will ever understand it and that's not something I care to explain.

"Wait," I suddenly say, attempting to pry his hands away from my neck. "Luke ... wait."

"No more waiting, *Mom*," he breathes, pulling back and giving me a dangerous look.

"Stop!" I screech, immediately regretting my reaction.

My lungs burn.

It's hard to take in air and stars are exploding before my eyes, but my son continues to apply pressure. He pulls his cock out of me and uses his other hand, wrapping it around the flesh of my throat that the other hand didn't cover, and pushes me deep into the bed.

I know that look in his eyes.

I've seen it in the mirror many, many times before.

I knew I could never save Luke because I only ever wanted to love him.

And now?

He's found a way to save himself.

EPILOGUE

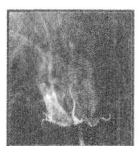

It's been a few years since Mom died and as I flip through her bible searching for answers, I have to keep focused on the task at hand. She was never right in the head after Trenton fucked her for the first time and I guess the only way she could keep what little bit of sanity she had left was to love me the way he loved her.

It wasn't a big deal to me the first few times, but when it became more of a demand than a loving moment between a mother and her son, I started to feel like I was being taken for granted.

I sigh irritably as I scan page after page, book after book, looking for something that might tell me that I did the right thing.

Nothing from the words that have been passed down for thousands of years from some great man in the clouds, but clues that

I know Mom must have left in these pointless scriptures.

Come on, goddamn it.

I keep flipping with a rage in my heart. Not for the

things she did to me because I know she only taught me how to love—how to truly love.

Even on the days and nights that I tried to fight her off, I knew it was the only way for her to convince me that her love was the purest thing she could offer me.

And I offered her nothing in return. Not a fucking thing I ever did was useful

to the woman that gave me life and it'll haunt me 'til the day I fucking die.

I think she spent so much time at that fucking restaurant because she hoped one day she would see Trenton again, and even Father Moore, but I'll never understand what she would have gained from those "chance" meetings other than spiraling further into her self-loathing.

With a sigh, I move from my knees and rest my back against her headstone, still searching for my answers on the flimsy pages of countless words that I'll never take time to read.

Trenton knew something was wrong the night he met us for dinner. When Taylee went to the bathroom, he asked me if there was anything he could do to help—to take me away from her, but I ... I couldn't. I couldn't leave her alone in a world she obviously forgot how to understand.

Did she deserve her end? I don't know, and I try not to think about it, yet I can't seem to feel proud of myself for stopping her before it became too late.

She told me that something was growing inside of her, but she was so goddamn paranoid that it could have meant anything, and I honestly didn't want to see what it was.

I raise my eyes to the bright blue skies for a moment and watch a cloud lazily drift by wondering if she's finally happy with her great man in the sky, before I look back down at the bible in my hands, ready to close it and give up.

And that's when I see it.

When I'm ready to give up and throw the book into the garbage can near her grave, I finally fucking see it.

It's Mom's unmistakable handwriting in the book of Revelation. Almost as if she knew that I would be looking for her to continue to guide me after she died.

I take a deep breath and smile as I run the tips of my fingers over her last words to me. The ones that will stay with me for the rest of my life and the lives of those that I choose to create and love in the same special way that she did to me.

You can be defined by this, or you can let it destroy you.

INFERNO

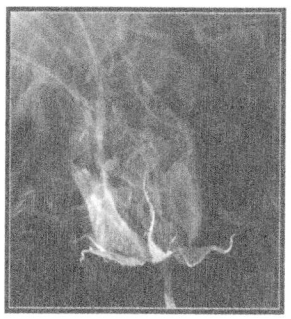

ACKNOWLEDGMENTS

My PAs, Lis Garcia and Linda Cotter, thank you for sitting through the headache that is Yolanda Olson and not quitting on me. You ladies kept me laughing through this entire thing when I doubted my sanity. You're the best!

Daqri Bernardo of Covers by Combs for this amazing cover that I knew I had to have the moment I saw it! Thank you for once again making my story come to life with the striking visual effect that only you can create.

Evelyn of Pinpoint Editing. Thank you so much for your hard work on this! Your comments made this fun to read through!

My Darkling Little Beta Team. I know I was driving you guys crazy, so thanks for putting up with this story in pieces. I appreciate it more than words can say!

To my readers...

I have no warning for you this time. Go in blind and come out on the other side with the light shining brightly in your eyes.

Good luck.

PROLOGUE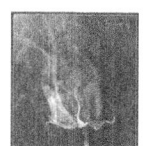

Everything makes sense now.

Why I'm here.

Why it had to be *me* and no one else.

I'm okay with it; as okay as I can be, anyway. I don't want anyone else to have to go through what I am enduring, so I'll gladly take everything he has to offer and praise him the way he tells me to.

Things are easier when I just comply with what he wants. He doesn't do me harm that way, and I even get food when I'm good.

I shake my head as I bring my dirty, bruised knees up to my chest and hug them close. He says when it's over I'll be canonized and that I'm doing this for the greater good, but I'm convinced he doesn't know what good is. It's so misconstrued that I sometimes wonder if he can tell the difference between reality and fantasy.

But it's okay.

I'm okay.

I'm used to the way things are and I'll make sure that, no matter what happens, he'll be happy. And in turn, I'll still be of use. Not that I really do much but stand and kneel when he tells me to. He says it helps him with what he needs to achieve and I don't question him. I just do as I'm told, and you would too if you could see his eyes go dark and cold when we enter his special rooms.

I've never been afraid of much before him, and I can honestly say that after being here for the years he's chosen to keep me, the only thing that scares me is telling him no.

That brings the worst kind of repercussion, and the weight of having disappointed him. Solitude and darkness for seven days and seven nights until he's had time to cleanse himself of my negativity. That's how he explains it: *a cleansing.*

Being alone was something I used to love and look forward to; now it's something that terrorizes me more than anything he could ever say when he puts on his displays.

I think I'm on day six of darkness now. I can't remember because everything just blends together after a while; time, tears, blood. Each time I'm dumped into this fucking hole, I come closer to losing the will to live. But I come out stronger each time. I don't want to disappoint him, and if I just lay down and died, it would be the biggest disservice in his eyes.

Besides, I haven't come this far, survived *this* much, just to fucking fall down dead. I don't have it in me to quit, and I have to make him proud.

The gate at the top of the makeshift dungeon opens and, shortly after, a shaky ladder made of rugged rope drops in. It must be the seventh day if I'm being presented with this gesture of freedom.

But I know that this is a treason punishable by death unless Pater has given permission for any of us to be removed from the oubliette.

Pater.

That is not his name but rather a title that he requires we address him by. He's earned it, he says, for putting up with us, for choosing to care for us in his own special way, and for all the years he spent studying his rituals.

I know his real name because he's whispered it into my ear during nights of unwanted lust and pain. I've survived as long as I have because I know that pleasure for him is not just physical; seducing his thoughts is the only way to stay alive, and even on nights when I wished that Hell would open and swallow me whole, I refused to leave the boys behind. I've stepped into their pain more than once to save them from things they shouldn't understand at such young ages, things they should never have to experience unless it's something they want, and he sees me as a prize for doing so.

I fear the day he gets bored with me though, because then there will be nothing left I can do to keep them as safe as I can. It's why I try my best to please him, to keep him happy any way I can, because nights spent down in the oubliette leaves them free to be tortured and fucked against their will.

With the strength I've managed to hold onto, I get up from the dirty, cold rocky ground, and walk over to the ladder. It's only being anchored by the strength of whomever is holding it, and I pray that it's the older of the two. He's the only one who can bear the strain of someone bigger than him, and if he doesn't hold on, the ladder will fall and send me back down toward a sure death.

If it were just me in this situation, then fine; let the ladder fall, let me die, but goddammit. I have to keep them safe and I have to get the fuck out of here to do that. I have to watch my mouth, I have to not speak back to Pater, and I have to do as he wishes at all times. If I don't, I'll know that the next time I'm in the oubliette, the others will suffer terribly, and it will be on my soul.

I *refuse* to die a failure. I *refuse* to allow them such a fate alone when I know that my part in this is simple and I just have to learn to accept it.

When he took me from my previous life, he told me he'd chosen me to be his wife; he'd even preformed some kind of ceremony to solidify this in his own mind, because I know that nothing we do here will be seen as such in the eyes of the law or anything above or below.

A hand firmly grips mine as I reach the top, shaking me from the thoughts of what I know I must do, but have so much trouble abiding by. In a matter of seconds, I'm looking into the solemn, brown eyes of Vaughn. He's lost a lot of the light and luster he had when he first arrived here and I can understand why, but beneath the solemnness I can see a sense a urgency, and I know that my early freedom was not orchestrated by Pater, but rather out of necessity.

With a final grunt, he pulls me over the top and begins to roll up the ladder as I start the long sprint back toward the house. I won't wait for Vaughn; I can't. If I do, Pater will know I was helped out of my prison and that will put Vaughn in danger. Instead, I'll just tell him I clawed my way out when he asks. I've been known to make it halfway to the top before breaking my nails as I slide all the way back down again.

He's seen me do it with his own eyes the first time he lowered me into this sensory deprived hell. But Pater is a complicated man and likes to see things as they are presented in the moment.

He'll believe me.

He *has* to believe me.

Because if he doesn't, we all die.

CHAPTER 1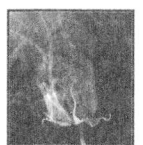

WHAT I STUMBLE upon when I enter Pater's home as I'm trying to frantically control my breathing is not what I expected from the urgency in Vaughn's eyes. The waiting room is empty, the living room just as hollow, and there are no trails of blood or anything hinting toward punishment on his dusty wooden floors.

So then why set me free ahead of schedule?

A silent answer is my reward when I turn in time to see him running up the long walkway toward the still open door. He puts a finger to his lips before leaning down and attempting to collect himself. I know he's scared, and I know that this must be important.

He tosses the neatly gathered rope toward the door and beckons for me to follow him. I trust him enough to blindly fall into step behind him, though I can't help but feel uneasy about where he's leading me.

Vaughn never has much to say these days. He lives in his own world most of the time, and he usually only ever comes to life when I'm around because he knows of my need to protect them. He does the same for me in his own way. Whenever I've been tossed into the little part of the world where Pater can forget about me for a week at a time, he sneaks out and drops scraps of food through the small cracks of the door.

It's not much, it never is, but it's enough to keep me alive and from starving to death as I think Pater wants for me sometimes. I don't know why he would want such a fate for someone he's taken as his "wife", but he has his reasons.

Maybe one day we'll find out what they are. Or maybe we'll die in the dark, confused as to what this all truly stood for.

As we near the opulent kitchen area where Pater eats like a fucking king, Vaughn turns to look at me and presses a finger slowly to his lips. A few steps later, we're both peeking around the door frame and now I understand why I was taken prematurely from my punishment.

Pater is leaning against the counter, his arms crossed loosely over his chest, with Eloy sitting in a stool. I roll my eyes at how pristine he looks and how we always look like we're mired in shit.

Eloy is the youngest of the three of us. He's thirteen and, for the moment, he's dressed as cleanly and beautifully as Pater. I hear the voice of someone I don't recognize and crane my neck to see if I can get a better look, but Vaughn pulls me back just as Pater's eyes start to wander in our direction.

"Get cleaned up," he whispers in his soft voice. "We have to go in and speak to that lady."

And as he walks into the kitchen, leaving me in the hallway, it's the first time I noticed since being pulled out of the pit that he's dressed like a prince, too. I'm the only one who looks like I've been through Hell, because I have.

A wide smile stretches over Pater's face as he sees Vaughn entering the room.

"And this is my other son," I can hear him say. I cringe at those words. *My other son.* If only this person who we're being presented to knew what kind of man Pater is, what kind of woman he forces me to be, she would take Vaughn and Eloy and run.

I could tell her.

I could weave a powerful tale of the horrors we face here, the things we're forced to endure, the evil man that Pater is, but I won't. If she doesn't believe me—and who would believe such a fantastical story—I go back into the oubliette permanently.

I sigh as I run toward the other end of the house. We are not allowed upstairs unless Pater requests our company because it's his home, and he deems that his personal space. It's how he keeps us separate from what he calls his 'normal' life, though there are times when he'll invite me upstairs, but never the boys.

That I know of, anyway. The only thing I ever pray for anymore is that they have never been forced to go with him into his room. They know they can trust me and tell me if they have, but I never broach the subject because they're afraid of me. Not as much as they're afraid of Pater, but they're still afraid.

I don't blame them.

I would also fear the person that's supposed to be like a mother to me, who instead decides to carry out painful and sometimes erotic punishments as directed to her in the most terrible ways.

This is why I know I never want to bear children of my own. If this is what I'm forced to do—to actually be capable of putting them through—then the only thing I truly deserve is a slow death at their hands.

But they fear me and will never raise a hand against me because I'm the only person who knows their pain and torture. I'm the only person that would believe them, and I'm the only person that can keep them as safe as possible from Pater.

I take their places as often as I can, but there are even nights when I'm so physically and mentally exhausted from the constant torrent of abuse that I can't save them. I believe that those are the nights that their hatred for me grows and the fear begins to slowly drift away.

If they did end up killing me, I would not blame or despise them for the deed. I would only hope that they allow me the opportunity to send Pater to Hell before me.

What do I wear? I don't even know who that woman is.

Pater, Vaughn, and Eloy were dressed casually but a little more presentable than normal when we have guests, so I assume she's of enough importance for me to wear a dress.

I just have to find one long enough to cover the scratches on my knees.

Pulling open the closet doors, I begin to quickly pick through my choices.

"I've always liked this one the best."

My body freezes under the weight of his breath, hot on my ear. One hand reaches forward and retrieves a blue and white floral sundress, while the other gently rests on my side.

He could crush me right now between his hands if he wanted to, but then he would have no wife to present to the woman in the kitchen.

"You know that as soon as she leaves you're going back

in." It's a statement, not a question, but I expected nothing less.

I nod as he lets his lips rest gently on my neck. "Maybe I'll fuck you before I throw you back. Or maybe I'll punish you a little more. Decisions, decisions."

"Whatever you desire, Pater," I reply quietly. That's the answer he likes the best, and I'm only here to maintain a happy home for him, which means he has to be happy as well.

"I don't think I'll ever get sick of fucking you," he whispers as he reaches down and begins to push my torn, dirty panties off.

I take a deep breath and use every ounce of bravery I have to gently push his hands away.

"We have a visitor, Pater. She must be important if you need me to be present. I shouldn't keep her waiting," I say softly.

He grunts in annoyance but he knows I'm right. Besides, the last thing I want right now is to have to lie on the bed while he uses me for however long he wants to. It's fucking degrading that I have to be so subservient to him, but it's how I stay alive. I'm willing to do it for as long as I need to be able to gain a safe escape for Eloy and Vaughn.

"Don't forget to cover that shit up," he warns, nodding at the cuts on my legs.

"Yes Pater," I reply unhappily.

"Hey," he says, turning me to face him and sliding his arms around my waist. Pater is a tall man so I'm staring unhappily into his chest, but he leans down to look into my eyes, cocking his head to the side so I can see his smile.

"I'm almost done with three of you. This won't go on for much longer, then I'll let you decide if you want to stay or go, okay? Smile for me, pretty baby," he says as I glance up slowly into his golden brown eyes.

The stubble on his face is black and has some gray in it, matching his hair perfectly. He looks so fucking normal, like a loving father, but I know better.

We know better.

I force a smile on my face, which makes him stand back up to his full height and kiss me on the forehead.

"That's my girl. Now get yourself cleaned up and come down as quick as you can. And keep that smile on your face; we're a perfectly happy family and I want her to know it."

I nod again, turn and grab the dress he picked out, and head toward the dresser. Once I've picked out some fresh underwear, I quickly make my way toward the bathroom and lock the door firmly behind me.

Fuck.

At least it'll be over soon.

CHAPTER 2

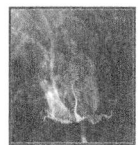

Twenty minutes later, I'm rushing down the hallway. Normally, after a week in the oubliette, my showers last for at least an hour, but I know I don't have enough time for that. As I round the corner into the kitchen, I quickly reach down and smooth out the hem of my dress, before plastering a huge smile on my face.

"There she is," Pater says, holding out an arm toward me.

"I'm so sorry I'm late," I reply brightly as I obediently walk over to him. He leans down and kisses me on the lips. It's a firm kiss and far from gentle, but it's hard for him to pretend he's something he's not.

"Laura, this is my wife, Jocelyn," he says, holding me close against him.

"Pleasure to meet you," she says with a warm smile.

"Likewise! Can I get you anything? Coffee? Water? Juice?" I ask, trying to remember what Pater lets me offer on the very rare occasion we have company.

"No thank you," she says, crossing her arms, the top of the island separating her from the boys. "I'm just about done talking to them, then I'd like to speak to the two of you privately."

"Oh, of course!"

Pater tightens his grip on me. Apparently, my acting is lacking today, but I was just in a fucking hole in the ground for six days. I'm hoping he'll cut me some slack when she leaves - instead of just cutting *me*.

"Would you like to wrap up with them without us here?" Pater asks Laura.

"Actually, that would be great!" she replies with an enthusiastic nod.

"Alright, we'll be just down the hallway then. One of you boys can bring her to the living room when you're done in here, okay?" he says, walking over and putting a firm hand on each of their shoulders.

"I will," Vaughn replies quietly, looking up at him.

Pater smiles at him and nods, before he turns and holds his hand out toward me. Without hesitation, I take it and let him lead me out of the kitchen, but I cast one last glance over my shoulder at the trio. Vaughn is speaking quietly to Laura, and Eloy glances at me with wide eyes. I shake my head once before I disappear from sight.

"So, who is she?" I ask Pater curiously as we head down the hallway.

"We'll talk about that after she leaves," he replies in an even tone.

Oh God, this can't be good.

"Okay," I agree softly.

Once we reach the living room, he walks over toward the window and pulls the curtain back. I watch him as he glances around until his eyes land on something and narrow. I won't question him any more. I don't even plan on speaking unless spoken to at this point. Something has Pater very angry and my leg is already shaking in anticipation of what it could possibly be.

Silence.

That's the only thing that sits heavily in the air between us as he walks away from the window and falls into the spot next to me on the couch. He has nothing else to say to me because, by all rights, I shouldn't even be in his sights until tomorrow night.

Pater irritably runs a hand over his mouth and crosses his arms behind his head.

"What the fuck could they possibly be talking about?" he mutters.

I don't respond. I know he wasn't speaking to me, and in his state of current anger, a response would most likely result in additional correction.

"It was so nice to meet the two of you."

Laura's voice finally echoes through the hallway as she's led to us. "Remember, if you ever need anything, you can call me and I'll do my best to help, okay?"

"Okay. Thank you," Vaughn's dejected voice responds. "Our parents should be in there. It was nice to meet you, too."

A few seconds later, Laura enters the room. Pater gets to his feet to greet her and I stay right where I am as she settles onto the couch across from us.

"You have wonderful sons. You must be very proud of them," she says brightly, taking a small notebook out of her purse.

"We are," Pater replies.

"Speaking of children," she says, turning her attention toward me, "Exactly how old are you? You don't look old enough to be their mother."

My body immediately begins to shake. My mouth opens and closes a couple of times, but nothing comes out.

"Old enough to have children," Pater says, putting an arm around my shoulder and giving me a reassuring squeeze.

Even if they're not mine.

"I'm sorry if I sounded intrusive. I was just hoping to get some beauty tips," Laura jokes, as she flips her notebook open and then produces a pen. "I just have a couple of questions for you, and then I'll be on my way."

"Fire away," he says, with that charming grin sitting on his face.

"Well, Eloy and Vaughn seem like sullen, but happy children. Are they usually like that?" she asks.

Pater squeezes my arm. He doesn't know how to answer the question, because he's never been near them unless it's for some kind of sadistic need.

"Vaughn usually doesn't have much to say; he's the quiet studious type, you know? And Eloy hasn't been feeling well lately so that could explain his mood," I say, leaning forward and clasping my hands in my lap.

She nods in understanding as she jots something down in her notebook.

"How are their studies?"

"Great! Like I said, Vaughn likes to learn things. He's very curious about how things work and if there's meaning behind every function. I expect him to be a scientist or something similar," I reply with a smile. "Eloy. Now, he likes his sports and he's happiest when he's outside exploring, so he's kind of like his brother in that respect."

Laura looks at me with a pleased smile on her face. Apparently, my answers are what she wants to hear, when

I'm really just telling her the truth. I do teach them when I'm not in the fucking hole, and I try to make sure they understand basic educational studies.

"And my last question is actually about the two of you. I would like if you could both answer me," she says, giving Pater a pointed glance. "How are things? Any worries you have that you may want to share with me? I'm not here to judge you, please understand that. I'm here out of concern and I want to make sure that you're both as equally happy as your children."

"Concern?" I ask her in confusion.

She smiled warmly. "I'll address that in a moment; first, I'd like to know how things are."

"Honestly, I couldn't be happier. Are things perfect? No, of course not. Perfection is a lie, an illusion. But my husband provides for us as best as he can and makes sure that we're well taken care of. I can't think of anything else I could possibly want," I reply with a shrug. *Except for you to take us with you when you leave.*

"Yeah, I agree. My wife maintains a tidy home as you can see. She keeps our boys educated and I don't think we've ever really had an argument. Any disagreements we actually have had have never been in front of our children, so I think we're doing okay," he adds, rubbing my back affectionately.

"Great!" Laura says as she jots what I assume to be her final thoughts about her trip into her notebook. I wait patiently, trying to still my jumping leg as she places her notebook back into her purse and looks up at us.

"So let me tell you the reason for my visit," she says, looking from me to Pater. His hand comes to rest in the middle of my back, almost as if he's expecting her to say it was *my* fault, so he could pull my spine out.

"For obvious reasons, any calls placed to me are anonymous, but I had a concerned parent reach out to me recently. It seems that Eloy has been spotted out in the woods behind your home, killing small animals. As a matter of fact, the parent that called me stated that they witnessed him skinning a snake and then attempting to eat it."

I lean back in shock, but Pater chuckles almost immediately. "Aren't snakes considered a delicacy somewhere around the world? What's the harm in it? He's just being a kid."

Closing my eyes, I decide it's best to let him handle this conversation because, judging by his response, I can tell that anything that comes out of his mouth next will be dripping with sugar. The only question I have remaining is whether Laura will buy it.

Well, maybe more than one question...

"Where did you say you were from again?" I asked her suspiciously.

"Oh, I'm just another concerned parent. I'm not tied to any official agency," she says nervously.

"Then what the fuck are you doing in our home? When *my* son comes to *your* house and tries to skin and eat *you*, then you have my fucking permission to show up with 'concern.' Until then, you can get the fuck out of here!" I shout, jumping to my feet. My fists are balled at my sides and I can't remember the last time I have ever been so angry.

Laura's mouth jumps open at my sudden outburst, but Pater laughs in appreciation. I'm not protective over many things in this world, because I really don't have anything, but those boys are my heart and he knows I would kill for them.

"I think you should listen to my wife," he says, as he rises from the couch to stand next to me. "And tell your 'concerned parent friends' that they can come over and talk to us about our kids anytime they want. Tell them we'll be waiting with an open door and a smile on our faces, because our boys are well fed, happy, cared for, and that's all that matters to us."

Laura nervously gets to her feet and nods, but as she begins to walk past us on her way toward the front door, something inside me tells me that if she makes it out, our entire family will be in danger.

And that's why when I grab the lamp off the corner table and follow her toward the door, I know Pater will let me put her in the oubliette in my place.

Because while she's now stumbling from the blow to her head, trying to stay on her feet, he knows what's in my heart. And he'll allow me to do everything I can for Eloy and Vaughn, even though I know he has to punish them first.

CHAPTER 3

"Why did you let her in?" I asked him as I begin to drag her back down toward the back door. "Did she show you some credentials?"

"Nah. I just thought it could be fun to fuck with the neighbors," he replies with a smirk. "I knew she wasn't anyone important. And you should be thankful I let her in. It got you out of the hole for a while and into a nice dress. As a matter of fact, a 'thank you, Pater' would actually be nice, instead of your bitching."

"Thank you, Pater," I say through gritted teeth. I take a deep breath and stand up straight for a moment, when the sudden severity of what I've done hits me.

"Oh shit. Oh *fuck*," I say frantically. "I can't believe I did that."

"It's 'cause you want to protect our little family as much as I do," he chuckles. "That's why you're my favorite of all the wives I've had. You would do anything to keep our secret and our boys safe, wouldn't you?"

"Yes," I reply softly.

"None of my other wives gave two shits about any kids we had. They all just wanted to fuck and stay out of the oubliette. It always got so boring. You, on the other hand," he says, walking toward me and taking my face in between his strong hands, "couldn't care less about fucking me. You're more invested in being a good mother, and *that's* why I appreciate you as much as I do. Now, if we could just do something about that mouth, maybe you wouldn't spend so much time in the ground."

It's the oddest feeling that's taken over me right now. Pride because of the praise I'm receiving as a mother, but anger because of the fact that I can't protect them as much as I want to.

Pater narrows his eyes and smirks, "I can't tell if that's a scowl on your face or a smile, so I'll just assume it's a little bit of both and be okay with it."

Laura moves next to us on the ground and begins her attempt to get to her feet, but I'm sure I hit her hard enough to keep her down a little while longer.

"What am I going to do with her?" I ask him quietly.

"Well. You got two choices. You can finish whatever it was you started..."

"Or?" I ask him, wringing my hands.

"I don't think you're going like this, but I think it could be fun," he says, flashing me his wide grin. I raise an eyebrow and wait. If he wants to fuck her, that's his prerogative, obviously, but I'm not joining in.

"Eloy!"

His voice booms throughout the house so unexpectedly that I jump in surprise and almost losing my footing.

"What are you doing?" I ask him curiously.

"Did you just ask me a question?" he asks, tilting his head, the grin widening on his face.

"No, Pater."

"I didn't think so," he says, turning his attention toward the sound of footsteps quickly approaching. "Hey there, son."

"Hello," Eloy replies nervously.

"I didn't know you liked to skin animals," Pater says conversationally. "I used to be into that when I was a kid, too. I figure we could have a little bonding moment if you're up for it. And to sweeten the deal, if you say yes to what I'm going to suggest, I'll make sure your mom doesn't have to serve the rest of her time in the oubliette."

Eloy's eyes widen hopefully as he glances quickly in my direction. He knows that the more time I spend *above* ground, the less time him and his brother are off Pater's radar.

"I agree," he immediately says.

Pater throws his head back and laughs. He knows that the boys need me as much as I need them, and that they'll do anything to keep me above ground.

"Good. Then what I want for you to do is drag that piece of shit out back. Hit her as many times as you need to to keep her quiet. I'll be out shortly. I just wanna finish talking with your mom," he says to him as he glances at me.

"Okay," he agrees, grabbing Laura by her hands and dragging her the rest of the way out of the house. A feeling of dread quickly cascades over me when it starts to set in. I have a terrible feeling that I know how he plans on bonding with Eloy.

"Listen, I can tell you've already got this figured out by the look on your face, but there's something I want to tell you. I feel like I owe it to you for being such a good mom," he says, rubbing his chin thoughtfully.

"Don't hurt him," I beg, reaching forward and grabbing

his forearms. "I can talk to him and tell him to be more careful. Please?"

Pater looks down at my hands and waits for me to pull them away before he responds. "We'll see what happens, alright? But I do need to punish him for being so fucking sloppy. You understand," he says with a wink as he starts to make his way outside.

I run to the door as he closes it behind him and crack it open. He probably heard the door open again, because he shakes his head as he walks toward the woods.

I find myself secretly hoping that whoever saw Eloy skinning and eating the snake will catch Pater doing whatever the hell it is he has planned - but I also hope they don't. My son shouldn't be punished for behaving like an animal, since that's how he's pretty much been brought up under Pater. He's only behaving as he's been taught, the way his father has conditioned him to. And for that, a nosy neighbor is going to die, Eloy is going to be "punished", and I have to sit here and hope for his life to be spared.

All because he blindly made a deal to keep me safe. Anything that happens to him will be my fault; Pater made that clear enough when he tricked Eloy by using me as a pawn.

I know I shouldn't do this because we're not allowed to without Pater, but I close the door and run as quickly as I can to the second floor of his home. I'll get a better view of the woods from his bedroom window, and that's how I'll know for sure if anything happens to Eloy.

Or, more painful still, what *will* happen to Eloy. With a lump in my throat and a sickened feeling in my heart, I make my way up the stairs and down to his bedroom door at the end of the hall.

I hope he doesn't see me because if he does, he'll take out his anger on the boy. If he doesn't, I'll know how to avenge Eloy if necessary. When the opportunity presents itself.

CHAPTER 4

An eternity.

That's how long I feel like I've been standing here, peeking through his bedroom window without a thing in sight, and I'm so fucking scared.

My husband is out there somewhere in the woods with our son, a nosy neighbor, and enough rage to punish them both with a smile on his face.

But what kind of father would that really make him? To punish his child for doing something that obviously makes him happy would be hypocritical of him, and Pater prides himself on being the very opposite of that.

But where are they? Why is there no sign of life between the trees when I know there are three people somewhere out there in the isolation?

I sigh unhappily and let the curtain drift back over the window again as I sit on the edge of his bed. This is not a place I've ever enjoyed being, and it seems to be more of a hell in the current situation of not knowing.

"Hello?"

My eyes widen as I run out of the room and find

Vaughn in the hallway peeking into doors. Neither of us should be up here, but it's more dangerous for him because if Pater gets a whiff of his scent having roamed through his private space, it makes him fair game.

"Go back downstairs *now*," I hiss at him frantically. He stares at me in confusion. He thinks the danger is not real because Pater isn't in the house, but I know better. I fucking know better and I have to get him back down to where he belongs.

"If he smells you up here, you're going to end up in his room," I say as I walk toward him, grip him firmly by the arm and begin to steer him back toward the stairs. "Get downstairs. Stay there; lock yourself in my room. I'll figure out how to fix this."

"But --"

"Now," I say again, firmly setting him on the staircase. I cross my arms over my chest and glare at him until he reluctantly begins his descent. I hate having to treat Vaughn with such false, overbearing anger, but if he believes he's angered me, he'll listen.

And it will keep him safe.

I don't know how Pater can tell when someone has been upstairs, but my curiosity got the best of me one day when he had been out buying groceries for himself, and I went up to his private floor. He found me later that night, curled up in my room reading a book, and quite literally dragged me all the way back upstairs and into his bedroom.

He told me he had been able to smell me in the place he told us was off limits; that he knew it was me because the hallways smelled of lavender and forgotten innocence. He told me that since I had broken his simplest rule, he had no choice but to break me in return.

I wrap my arms around myself and shiver as memories

of that first night in his bed threaten to wash over me and drown me where I stand.

Pater is an evil man in everything he does, and that night was no exception. However, I cannot allow myself to be lost in those thoughts. I have to rid the upstairs of Vaughn's scent, then go back to the window and hope that I'll finally catch a glimpse of Eloy.

It honestly worries me that I'm so invested in being an actual maternal figure to them now more than ever. It means I've accepted Pater as their father and as my husband, but I will do what I must to keep them safe from his misplaced sexual desires. I will take the brunt of his devious needs, and I will make sure they're kept safe from things they shouldn't have forced upon them.

They shouldn't be here and neither should I, but this is the hand we were dealt and he chose us specifically for this very reason. At least, that's what he's told me before, though I don't know how much I believe of his story.

As long as it keeps Vaughn and Eloy out of his bedroom and out of his special rooms, I will gladly be the sacrificial lamb. It's what a mother would do, isn't it? Lay down her life for that of her children? I know I'll find out soon enough, but for now I just want some sign that Eloy is alive, and to rid the upper floor of Vaughn's scent.

I've made it as far as his bathroom when I hear the front door of the home open. He's laughing loudly, the echo booming throughout the downstairs of the house, and I know I'm too late. I won't be able to do much to deflect his knowledge that Vaughn transgressed him, but I will still try my damnedest.

But as I leave his bathroom with a can of air freshener in my hand and begin to vigilantly spray the hallway as I run down its length, something slows me down. Pater is still laughing, yet there's no other sound accompanying him. No sound of an upset young boy being mocked or praised, no sound of the additional set of footsteps that *should* have entered in the house with him.

And as he begins to ascend the staircase, I try my best to steady myself against the wall next to me. Is he laughing because of what Eloy has done? Or because of what *he* has done to Eloy?

CHAPTER 5

By the time he reaches the top stair, I've saturated the hallway as best as I can and I'm standing in a choking fog of ocean breeze. I don't care that he'll see me here, as long as I've done my part to keep Vaughn off his fucking radar.

He stops when he sees me standing just beyond the landing and his laughter gives way to a grin. I watch as his head tilts to the left and begin to shiver as his eyes travel up and down my body before resting on the can I'm holding.

"What are you doing up here, Jocelyn?" he asks in a quiet, sickening tone.

"I ... I ..."

He chuckles and walks toward me, jerking the air freshener out of my hand and takes a deep breath. He narrows his eyes for a moment and looks behind me before he nods in understanding.

"Bad, bad, bad," he chides, shaking his head slowly. "Why are you all behaving so badly all of a sudden? Do you like being punished?"

The slight bounce in his step tells me that, regardless of my answer, he's going to do whatever he deems necessary to correct my misstep, and I can't fight him over it because it would mean Vaughn would have to take my place.

"Pater?" I begin slowly. "Where's Eloy?"

"Did you ... Did you just ask me a question?" he inquires in a mocking tone as the grin fades from his rugged face.

Normally, I would back down. I would tell him *no* and I would await whatever punishment he deemed necessary, and allow him to take the appropriate corrective steps against me. But Eloy is missing now, and I want fucking answers, no matter the cost.

"Yes," I reply defiantly. "Where is he? Where's the boy?"

Pater walks quickly toward me and I can feel my body stiffen, but I maintain the defiance in my eyes that I feel in my heart for him as he stops in front of me. His breathing is uneven and I can see the fire burning in his gaze, but I refuse to let him consume me in those flames; not until I know where Eloy is.

His hand flies through the air and lands firmly across my face, almost knocking me to the ground. The sting of it makes my eyes water slightly and I stumble, but don't fall. This isn't what he wants. He doesn't want me to oppose him; he's told me that so many times before, and that's why my second home is that abandoned fucking hole in the ground.

I wish I had the will sometimes to not fight him and just let him kill me, but these boys – who would fight for them if I lay down and died?

"Now, I'm going to ask you again," he says in an even tone. "Did you just ask me a question?"

I put my fingers gingerly to my lip and wipe away the blood from the small cut. He's never hit me hard enough to draw blood before, because he cares about my outside appearance. I use my tongue to quickly lick away the copper tasting drops still lingering on the corner of my mouth before I answer him.

"Yes. *Where is the boy?*"

His mouth tightens into an angry line as he stares down at me. He should expect this from me by now when it comes to the welfare of the children, and I find myself wondering if he left his common sense out in the woods as well.

"Let's get a couple of things straight here," he says, after letting out a deep sigh. "First of all, he's not your son. Neither of them are; you're just the stupid little bitch I chose to play mommy to them. What I decide to do with them, or *to* them, is really not your fucking concern. Remember that."

Pater crosses his arms over his chest and the grin begins to return. He likes to use words to cut me down; he always said that words would leave a deeper cut than any blade. Words – the ones spoken to inflict harm – will stay with you much longer than any scar worn on the skin.

If Pater is anything, he's a master of cutting deeply with his words.

Don't let him do this while you still don't know where Eloy is.

"Secondly," he says, dropping his arms to his sides, "You can't keep secrets from me. Even when you think you've got everything figured you, you should know better by now. Which begs a question. You haven't been up here alone, have you? No amount of that shit you sprayed can hide it from me, which means I'll give you an option. Even though you don't deserve it, even though *he* doesn't deserve it, tell me. Who's keeping me company in bed tonight? You, or the nosy little fuck that can't do as he's told?"

"Neither," I reply, my voice wavering slightly. *Fuck. He'll know he's getting to me now.*

Pater runs a hand irritably over his face before he chuckles. "I don't know why you think you have a say in the matter. Now, either you pick, or I will."

I let out an unhappy sigh as I turn and begin to walk back toward his bedroom. He knows that, given the choice, I'll always place myself in harm's way to spare them.

"Not so fast," he says, in a tone that stops me in my tracks.

I don't turn to face him immediately because I'm worried about what it is he wants before he subjects me to the level of correction he feels I deserve for talking back to him. For standing my ground against a tyrant and exercising a basic human right that I was stripped of the moment I willingly walked through his door, because I agreed to be less than human. I agreed to be this empty marionette to do his will and now, after all this time, I find myself rejecting the idea, even though it's too damn late.

"Yes, Pater?" I ask quietly as I finally turn my body toward the wall. It still can be seen as an act of defiance because I'm not facing him completely, but it's enough of a submission that he won't add anything extra to the punishment he's ready to bestow upon me.

"I want you to do a few things for me before I do a few things to *you*," he says, a wicked smile starting to spread across his lips.

"Yes, Pater?" I inquire again curiously. This isn't normally how he does these things, and the worry that has washed over me is being overshadowed with doubt and wonder.

"Let's call this little game *A List of Tasks*. For each task you complete, I'll go a little easier on you tonight. Of course, if you complete them all, you're still going to be punished, but not as severely. Questions?" he asks.

I don't respond. Not verbally, because I've already talked myself into enough shit to have to add more to drown in. Instead, I shake my head and nervously begin to wring my hands while I wait for his first task.

"My God. If only you knew how beautiful you are when you just stand there with your mouth shut," he remarks with a wistful sigh. "Alright. Task number one; it's going to answer your question."

My question?

"The first thing I want you to do is go out into the woods behind the house. Find the mess the boy made and clean it up. I want it so spotless out there you'd never know that anything other than animals shit between those trees. When you're done, you come back up and we'll talk about your next task."

I run past him and damn near fall down the stairs. If he wants me to cover Eloy's tracks, then chances are he's still alive. He may be bruised, battered, and beaten, but he's still alive and now I have the chance to be the mother he deserves and help him.

But I can't shake the chuckle Pater let out when I ran past him, and I know this task won't be as simple as finding some shit to clean up.

Whatever it is I find is going to break my heart, mind, and soul.

CHAPTER 6

THE MOST DAMNING thing about what Pater has set as his first task is that I know it will easily break me if something has happened to Eloy. If I'm broken, I can no longer fight for them. I don't care about myself; I am disposable because I'm not the first wife he's had, just the one that has survived the longest.

But for Eloy and Vaughn to be left alone in his care again until he decides he wants another wife is more than I can take. It's a weight on my shoulders that's been threatening to crush me for quite some time now, and while my foundation may be slowly crumbling, I will not collapse until they're safe.

I'm my own worst enemy in all of this. My constant fear of failing the children is starting to undo me, and the nights I spend in the oubliette would be much more bearable if I didn't have them to worry about.

I can see him now as I quicken my pace, the grass crushing beneath my feet. I can see Eloy standing naked, almost completely hidden in the brush that leads into the woods. He has marks on his back, and from what I can tell, they aren't severe.

"Eloy!" I call out as I run faster.

His body is shaking; I can see it now the closer I get to him. The marks on his back look like a series of scratches, but I can plainly see where he has been lashed with a switch. I call his name again, but he doesn't turn to face me. Instead, he balls his hands at his sides and lets out a sob.

"I'm here now, it's okay," I promise as I finally reach him and put a hand gently on his shoulder. I guide him into the woods to keep our conversation hidden from any eyes that may be watching. Even though I know we can't be heard out here, I also know he'll use our body language to deduce whatever the fuck he wants, and punish us accordingly.

"I'm sorry. I didn't want to. I'm sorry," he wails miserably.

"Nothing we do here is by choice; you know that. Whatever you've done, it was because you were made to. I'm just happy you're okay," I say, trying my best to comfort him, but the fact that he's shaking his head and still refusing to face me destroys any hope that Pater hasn't already defiled him.

I push my way through the brush as I move around to the front of him. His teeth are grinding together and he lowers his face so that I don't see how much he currently resembles a wounded animal.

"What did you do, Eloy?" I ask gently. I place a hand on either side of his face and pull him toward me. His body is covered with lash marks, and the haunting sound of Pater's malicious laughter when he reentered the house begins to taunt my memories.

"It's okay. I promise. I'm here to help you. I'll fix whatever you've done; you just need to tell me where to go, and I'll fix it."

"I didn't want to. I didn't want to, but he made me do it," he repeats desperately. What could he have been forced to do that's rendered him a babbling mess? I would imagine Laura was already dead by the time they had dragged her out here.

Wasn't she?

"He made me fuck her. He made me do it. I didn't want to and when I refused he started to whip me. Then he told me--" his voice broke into another anguished sob as he buried his face in my hair and finally wrapped his arms around me.

"What did he say? He can't hear us right now, and I swear to you I won't repeat it. What did he say, Eloy?" I press gently as I run a hand softly over his hair.

Eloy takes a small series of deep breaths to try and calm himself, and it works long enough for him to tell me what the price of his refusal was.

"He said that if I didn't fuck her, he would make me fuck you. He said he would make Vaughn watch us and then he would kill us all. I'm sorry," he says, as he resumes his uncontrollable sobbing.

"Don't cry. It's okay, I promise it's okay."

I feel a rage starting to intensify deep within. Pater's sexual appetites are unrivaled and his devious words are always enough to get us to do what he wants, but doing this to Eloy – he's crossed a fucking line, and he knows it. That's why he made me come out here; not to clean up a physical mess but to fix a psychological one he knows I don't have control over.

"Listen very closely to me right now. Eloy? Look at me,

please," I say, stepping back and gently removing his arms from around me.

He uses the back of his hand to wipe the tears away from his face, but does as he's requested and locks eyes with me. My heart hurts for him when I look into those beautiful brown eyes. They're so devoid of any meaning - so dead and hopeless that nothing will ever bring life to them again.

"I'm going to help you escape," I say, pulling off my shirt. I quickly wrap it around his waist and tie it securely. "This isn't much, but at least you won't leave as degraded as he's made you. Follow me."

He nods as we walk back toward the line that divides Pater's property from the woods and I glance at the door.

Empty.

Good.

"When I get to the door, I want you to run as fast as you can. Do you understand? Run away from this terrible fucking place. I'll cover for you. I'll tell him that you were far beyond reproach and I killed you as a mercy. I'll tell him I buried your body under Laura's. He'll believe me. He has to believe me."

With as much as I hate to admit it to myself, killing Eloy would actually be the kinder mercy than letting him run away. He has no chance of a normal life outside of Pater's rule and he won't know where to go, but I have to try.

"Come on, this is our only shot at this. Don't worry about any of us, just fucking run as soon as I get to the door, okay?"

He nods and slowly begins to follow me toward the back of the house. As soon as I reach the door, I turn slightly and nod, but just as Eloy begins to run, an upstairs window opens.

"That's a bad fucking idea, kid."

Nausea quickly overcomes me as I glance up and see Pater at the upstairs window. What makes my blood turn cold, what makes Eloy stop running, is when we see he has Vaughn in the window with him.

"Come on up. It looks like we need to have a family meeting. And you should probably get a move on. I'm getting hard just thinking of all the possibilities," he says, giving me a menacing smile.

"No!"

I push the back door almost off its hinges and begin to run back up to Pater's room. Eloy is behind me. I can hear his feet slapping the floor as he desperately tries to keep up with my frantic pace.

And just as I make it to the top landing, I can hear Vaughn let out a pained scream.

I'm too late.

CHAPTER 7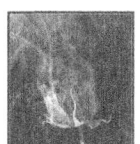

I DAMN near end up barreling through the door, and I would have been successful had Pater not left it open. Instead of entering heroically, I end up stumbling over the surprise of a door slightly ajar and almost fall on my face.

"Are you okay?" I ask Vaughn once I regain my balance.

He glances quickly at Pater and nods. Eloy enters the room behind me and walks toward his brother. They embrace each other as he begins to quietly weep into his arms.

"You're a man now, kid. Finally got some hair on your balls! How does it feel?" Pater asks him with a wide, shit-eating grin on his face.

I shoot him a dirty look which he chooses to ignore as he sits down on the window ledge. It wouldn't take much to rid us of this plague. I could run at him and shove him out the window and he would break his neck when he hit the pavement below, but would he die? Would it be enough to kill him?

"Oh, you've got that look on your face again, Joce.

Thinking of a way to kill me, huh?" he asks with a chuckle as his grin widens, and he crosses his arms over his chest.

Pater has always said that he can read our minds, that he knows what's in our deepest thoughts, and that there are no secrets we can keep from him. Every time I've thought of ending this so far, he's proven his word on that.

"No," I reply, letting out a long suffering sigh.

"No..." his voice trails off and he raises an eyebrow. I have to fight the urge to roll my eyes so that he doesn't end up smacking them out of my head.

"No *Pater*," I amend through gritted teeth.

"You're so pretty when you're behaving," he remarks in a much softer tone. The way the words slide from his tongue, knowing the venom that he usually spews, doesn't move a goddamn thing inside of me. To be honest, I think it's meant to be a compliment, but coming from him it has about the same effect as salt in an open wound.

"Come here, baby girl," he says, holding a hand out toward me.

I don't move right away. In fact, I'm hesitant because I don't know if he plans on throwing me out of the window, like I did him.

"I'm not gonna hurt you, Jocelyn. Come here," he says again, his tone hardening slightly. I shoot a quick glance at Vaughn and Eloy before I make my way toward him.

I take his hand and allow him to intertwine his fingers with mine as he looks into my eyes. There's almost a soft calmness to them, like he wants me to learn to trust him. Like he hasn't spent the entire time here trying to destroy the three of us. Like he's worth so much more than just being feared.

"Hi," he whispers softly. I'm afraid for the boys and myself, because I've never seen this almost human side of

Pater before. He seems more like a man now than someone consumed with being a completely jaded and sick motherfucker.

But what honestly worries me the most is that the way he holds my gaze and gently strokes the top of my hands with his thumbs is causing my body to relax. My guard is going down and I find myself feeling safe for the first time since I've been here.

"Hi," I reply, almost shyly.

Look away, Joce.

I turn my eyes down from his gaze and let out a small, shuddery sigh. I don't like this feeling, not when there's so much he needs to be held accountable for. And definitely not when I still have children to protect from his insane Messiah complex.

"I wanna talk to you privately after we're done here," he says, pulling me against him and nuzzling my ear with his lips. The stubble makes me shiver slightly and I nod. I feel the smallest glimmer of hope that maybe he'll let us all go without punishment, but I know better.

He chuckles as he spins my body around, almost in a pirouette, then moves over to sit me next to him on the window.

"Eloy," he begins in his fatherly tone, "Where were you off to just now?"

"I just wanted to see how fast he could run," I interject, wringing my hands.

"Let him answer for himself," Pater says sternly, giving me a side-long glance. I bite my lip and nod, watching the grin return to his face as he looks back at Eloy expectantly.

"I've never really been outside by myself," he replies quietly as he wipes away the last of his tears. "I just wanted to look around."

"And you encouraged that, huh? Damn," Pater asks, shaking his head slightly as he looks at me, the grin slowly starting to fade. "I expected better from you."

I've disappointed him and it cuts me deeply that he's suggested as much. I don't want to be here, I don't want to be his fucking slave, and I don't want the boys to be harmed, but to know that I've disappointed him completely decimates the little bit of hope I have left.

"Alright, well," he says, as he gets to his feet, "I'm not going to do anything to you tonight, boy. You can go back down to your room and you can fucking stay there until I decide I want to see your face again."

Eloy lets out a sound of relief that resembles something like another strangled sob, and Pater sighs loudly.

"Stop fucking crying already!" he shouts at Eloy as he quickly makes his escape from the room.

"He's just a child," I say quietly.

"Jocelyn, I'm trying really hard right now, so shut your fucking mouth," Pater barks at me. "You - get out. I'll come talk to you later about something. You get to bear the brunt of the bullshit these two tried to pull," he says to Vaughn as he nods toward the door.

I can see the color drain from the older boy's face, but he nods and leaves, giving me one last glance over his shoulder on the way out.

As soon as Vaughn is gone, Pater walks toward the door and closes it firmly. He lingers there for a moment, his hand on the white wood, and hangs his head. I don't know what he plans on doing to me, but I have absolutely no problem throwing myself out the window.

"But you won't, because you won't leave those boys behind," he says, straightening himself up and turning to face me. He leans against the door and crosses his arms over his chest, a vacant expression in his eyes.

"How do you do that?" I asked him quietly.

"No questions. Don't do that. Don't be a bitch right now, not when I'm trying so hard to be a good man," he says, shaking his head vehemently.

"I'm sorry," I say again, for what seems the millionth time in my captivity.

"I'm going to tell you right now that when I'm done with that little shit, you're going to hate me. More than you already do. And don't tell me you don't, because I can see it in your eyes. You've been plotting against me for a long time, Jocelyn, but we've still got our *List of Tasks*, don't we? We have to finish our little game before you decide to get brave enough to make a move against me."

"I'm not going to," I say, shaking my head. "I'm not! I wouldn't!"

"You won't while they're still alive. *They* give you a reason to hold back, but I don't want that anymore. I don't want a wife that doesn't know how to take what she wants. I want you to show me you're strong enough, that you're capable of this life. We can always have more kids, but I can't have another *you*."

Pater moves away from the door and walks over to where I'm still sitting. His steps are slow, deliberate, and so fucking enticing.

"Do you really want to die before I've had a chance to fill your womb?" he asks in a whisper as he places his hands on my sides. "Don't you want to know what it's gonna feel like to grow swollen with my child? Hm? Don't you want to know what it's going to feel like when I cut the little bastard out of you?"

"What?" I ask, looking up at him. I couldn't have heard him correctly. That's too sick, even for him.

"The only reason I kept those two around was to see what kind of mother you would be," he says softly, his lips curling into a smile. "And you'll be a damn fine one if I do say so myself. We just have to get rid of them, and then we can start over. Just the two of us for a while."

"Why?" I ask, my voice shaking.

"Because that's how it's always been, baby girl. Now when I go visit Vaughn later, I don't want you to cry or be upset or even think about it. I do want you to take care of another task for me, though. Can you do that for me?"

His breath is hot on my face as he rubs his lips gently against mine, before pulling back and leaning down to look into my face.

"I want you to get rid of Eloy. We don't need him anymore."

I let out a shaky breath and choke back my sob. If I do this, it'll be merciful, I know it will. If I don't, he's going to die anyway.

"Yes, Pater," I agree in a shaky whisper.

CHAPTER 8

He looks so peaceful as he sleeps; like a cherub, ignorant of the dangerous plot that's been laid out behind his back. He doesn't know that his life is meant to come to an end soon, and I won't wake him to tell him either.

I gently lay a hand on his leg and his body shivers, but he doesn't wake up. It's a natural reaction to being touched in this godforsaken place. You can wince, you can shiver, you can whimper, and you can cry, but you can never say no.

It's been a couple of hours since I've entered the boy's room, and this is the first time I've actually touched him since being here. I've only just sat on the edge of his bed, watching his chest rise with each breath he takes in, and lower shakily with each breath he lets out.

To know that I'm here to make sure his breathing comes to an end is more of a psychological pain than anything else, but that's always been the main point of any game Pater decides to play.

"I'll either break your mind or I'll break your spirit, but rest assured that I will fucking break you."

Those words have never left me. Ever since I ascended, so to speak, to the role of wife and mother, it was a credo he would repeat to me almost daily until I accepted the fact that I would never be able to leave him.

Not on my own terms, at least.

Of course, his warnings have always been sugar coated with assurances that he would never harm me more than I can bear, but what he asks of me now is just too cruel to comprehend.

I hate myself for agreeing to this, but he'll go much more peacefully at my hands than he would Pater's.

Leaning forward, I brush his hair out of his face and give him a gentle kiss on his cheek before I reach for one of the pillows on the bed. The one lying next to his head. The one that won't wake him if I try to pry it out from beneath him. The one I'll use to steal his last breath.

"Good night, my sweet boy," I whisper, a tear rolling down my cheek.

With one swift movement, I place the pillow over his head and press down as hard as I can. Since he's asleep, he's unaware what's happening, but it doesn't take long for his body to react to the lack of oxygen and his will to survive surfaces.

Eloy attempts to fight me off and he's so valiant in his efforts that I almost stop. But I know this is what Pater wants, and it might spare Vaughn a similar fate, so I get onto the bed and straddle him, pushing down with the weight of my body to hold him in place.

"Please. Don't make this harder than it has to be. Go back to sleep, sweet boy," I whisper, pushing down harder.

His muffled cries for help are starting to fade, but he's not resigned to his fate; not yet. He continues to claw at my hands, trying his damnedest to get me to stop.

"I'm going to miss you so much," I manage to choke out as I push down even harder. "Please remember that I love you. Please."

His body is beginning to relax now and his breaths come in three more heaping gasps before there's silence. There's no more fighting, no more hoping that this isn't really happening to him. And one less son to keep safe.

A wail escapes from deep within me. It's loud and desperate, and so heartbreaking that when I collapse against Eloy's lifeless body, I know it will take the strongest of men to pull me off him.

The door opens a moment later and I can hear the heavy footsteps of Pater as he walks toward the bed.

"Come on. Off," he says quietly as he grips my arms and pries the pillow from my hands. His small act of kindness is to leave it balanced on Eloy's face so that I don't have to see what I've done to him.

"Alright, stop crying," he says, as he uses all his strength to pull me off the boy. He struggles a bit and I can attribute that to a mother's love for her son. For not wanting to be parted from him. Even though it was my own hands that extinguished his life, I felt I needed to still keep him safe from Pater.

"Joce. A little help here. Come on," he grunts as he gives me one hard, final yank and rips me away from the shell of Eloy.

He envelopes me in his arms and gently places a hand on the back of my head, holding me closely against his body. He's rocking slowly in an attempt to soothe the pain he's put me through, but nothing will ever be enough to wash this horrendous misdeed from my hands.

I've earned my place in Hell for this and I will gladly burn for as long as I need to purge myself of this sin.

Pater pulls me off the bed and walks us toward the door. He has to use his foot to push it all the way open because he knows that if he lets me go, I'll attempt to take my life in any way I can.

"Vaughn!" he calls out.

I begin to cry, a brand new cascade of heartache washing over me, as I try to take some comfort in knowing that my oldest child is still alive.

"Yes Pater?" his voice calls out vacantly as he approaches us.

"Take care of that," he says to him.

I dig my hands into his chest, crumpling his shirt between my fingers. A silent plea to spare Vaughn from having to see his own brother dead, but it will fall on deaf ears. It always does.

"E...Eloy?" Vaughn asks uncertainly, stepping into the room.

"He can't h...hear you," Pater mocks. "Now clean this shit up. I've gotta take care of your mother. Meet us downstairs when you're done. And if you try to run," Pater breaks off with a chuckle, "well. I'm sure you know the price now."

I pull away from his chest and look at Vaughn through eyes hazed with tears, attempting to catch his glance, but he refuses to look at me.

I don't blame him.

I'm supposed to be the one keeping them safe, and now he knows I'm just as dangerous as the man keeping us here as his prisoners. And that makes us all as equally responsible for the torments that will unfold next.

CHAPTER 9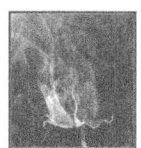

I'VE FALLEN into a world of half sleep. A place where Eloy is still alive, but the hand of Pater still keeps me awake as he gently strokes the side of my face, reminding me that the world I'm trying to surrender to is nothing more than a lie.

My head is resting comfortably on Pater's lap and I can hear him whistling softly. It's just another ploy to keep me awake, but I don't want to dream. I honestly don't want to be in a place where the life I've just taken stares at me with damning eyes, asking me why I betrayed him.

It's a bit of a conundrum, really. To be in the realm of sleep where I can hold Eloy safely in my arms is more of a punishment than anything the man that helped give him life could ever dream of.

Keeping me as awake long as he possibly can helps me hold on to the thin shred of sanity I have left, but I don't know how much more I can take of these endless games. These *Tasks*, as he calls them; only two have been accomplished, and I can tell there's still so much more that needs to be done.

"Took you long enough," he says quietly.

I don't attempt to sit up to look at Vaughn. The whole point of him coming into the room and seeing me in the distress I had left myself in was part of Pater's plan. He'll never trust me again, and I can't fault him for that.

I'd take my own fucking life if it weren't for Vaughn.

"Sit down," Pater said to him, still gently stroking my hair. "I've got a little job for you."

"No," I say softly. It takes every last ounce of energy I have to push myself off Pater's lap and sit up, but when I look into his eyes, I know that any anger I incur over what I say will be worth it. "No more games. No more tasks. No more jobs. Please, just let this be the end."

"That's not how this works and you know it, Joce. It's what you signed up for and until I say it's over, we keep going," he says, shaking his head at me. He turns his gaze back toward Vaughn as he scratches his chin. The gaze isn't returned; if anything, Vaughn looks like he's already given up and would happily collapse and die if it were allowed.

"Pater," I plead, putting a hand on his thigh. "Just me. This can all end right now with just me. I surrender to you. Let the boy go."

A grin starts to slide over his lips. I used the words he's been trying to get out of me for so long, and I hope that by giving myself over completely to his fucking whim that it might spare the only child we have left.

"Oh yeah?" he asks, leaning back against the cough. "And all I have to do is let the boy go?"

"Yes," I say quietly.

I hope that if he agrees to this, one day Vaughn will look back on me as the mother that tried to protect him for as long as I could. Not as the mother who murdered his brother and became no better than the man he fears so much.

"I'll think about it," he says brightly, getting to his feet. "Come on, kid. Time to put you to work."

"Wait!"

I quickly get to my feet and Pater lets out a sigh before pushing me back down.

"Stay," he commands, holding up one finger. "I'm not gonna hurt him, so I need you to just calm down and stay fucking put. I'll be back."

Vaughn quietly begins to follow Pater out of the room, and even though I know it'll fall on deaf ears, I can't let this possibly be the last time I see him without saying what I feel in my heart.

"I love you, Vaughn," I call out to him urgently.

He doesn't return the sentiment. He doesn't even cast me one final glance, and even though Pater said he's not going to hurt him, I can't help but feel like this is the last time I'll ever see him again.

"Wait," Pater says to him sternly. "Your mother is talking to you; show a little respect, huh?"

Vaughn clenches his fists by his sides and turns slowly to look at me. We finally lock eyes, but the look he gives me tells me I've lost him.

"She's *not* my mother."

CHAPTER 10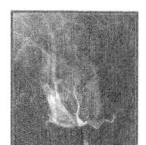

THE PAIN of his words wounds me as deeply as what I was forced to do to Eloy, but it's because he speaks a bitter truth. An honesty that is so raw and uncommon in this house that hearing it for the first time since this entire charade started is like a blow to the heart.

I don't know how long it's been since they've left this room. Time means nothing when everything you love has collapsed around you because of your own actions. When your will is no longer your own and you're forced to survive by any means dictated to you, you do what you must.

What happens when you choose to fight against the will of Pater is far worse than what I did to Eloy, and what he's most likely doing to Vaughn. For now, I'll comply. I'll listen. I'll take every blow to my heart until it finally gives out, and because of my choices, I'll survive.

"Hey, you alright?"

A strong hand rests gently on my shoulder and I shudder. Not out of revulsion, but the need to feel his touch comforting me. Pater may be an evil man when it comes to many things, myself included, but he always attempts to make sure I'm okay.

"I'll be fine," I whisper as a tear rolls down my cheek.

He crouches down and uses his hand to gently lift my face up. He's searching my eyes, looking for some sign of deception, but he'll find none.

I *will* be fine.

I always am.

"Come on. You can stay in my bed tonight," he says, gently pulling me off the ground.

"I don't..." *want to,* I finish to myself. While I appreciate his comforting hands on me, that's all I want. I don't want to feel him roughly moving inside of me until he's satisfied himself with no regard for how much it hurts me.

"I'm not looking for anything tonight, Joce. Especially not any arguments," he replies tiredly. "I just want you to have somewhere comfortable to sleep."

I let him get me to my feet, but he can tell I have no intention of following him.

"Alright, you've got two choices," he says, rubbing his stubble irritably. "You can sleep in my bed, or I can throw you back into that hole. Ladies' choice."

Normally the answer would be simple and instantaneous, but there's nothing normal about this anymore. Eloy is dead. Vaughn is... I don't even know where the hell Vaughn is. And the man that took him from me doesn't seem like he's going to talk about it, either.

My heart is telling me to accept the oubliette. After all, I still owe him a day in the darkness and solitude, but my mind is telling me to stay in his bed. I won't be of any use to Vaughn if I'm tired and hungry, and being in the house will afford me the chance to rest and eat when Pater falls asleep.

"I have a condition," I say, as I wipe away tears. "Will you meet it?"

Pater looks at me through narrowed eyes, but nods in acceptance. Since this is his home and we abide by his rules, he's not bound to any promise he makes. I know it just as much as he does, but I can only hope he'll allow me this small token of kindness.

"I want to know what you've done with Vaughn," I reply, crossing my arms over my chest and meeting his narrowed eyes with a stubborn stare.

A slow, malicious grin spreads across his handsome face and I can feel myself starting to waiver in the mock confidence I've presented.

"I dumped him," he says, chuckling. "If he doesn't have respect for his mother, he definitely doesn't have any for his father. Can't keep a little shit like that around."

In an odd moment of clarity, I'm surprised that I feel nothing. No more sorrow, no more hope, no more hatred toward Pater. And what I feel least of all as his words ring through my mind is my soul.

It's gone now.

All of it.

By taking both the boys from me, he's taken everything. It's just me and Pater now, and by his assuming that he's relieved me of the duties of being a mother, he's given me something else I haven't felt in years.

The will to fight.

CHAPTER 11

Pater has his arm wrapped tightly enough around me that I can't leave the bed without him knowing, but loose enough that I'm free to move around until I'm comfortable.

"Hey, Joce?" he asks, punctuating his question with a wide yawn.

"Yes Pater?" I ask tiredly.

I'm holding his arm tightly, almost as though I'm trying to pull something good out of the cesspool that he's become, but I know it's all in vain.

"When I said I dumped Vaughn? You didn't ask where."

"It's not my place to question you, Pater," I reply quietly.

He chuckles as he nuzzles up closer to me. "I'm glad you chose to come with me. I didn't want to put you in the oubliette. It would have made things too crowded."

"What?" I ask in confusion.

"And I'm not exactly sure he's alive, anyway. I did give him one hell of a push, after all," he admits sleepily.

It's another mind game; a trick. If I believe that Vaughn

is alive, he knows I won't resist him, but if I believe he's dead, I'll gladly go to my death and take Pater with me.

"What's a girl to do?" he asks in a sing-song voice. He chuckles as he begins to run his fingers up and down my arm. The slight tingling sensation, the shock-wave his touch sends throughout my body, makes me both sick and almost happy.

Almost.

"I guess we'll just have to wait and see," I reply as evenly as I can. It takes more bravery than I've ever mustered before to lay a challenge so boldly at his feet, and another chuckle is his response. He's accepted I'll do what I must in order to end this entire fucking charade, and I know he won't make it easy.

"Tomorrow, baby girl. We'll worry about all of this tomorrow," he says, sliding his arm around my waist and pulling me closer to him still.

"And the day after that?" I ask, turning to face him.

"Will there be another day?" he inquires, looking into my eyes.

"You're leaving it up to me?" I ask in surprise.

A smile spreads across his full lips. He turns himself onto his back and folds an arm underneath his head. Taking a deep breath and letting it out, he keeps his eyes trained on the ceiling and I can tell he is very carefully picking his next words.

"Honestly? No. I prefer if you would just go along and say there will be another day after tomorrow, and a day after that. I know this hasn't been easy for you, but at some point, I'm really gonna need you to just *try*. Think you can do that for me?"

The truth is that I *have* been trying. I've done everything Pater has asked of me, and he still wants more. There's no satisfying a man of his appetites, regardless of what they are, and my only reasons for even caring are either dead or dying.

And here I am: lying in his bed like a whore, ready to please the man who bought her affections for the night.

"Pater?" I ask, as I sit up in the bed and pull my knees up to my chest.

"Yes, Jocelyn?"

"Can I speak freely?"

"Yes."

I take a deep breath and wrap my arms around my knees, resting my face against them so I can look at him. His reactions never lie; he may have a serpent's tongue, but his face will always betray him and tell me the truth.

"Why are you doing this? Wouldn't it be so much easier to kill me too?" I ask quietly.

He closes his eyes for a moment and when he opens them, I can almost swear I see tears forming. But Pater doesn't cry; he's the man of this house, and the only emotions he's ever shown us are the ones he chooses. Crying is for the weak, according to him, and Pater is far from weak.

"Because the three of you have always been my favorites," he replies irritably. "Now go the fuck to sleep or I'm dumping you in the fucking ground with Vaughn."

His attempt at a threat actually makes me laugh. To think I would fear death at this point when I would gladly decompose by my son's side is laughable to me.

"Don't bother. I'll throw myself in the fucking pit," I say, getting off the bed and walking toward the door.

"Hey. HEY!" he bellows as soon as I open it.

I turn and give him a sharp glare, watching his face go from anger to amusement in a matter of seconds. He pats the empty side of the bed next to him where I was sitting not moments before, and I sigh.

A part of me wants to see tomorrow and the day after, but the heroine in me wants to see this come to an end.

"You coming? Or do I have to fetch you?" he asks, tilting his head to the side, the grin widening over his face.

It's maddening.

This entire fucking thing is maddening because I do love him in a way, but I loathe him just the same.

One more night.

One more day.

When I wake up in the morning, I'll have decided if it's worth seeing the day after.

CHAPTER 12

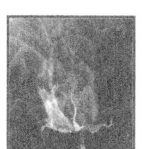

I WAKE up with a terrible headache and the weight of the world on top of me. It's astounding to me that I was able to sleep at all, but now I'm awake I find myself in a terrible situation.

Pater's face is hovering inches from mine, and his breathing is slightly labored. It's not the weight of the world I feel lying on top of me, it's the weight of the man that holds me here against my will. He's pushing his cock inside me, slowly, deliberately; in a way that only Pater can. He wanted me to wake up to find him on top of me. He wanted me to feel every thrust he's been lovingly pushing into me while I slept.

He wanted me to experience everything he promised me he didn't want the night before, and it's because he wants me to understand that he's the one who will decide if tomorrow comes or not.

"You're so pretty when you sleep," he whispers, brushing his lips against mine.

I hate my body for reacting to this. I didn't consent to this. I didn't want to wake up to him fucking me, but I did consent to be in his bed, so I shouldn't have expected anything less.

"Pater's almost done, baby girl," he says softly, as his breathing becomes even more labored.

He gently places his forehead against mine as I lie beneath him, pinned to the bed and waiting for him to fill me with his seed. It's what he wants most of all. He wants me to become a mother – he always has – I've just been able to convince him otherwise, since we still had Vaughn and Eloy.

It takes no more than three thrusts before I feel the warmth of him spilling into me. He lets out a loud moan as he finishes and lets his body fall on mine, his head lying on my shoulder.

"You're going to make such an amazing mother again someday. You did such a wonderful job with those two little bastards," he says gently.

"Thank you, Pater," I say quietly, fighting tears that are dangerously close to spilling over.

I place my hands on his shoulders and attempt to give him a gentle shove, but he's still hard and still inside me, showing no signs of moving.

"Not yet, Joce. Let's just lay here like this a little while longer," he says happily, turning his head up toward me and nuzzling my neck with his lips.

I can't help but wonder if this is what love is like. To have someone who would do anything to keep you, no matter the cost, with no care of what the outside world would think.

I finally feel him become flaccid and he pulls himself out of me, turning his back to me as he gets comfortable on the bed.

Maybe it's not love, after all.

"When did you start to hate me?" he asks quietly. "And don't lie to me, please."

The question takes me by surprise, because I was always so damn sure he never cared what I thought of him. His demand for the truth tells me he'll do his mind reading trick that still fascinates me.

"When you made me your wife," I reply bluntly.

Pater sighs loudly and rolls onto his back. "Would you have preferred that I just killed you instead?"

"Yes," I admit softly.

"Sorry to disappoint you," he spits back bitterly. He sits up and runs his hands over his face, then sighs as he glances at me. "You have to understand something. I've always loved you the most. That day that I cut you from your worthless mother was the happiest day of my life. You stopped crying as soon as I held you against me, and the way you looked at me..." Pater's words trail off for a moment as he shakes his head, "I knew right then and there that we would be something great someday."

"If I knew that this is what my life was going to become, along with Vaughn and Eloy's, I should have just drawn the blades across our throats when you took us out of Mama," I spit back.

His desperate attempt at trying to become some kind of human right before my eyes are falling on deaf ears. I've had enough of these fucking games, and with as much as I want it to be over, I want my pound of flesh first. The only way to get that from him is to antagonize him to the point of no return.

"'Mama,'" he repeats in a mocking tone. "She was worthless. The only thing that bitch was good for was giving me three kids, and then, once Eloy was born, I was done with her. She died the way she came into this world: screaming and covered in blood."

I attempt to push myself off the bed, but he grips me by my arm and pulls me right back next to him.

"It doesn't have to be this way with us, Jocelyn. Ever since I put you in your mother's womb, I knew you would take her place. Like she had taken the place of the wife before her. I think we work, don't you? You're a pain in the ass and I know how to handle you accordingly. I like these games, and being inside you is the most amazing thing I've ever felt in my life. Fuck society and their rules; we're meant to be together," he says with his damn grin sitting on his ruggedly handsome face.

The same face that was vaguely reflected in Vaughn, and almost an exact match to Eloy's. The eyes I'm looking into are passed down through blood, and that smile is something I used to wear before all this started. But I have to remind myself that this hasn't been the face of my father for a long time; it's always been the face of the man who destroys everything he can't control, and uses people until he gets bored with them.

"How much longer is this going to drag on, Pater? How much longer am I stuck here being your wife?" I ask him irritably.

"Until you have my baby, of course," he replies as his grin widens. "Then we'll see what fate has in store for you."

That's been his plan this entire time. That's been his motive in every wife he's taken.

Isolate the body.

Break the soul.

Break the spirit.

Fill them with his child and if the child is up to his standards, kill her and replace her with the next one.

CHAPTER 13

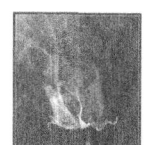

PATER IS SITTING at the dining room table, reading his newspaper and occasionally sipping on his coffee. He's invited me to sit with him, but so far the offer of food has not been made, and I'm close to snatching that fucking paper from his hands and eating it.

I don't know when the last time is that I ate. It must have been a few days ago, when one of the boys dropped some scraps into the darkness, and with as unbelievable as it may seem, that's usually enough to hold me over for a little while.

I have to check the oubliette.

Clearing my throat, I begin to drum my fingers along the tabletop. It's a small enough distraction that he peers at me over the top of his newspaper, before he reaches over and puts his hand on mine to stop me.

"What's up?" he asks curiously.

"I'm more worried about what's down," I reply tiredly.

"What?"

A rare look of confusion crosses his face, and I sigh as I slide my hand away from underneath his. I glance out the window behind him, and don what I hope is a meaningful look, but if he understands what I want, he's choosing to ignore it.

"Well?" he asks, shaking out his newspaper. He licks his thumb as he flips the page and keeps his eyes trained on me expectantly.

"I'm hungry," I admit quietly. It's not exactly a lie, but it's not the entire truth. I *am* hungry; however, I'm more concerned with taking my scraps to Vaughn.

If he's still alive.

"You can eat," he says with a nod as he turns his eyes back to his article. I almost faint with relief, because he's never given us food so easily. I think it has to be because he's already attempting to make me pregnant, so it makes him slightly kinder.

I know better, though. I know that trusting a man like Pater, no matter what the circumstance, is a more dangerous game than anything he could possibly dream up.

"Thank you," I reply softly.

I get to my feet and walk toward the counter where there is still one steak left on a greasy plate. There's a spoonful of home fries and one strip of bacon, too. I quickly pile it onto a clean plate and, as I'm placing it into the microwave for a quick reheat, I hear Pater slide his chair back.

In a matter of a few steps, he's standing next to me, washing his hands in the sink, and I can feel myself start to tremble again. I know he feels my fear when he gives me a sidelong glance and smirks. He doesn't say anything, though. He dries his hands off on a dishtowel, pulls the drawer open next to me, and fishes out a fork. Once the microwave dings, he opens the door, pulls out the plate and takes it back to the table.

I'm two seconds away from throwing the mother of all tantrums, when I see that he's set the fork and plate where I had been sitting. As he makes his way back to his seat and newspaper, he clears his throat and continues to read.

"Make sure you eat every last thing on that plate, baby girl. I know you kids had some kind of system with whatever you swore you just couldn't eat, but don't forget: you're the only kid now."

He's lying.

I know he's lying because I can still feel something in my heart that's only lived there since I was put in charge of Eloy and Vaughn.

"Hey, don't you have a birthday coming up soon?" he asks conversationally.

"Yes."

"Any idea what you'll be wanting?"

"I haven't thought about it," I say, finally taking a bite of the steak. My stomach growls loudly and Pater chuckles, but makes no further mention of the disruptive sound.

"Well, how long do we have until it's time to celebrate, Joce?" he asks, setting his paper down and smoothing out the pages with his hands.

With another sigh and shrug, I take a second bite of the steak. It doesn't matter how long I feel we have, or how long it will actually be until my birthday. The only thing that matters is when Pater will be ready to dedicate a moment to the day. It doesn't hold any special meaning to me anymore, my birthday. If anything, it's a day I've come to loathe. I wasn't born into normal surroundings.

I was born into a world where evil existed long before I was conceived, and where innocence goes to die.

"How old are you these days, Jocelyn?" Pater asks, resting his chin in the palm of his hand. He glances up at me when I don't answer him right away, and I'm terrified he's caught me scraping food off the plate into my lap.

"I'll be twenty, I think," I reply, as I grab the fork and slice another piece off the steak. I'm not sure what it was exactly that I managed to scoop off the plate, but I hadn't expected him to ask me something so personal. It's not like Pater to give a shit, and he should know the answer to that question anyway.

"Huh," he says indifferently. "That's about the same age your mother was when she had Vaughn. Eh, I might have to sit through more boys again."

"Pater?" I ask carefully. Now he's mentioned Mama, I have a few questions of my own. "May I ask you something?"

He looks at me for a moment as he considers my request. He sucks his teeth before turning his eyes back down to the newspaper.

"Sure, kid."

"If I'm the oldest, why *did* you keep getting Mama pregnant?"

Pater lets out a sigh as he closes his newspaper and runs a hand over his face. The good thing is that he doesn't look angry at my question; he actually looks thoughtful.

"Nothing in the world is more beautiful than seeing the woman you love swollen with your child. Your mother was definitely a good looking gal, and even though I had already fallen in love with you by that point, I wanted to be able to get a couple of more years out of her. I knew I would have to wait a long time before I could make you my wife, and she knew it too, so she did everything she could to keep me satisfied until I was bored with her. There's only so many times you can keep fucking the same hole before it becomes redundant, you know?"

He's looking at me knowingly, and I know I've still got at least one seed's worth of growing to do before he decides if he's going to kill me or keep me.

"Don't worry about that shit right now, though. I just told you I've been in love with you for your entire life. I have no intentions of getting rid of you. I think my grooming the next bride days are done. It'll be you and me and our children until we both die," he says, with that damn wide grin spreading across his face.

I sit back and fold my arms over my chest, taking him in. Years mean nothing to me, because I stopped counting them when I turned fifteen. That's when he took me as his wife and I lost the title of daughter, but I'm becoming more and more curious the older I get, and I have one more question for him.

"Pater?" I ask softly.

"Yes, baby girl?" he asks, still grinning.

"How old are you?"

He chuckles and hangs his head for a moment, before glancing back up at me. His grin has faded into a simple smile and he doesn't answer me right away.

"Well, that depends, I guess," he replies mischievously.

I raise an eyebrow but say nothing. I don't want to continue to ask him questions and anger him instead of just getting a simple answer.

"Will it make you love me any less? Assuming that you do love me, that is," he says with a smirk.

I *do* love Pater. I will never deny that, but I don't love him in the manner that he wants me to. I love him as a father who lost his way long before I was born and needs saving, even though I know he doesn't want to be saved.

"No," I say softly.

He grins, gets up from his chair, and walks around the

table toward me. Pater puts an arm around my shoulder and kisses the top of my head gently.

"Good girl. I knew you'd always love me as much as I love you," he says gently. "You about done with that?"

Before I have a chance to answer, or save any more food for Vaughn, he takes the plate from the table and dumps the remnants into the trash can. I use his distracted moments to shove the bit of food I've managed to scavenge into the bottom of my shirt, and roll it up just enough to make sure it can't fall out.

"You can go out and throw him what you've saved," he says with a tired sigh. "If he's still alive, I'm sure he'll appreciate it."

And with that, he walks out of the kitchen leaving me with one last unanswered question, and the moment I need to go save Vaughn.

CHAPTER 14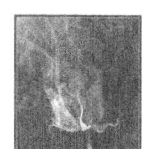

He's going to kill me.

I know he is, because that's the end game. No matter what he says, no matter how much he professes his love for me, I know it's the only thing that can come of this.

I'll never be the wife he wants me to be, and I'll never be more than a scared child praying for the safety of the children forced underneath her rule, instead of being by her side as it should have been in a normal world.

To survive much longer than I know I'm meant to, I'll have to be more careful. He knows too much, sees more than I think he does, and he'll stop me when he feels I'm getting ready to strike.

He'll be the end of me. He'll send me to the afterlife with a smile on his face once he has another child to hold in his arms, but I will take a part of his soul with me.

I won't think about it now. I still have Vaughn to worry about, and I don't think he knows that Eloy is still alive somewhere in the woods. That's where Vaughn would have taken him, because that's their safe place away from this hell we have to endure.

I can see the top of the oubliette from here and I stop walking, taking a deep breath. I have to prepare for the worst, because if I hope for the best and it's not there, it'll crush me completely.

I've managed to save one son so far by putting on one hell of a show, and I know I won't be able to handle not saving the second.

Please, I pray silently as I kneel down by the broken door that sits on top. I close my eyes for a moment, trying to find the courage to do what I know has to be done, to calm my nerves and steel myself against what I hope I don't see, before I finally pull the door open.

It's dark in the oubliette, but that's the point. To be encased below the ground in the darkness, with only the occasional chirping of birds, or the crickets at night; the punishment always fits the crime, and if Pater has banished you to the underground dungeon, the transgression must have been severe.

It's my second home because I defy him so frequently to protect Vaughn and Eloy, but I don't mind it as much as he thinks I do. From what I know so far, he hasn't laid his hands upon them in any form of sexual deviance, and because of that, when I'm in the dark, I sleep more soundly than I do in his bed.

It's the days leading up to my freedom that always make me anxious. That's when I lose the most sleep, because I have to face my children and hope they're still safe from having to feel his touch.

A pocket of air was enough to save Eloy; maybe the will to survive the fall will have been enough to save Vaughn.

I let out my breath in a rush of quick air as I lean over the side. I can't see him from the top of the pit, which means he's huddled in a corner, or dead where he's fallen.

"Vaughn?" I call down quietly, my voice cracking. I take a deep breath, clear my throat, and try again. "Vaughn? It's me; Jocelyn."

Silence greets me in return. I blink furiously to keep tears from falling and call out his name again.

"Vaughn?"

I feel like the world is slowly starting to crush me into the ground when I still receive no answer, and just as I'm ready to accept that he's gone, I can almost swear that I hear a slight shifting sound at the bottom of the pit.

"I have food!" I call back down as I unroll the bottom of my shirt and drop it into the pit. The sound I heard could very well be the rats that make the inside of the walls their home, but I'm too stubborn to give up all my hope until I know for sure.

My entire problem is that I'm blinded by the one thing I refuse to let go of. Hope that Vaughn is still alive. Hope that Eloy is safe, wherever he is. Hope that Pater will see the madness in this entire scheme and let us go.

My own worst enemy is the only fucking thing I keep hanging on to. If I learn to let go, I know things will become clearer; this will all end the way it's meant to, and not how Pater wants it to.

There are no further sounds coming from the darkness below, and there's no sign of movement. If Vaughn is still alive down there, he doesn't trust me enough to let me know.

I can't blame him.

He walked into a nightmare, thinking that his younger brother was dead at my hands, but even when he realized he wasn't, he couldn't find it in himself to forgive me for tricking him into thinking otherwise.

I'm okay with it.

I have to be.

If he doesn't trust me, it will only make his will stronger, and maybe it's him and not me who will be the one to end all this.

"Find what you were looking for?"

I jump in complete shock at hearing Pater's voice coming from above me, almost losing ground and falling into the pit, but he's faster and much stronger than me, and manages to pull me back before it happens.

He gets me to my feet, giving me an unbelievably harsh glare, prompting only a nod in return. I won't attempt to mimic the look he's giving me. He's won this round and he knows it, because if he thought otherwise, he would be smiling at me instead of sneering.

"Why are you always so content to defy me?" he asks in a low, even tone.

"What? You told me I could--"

Pater smacks me so violently that I fall back onto the ground and come dangerously close to plummeting into the darkness. He gets on his knees in front of me and grips me tightly by the arms. He makes no move to pull me away from the abysmal opening, instead leaning my body further into it.

"Don't play dumb, Jocelyn. And drop the fucking innocent act. I thought we actually understood each other at this point, but you still seem to be full of games, and we can't have that," he says, as he tips me a little further back.

My hands immediately clench his wrists. If he throws me in, I'm going to make damn sure he comes with me. Ending this now would be premature, but why does he deserve to breathe another breath when those of us that were chosen for this are considered so easily disposable?

I take a deep breath and clench my jaw tightly. The

pressure of being bent in such an unnatural manner is starting to hurt me, but I refuse to let go of his wrists. I'm not as strong as Pater, and I'm not as fast as him, but I hold an equal amount of determination as him, if not more.

"I think we need to go back to the beginning here, Jocelyn. I think we need to go back to the very first Task I gave you, and complete it together," he says meaningfully.

I close my eyes tightly and do my best not to cry. He knows; of course he knows. I was stupid enough to think about how I saved Eloy, and Pater picked it out of my brain.

"Where is he?" he asks, pulling me back toward him. I'm inches from his face now. I know because I can feel his breath on my face, as well as the rage radiating from his body. It's equally terrifying and intoxicating.

"I don't know," I reply truthfully.

"Do you really want it to end like this?" he asks me angrily, giving me one hard shake. "We have plans, Jocelyn, and you're willing to throw it all away on some bastards that aren't worth more than dog shit on the bottom of a shoe? Give me one good reason I shouldn't drop you into this fucking hole."

I take a deep breath and open my eyes. Pater's face is twisted in hideous rage and genuine confusion, and for the slightest of moments I feel bad for betraying him.

My heart aches slightly when I'm confronted by the complete and utter hurt on the face of my own personal devil, knowing now that he's been betrayed.

"Because I'm the only hope you have for a new family," I respond quietly.

He lets out a guffaw, and his hands begin to shake. He knows it's the truth, and that's why I can now openly go against his will. He's laid his cards bare on the table and foolishly told me he needs me, allowing me to use it to my full advantage.

In the rare moment Pater tried to be nothing more than a man in love, he sealed his own fate. He showed me that I'm his weakness, and that he needs me now more than I need him.

Even though the realization hits in this moment, holding me on the brink of life and death, I don't plan on using it to my advantage. Not until I can get Vaughn out of the darkness and make sure that he and Eloy can find their own safety far away from this place.

CHAPTER 15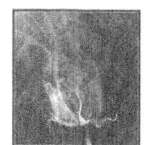

THE SOLES of my feet are scraped raw from walking the property barefoot, since I've agreed to go into the woods with Pater and try to locate the young boy. I figure it's a small price to pay. He says if we find Eloy and finish what I should have done together, he'll assist me with getting Vaughn out of the oubliette.

"I really think we should have Vaughn with us right now," I grumble. "I don't know where he hid Eloy. I don't know if he's even still *here*."

Pater tightens his grip on my arm and shakes his head. "He's still here. Know how I know? Because you don't want to help look for him. You want to pawn this off on Vaughn, and you hoped I would fall for it. I'm not as stupid as you'd like to think I am, Jocelyn. Vaughn earned his time in the hole. Eloy earned his punishment. And you're going to be a good little wife and follow through on what you've promised me."

Pater stops walking abruptly and glances down at me with a devious smirk on his face and cruel intentions in his eyes.

"Tell you what," he says, licking his lips and pulling me toward him. "You help me take care of this, make it all the way it should be again, and I'll take you to see your precious Mama."

I stare at Pater with wide eyes and the most doubt and confusion I've ever felt in my life. How can he take me to see her when he's already told me she's dead?

It has to be where she's buried. That's the only thing that would make sense with a promise like that, isn't it?

"How far in do you think he is?" Pater asks, running his hand down the length of my arm and intertwining his fingers with mine.

I shake my head. I don't know; I really don't. I only assume, as he does, that this is where Eloy would be because it's his favorite place to go when he's allowed outside. Of course, after the debacle with Laura, I honestly doubt that he would want to wallow in whatever memories his mind was forced to create.

"Alright, then you can go first," he says, letting go of my hand and pushing me in front of him. It's not that he's afraid; nothing scares Pater. His intention is that if there is a boy to be found and I'm seen before him, then the confidence would be there to make himself known.

It's a fucking trap, and I'm the bait. What will happen if Eloy steps forward unknowingly? Will Pater end him right then and there, or will he leave the task up to me again? He'll watch, I know he will, and he'll make sure that this time it's done to completion, and the blood I've tried so quietly to save will flow freely over my hands.

"May I have a moment first?" I plead, turning to face him. My hands automatically go to his chest, the safest place I knew as a child, and I can see it still has an effect on him by the rapid way he blinks.

"Only a moment," he agrees with a sharp nod.

I pull away from him and immediately begin to push through the low hanging tree branches and overgrown brush. Pater won't give me more time than he feels is warranted, and I haven't even earned these precious moments he's given me.

He should have just thrown me back into the darkness. If he had thrown me back in after Laura was disposed of, this wouldn't be happening. This is all my fault.

A sob escapes me as I reach the clearing. There's a rather large circle of trees that span a patch of dirt in the woods. A large stone sits in the center of it, with smaller rocks scattered about, almost like a tiny village of sorts.

In the large stone, there's a makeshift chair; a throne. It was there before me and it'll be there after me, because I do not believe him when he tells me I'm the last. It was the chair I sat in after he bound us together as husband and wife. He said the chair held special meaning, that it would help us survive any obstacle set before us, and yet I can't help but find only lies in a truth only he believes.

In that stone chair, there's now a body, slumped over and bleeding. I can't tell if there's still life inside it or not. It's hard to even tell if it's human from where I am, and since I don't have time to waste, I run over and stop just short of it.

It's Eloy.

Bloodied, bruised, damn near mangled, with a pile of rocks sitting around him. He's not alive; he can't be. Vaughn did the one thing I couldn't do. He saved his brother from a life of anguish, misuse, and deviance.

By stoning him to death.

Placing him in the chair afterwards was symbolic. It was his way of saying that the bond between Pater and I isn't real, that I could have saved all of us had I only managed to muster up the courage he was forced to have.

Did he tell his brother he loved him before he killed him? Did he tell his brother that even though this isn't how life is supposed to be, I tried my best and loved him too? Did he tell his brother that, no matter how long it takes, we'll rid the world of Pater and his evil ways? Did he tell his brother that he'll never have to see either of us again in the afterlife?

Did his brother believe him if he did?

Vaughn was the only one he could trust, and since I don't see any evidence that he was bound to the carved chair, I know he willingly gave up his life so that Vaughn wouldn't suffer if Pater found him alive.

He sacrificed himself to save his brother and give Pater one less person to deal with. He saved himself by welcoming death, and I stand here a coward, unwilling to go down as easily because I'm wracked with thoughts of vengeance.

But the first Task is done to completion, as Pater would have seen it, and as I turn to walk away from Eloy's lifeless corpse, I feel rage in the empty spot of my heart that once held unconditional love for him.

My son is dead for the second time, because I wasn't strong enough to put an end to the monster that holds us here.

CHAPTER 16

"Damn."

Pater has finally made it into the clearing and is shaking his head in what looks like appreciation.

"Rocks, huh?" he asks, crouching down in front of Eloy's torn body. "I wonder which one of them chose that. Must have hurt like hell."

"Eloy," I say softly, a single tear slowly trickling down my cheek. "He always liked looking at nature. It's only fitting that he chose it as his end."

"Guess I really should've got to know him. I always feel so damn bad when you tell me things about these kids that I didn't know," he says, reaching up and pushing his face back. I can see the cuts and scrapes on Eloy's face now. His eyes are still open, but vacant. They're looking into a void that neither of us can see, one we should have gone to in his place.

"What's your next Task?" I ask Pater. He glances up at me curiously as he lets the boy's chin fall back onto his chest and stands back up. I wait patiently as he crosses his arms over his chest and looks up at the trees.

"They weren't really tasks, Joce. They were tests of your loyalty to me, and as much as I hate to say it, you failed, baby girl."

"So kill me, and fucking get it over with," I shout in desperation, shoving him as hard as I can.

Pater rolls his eyes and reaches for my arms as I try to shove him again, forcing them to fold over my chest.

"If I kill you, we can't have forever. I promised you forever, and I plan on keeping that promise," he says in a soft voice.

"You promised Mama forever. And the one before her the same thing, and the one before *her*. What makes me so fucking special that you have to keep doing this to me? Haven't you destroyed me enough?" I scream at him as I try to rip my arms away from his vice grip.

Pater gives me one firm shake to stop my hysterics, before wrapping his arms tightly around me and holding me close to him. He looks deeply into my eyes, almost soulfully, and I can tell that whatever words he chooses to speak next are of some meaning to him. Whether *I'll* find any meaning in them is of no consequence. Anything I could have ever felt for this monster is as dead as the boy listening to us with hollow ears.

"If you want me to answer you honestly, I'm gonna need you to calm the fuck down and listen," he says sternly. "If you insist on flailing around like a fucking lunatic, I'll just tell you what you want to hear and make you believe it. It's up to you."

With that, he releases me and steps back, crossing his arms over his chest and waiting for me to make my choice. Pater is a patient monster, and he's used to always getting his way. This time will be no different, I decide, as I push my hair back from my face and nod in agreement.

Pater clears his throat and runs a hand over his chin. There seems to be more gray hair than black now, and his eyes look so tired that I almost feel bad for him. He's been through a lot, not as much as the three...two of us have, but he seems to be feeling the weight of his decisions finally starting to press down against whatever humanity he tries to hide deep inside of him.

"Alright. Yes, there were others before your mother, but she was the first one that actually gave me kids. The others before her tried, but could never conceive. Either that, or they aborted and never told me - I don't know. Since you were my first born, you held so much more meaning to me than anything else in the world. You're a symbol that I actually did something right for once in my life, and I tried not to fuck things up, Jocelyn; you have to believe that. I *tried*." He takes a deep breath for a moment and closes his eyes tightly before opening them again and looking back into mine. "Did I mean for all of this to happen? Yeah; I honestly did, but not like this. I wanted those boys to stay alive even though I didn't have any fucking use for them, because I could see that they made you happy. And once I realized that you could make *me* happy in every way a man could feel, I got rid of your mother. She would have just gotten in the way and tried to stop us from being together. Don't you wanna be with me, Joce? After everything we've been through?"

The tone of his voice is bordering on pleading, but he doesn't change his demeanor to match, and it leaves me confused.

Would I have ever thought this way of living was okay? At one point, I didn't know any better. I thought this was how a father loved his children, because when he plucked my innocence from a garden I've long since burned to the ground, I did love him. In every way he wanted me to, I loved him.

The older I became and the more he pushed Vaughn and Eloy away, the endless nights spent in the oubliette, and the constant having to stay awake to keep the boys safe wore down every thread I was hanging onto that made me believe, once upon a time, that Pater was worthy of my love.

"We've been through nothing together," I begin quietly. "You forced this life on me. On Eloy. On Vaughn. We didn't have a choice in any of this, and because your love is so weak that you chose only one of us to care for instead of all of us, I can't say that I want anything with you, much less forever."

He puts his hands on his hips and looks away. I can see it now, the monster inside of him coming to the surface, but I don't stop. After all, he offered me honesty, and I feel it's only fair to offer him honesty in return.

"This *will* come to an end someday soon, and one of us won't survive. The only question left to answer between us is who."

"Don't do that. Don't make idle fucking threats when you know I can snap your neck any time I want to," he warns, shaking his head vehemently.

"But you won't. You want another child, and I refuse to give you one, knowing what you're going to put it through," I spit back stubbornly. "Now, if you'll excuse me, I have to go back to that fucking hell in the ground you're so keen on keeping us in, and retrieve Vaughn. Dead or alive, he deserves to be with Eloy, and that's exactly where I'm going to put him."

As I spin on my heel with fire in my veins, I can hear Pater call my name out, but I don't stop or turn toward him.

He's had too many chances to make this right again, and

he's always chosen the path that best suited his needs. His disregard for us, the death of Eloy, the possibility of finding Vaughn dead in the pit will be his downfall. His reckoning is coming, and I will be the hand that delivers it, so help me God.

CHAPTER 17

I DON'T GO DIRECTLY to the oubliette. Instead, I walk back into the house, making my way down the entire length until I reach the front door.

A-ha! It's still there.

I gather up the rope ladder that Vaughn had used to rescue me, and open the front door. I can hear Pater calling my name as he makes his way toward me. He sounds damn angry at being disregarded, but it's time he knows what that feels like for once.

Pater's taller and much faster than me, so I know he'll catch up to me if I don't quicken my steps. I throw the rope over my shoulder and begin to jog toward my destination. If he won't tell me what's really happened to Vaughn, I'll climb down into the abyss and find out myself. Besides, seeing it with my own eyes will serve my intentions much better than hearing a story venomously packed with sweetened lies.

"JOCELYN!"

Pater's booming voice as he exits the front of the house

almost stops me, but I need to know what happened to Vaughn, and I need to know now.

I break into a run. As fast as my legs will carry me, I fucking run. I reach the top of the dungeon in no time and flip the door open. I quickly wrap a large part of the rope ladder around the cylindrical stone and pray that it holds as I toss the rest of the ladder over the side. I give it one hard tug and I'm over the side, descending into the darkness.

"Goddamn it!" Pater yells angrily.

I glance up momentarily to see him leaning down into the oubliette, attempting to reach for me, but I'm already too far down for him to snatch me back up.

"Fucking kids," he shouts, slapping his hand against the door before he disappears from sight.

Good.

He's angry and he knows he can't reach me, because there's no way in hell he'll crawl in here to retrieve me.

Pater is afraid of the things he can't control, and the darkness is *my* home, not his.

There's not a lot of room to move down at the bottom, but what little space there is I know like the back of my hand.

"Vaughn?" I call out as I come closer to the bottom.

Please be okay, I will desperately.

I'm nothing like Pater; I can't think of things and make them happen. I can't read minds, and I can't take control of people's lives, but what I can do that he can't or won't do is help those who need it the most.

I don't deserve help, because I should have been able to save us from this, but I was too blinded by his deceptions for so long that I welcomed everything he did to us.

I don't know if I'll ever be able to leave Pater. My world would crumble without him and I know it, but if I can just save *one* of these boys, then I'll be okay with being left behind.

The ladder is too short to get me all the way to the bottom, since I wrapped a good portion of it around the opening, so I hop down the last couple of feet and hope that if Vaughn is alive, he'll either be capable of pulling himself up, or give me enough help to get us both out of here.

"Vaughn?" I ask into the darkness. I rub my hands together before wiping them on my thighs and narrow my eyes.

I'm not a nocturnal animal, but it's easy for my eyes to adjust to the darkness they know so well, and from what I can tell, he's not standing if he's down here. Dropping to my knees, I begin to crawl in a small circle, following the pattern of the constructed abyss, and it finally dawns on me.

Pater lied.

He never threw the boy down here, and I blindly followed my heart to save someone who wasn't even here to save.

CHAPTER 18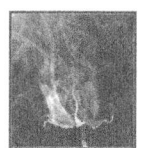

I DON'T KNOW how long I've been down here. The sun has already set, which leads me to believe it's been a few hours, but I could be wrong. I don't know where Pater is either, and because I chose to defy him, I know he won't do a damn thing to help me if I can't reach the ladder.

I haven't tried yet. I'm too full of rage at myself for trying to be something I'm not, and failing Vaughn yet again. Maybe he'll be better off if I just stay here. After all, the only thing I've managed to do is consistently fuck up every attempt I've made to help these boys, and because of it, one of them is already dead.

It would be so easy, almost too easy, for me to die right now. I could simply tie the end of the ladder around my neck and sit down, letting the weight of everything I've allowed to happen crush my neck.

I stand up and walk over, touching the tip of the ladder, and sigh. I deserve far worse than this, and that's the only thing that stops me.

That, and the hope that maybe Vaughn is alive out there somewhere. He's already deserted me by rebuking me as his mother, but I don't hate him for it. Had I been the one in his shoes being rejected at every turn, I would harbor the same feelings he does toward the "favorite."

I let go of the rope and sit back down on the cold, stone ground, wiping away bitter tears. There has to be some way to stop Pater; I just can't see it. I'm willfully blind to it because I need him as much as he needs me, even if it's not in the same way.

He wants to give me my own child, but then what? Will he do the same thing to me that he did to Mama if it's a girl? He said he'd never discard me, but what if that's the only way? To give him what he wants, pray for survival for the next fifteen years, and then allow him to finally end me when he takes the child as his new bride?

I've been in love with you since I first held you.

How is that possible? How can such a monster feel love for anything? And while I know I'm not better than Pater, I'm also not his equal. My love for the boys came from a need to protect them. The nights I've spent in Pater's bed, feeling his touch, were out of necessity, to keep them far from it.

I'm afraid part of my needing Pater is that I've learned to feel as much safety in his hands as I do down here in the darkness.

If there's an end to this, I can't see it; I don't *want* to see it. Maybe he'll be willing to come to some agreement of sorts, if what I have to offer is enough, but what can I give him that he hasn't already taken?

I rest my head back against the hard stone and almost laugh in relief. The answer is so clear to me, in a place where it's damn near impossible to see your own hand in front of your face. I *do* have something to offer Pater. Something he can't take unless I give it willingly, and it's the only way to get him to let his guard down.

With a renewed conviction, I get to my feet and wipe the dirt off on my legs, before I reach up and begin to pull myself up the rope. I'm better at this than I should be. Even though I've spent countless nights out here alone, I've also had rare moments alone with Eloy and Vaughn when they've been able to sneak out unnoticed and throw the ladder down to me.

In a way, I feel like I'm clawing my way out of hell, and to be quite honest, maybe I am. The darkness no longer wants me because I'm no longer pure of heart. I have blood on my hands. Even though not spilled by my own hands, my misdeeds have caused the death of an innocent, and I'm being rejected by my safe place.

I understand it and I accept it.

I'll make my way back down here again once I've purged myself of that malady, and the only way to do it is to give myself completely and unconditionally to Pater.

I have to love him, *need* him, the way he loves me. It's the only way to earn his trust, and the simplest way to bring a tyrant to their knees. It's not an easy thing to topple an empire as an enemy, so I'll be his willing lover until the sun sets over the both of us for the last time.

CHAPTER 19

I DECIDED to sleep in the clearing behind Pater's house. I don't want to give him the satisfaction of knowing where I am just yet, and I still have to convince myself that being his perfect little wife is worth the price I'll end up paying in the end.

I'm only awake now because the sun is breaking through the trees, and slivers of sunshine are hitting me in the face. I sit up with a sigh and look at the now empty stone chair. Eloy's mangled body is gone, and I'm sure Pater is the cause of it, but I can't worry about that now. He's not here to save anymore, and perhaps, in his brutal death, he's already received more salvation than I would have been able to provide for him anyway.

Today is the day I crawl out of my cocoon and become the delicate creature Pater has always longed for. The one he crushed when he decided Mama wasn't good enough for him anymore. The one he worked so vigilantly to destroy on the nights he needed to feel another's touch.

And I will become this. I've already decided it. The

only thing I need to do now is stick to my plan, and hope he doesn't see through me.

It shouldn't be too difficult, but I have to remember that I'm dealing with a master of deception, and he's more than likely already plucked the thoughts from my mind.

I lean down and scoop up one of the bloody stones, slip it into my shirt, and secure it safely so it has a place near my heart. It will serve as a reminder of why I will do these vile things I've committed myself to.

With the memory of Eloy tucked closely next to me, I make my way toward the back door of the house, and to my utter and complete fucking shock, feel like I've walked into a almost a do over of a few days before.

There's a young woman and man I don't know standing on one side of the island in the kitchen. Pater is leaning against the counter, and Vaughn is sitting there quietly, speaking to her.

"There she is," he says with a warm smile, holding an arm out toward me. "This is my Jocelyn."

I walk dutifully over to him and let him wrap his arm around me, then turn and smile at the young couple who greet me with wide grins.

"Your dad was just telling us about you!" the young woman says brightly.

"My ... Dad?" I ask, stealing an uncertain glance toward Pater. The stern look he returns to me tells me he's already rejected me. I've defied him one too many times, and when he's ready, I'll have to pay the price.

"From what he tells us, you seem like the perfect person we'd love to hire to babysit our son. Your brother said he's willing to help out too, if you need it," the young man explains, placing his palms on the island top with a smile.

"Oh. Yeah, I'd love to," I reply quietly.

"Joce will be an excellent babysitter. She helped raise her brother, and she hopes to be a mother herself one day, don't you baby girl?" he asks, giving me a gentle squeeze. Another stolen glance up into his eyes and I can see the soft yearning that was once going to play a part in my failed plan.

"I'd love to be a mom!" I gush happily. "How old is your son?"

"Seven," the young woman replies with a smile. "He's our fur baby, but we still consider him our son, you know?"

"A dog?" I ask curiously.

They look at each other sheepishly and nod. A small smile curves my lips. I always wanted a pet, but Pater never allowed it for fear that the animal would attack him on the nights he attacked *me*.

"Can we bring him by tomorrow so you can meet him? He's really playful, so maybe a test run would be best before we commit," she says thoughtfully.

I turn and give Pater a hopeful glance, hoping it will soothe the anger I know he's feeling at the baby not being human, but he grunts and nods in agreement.

"Perfect! How does, say, seven o'clock sound?" the young man asks, glancing at Pater.

"That'll be just fine," he replies, in a bored tone.

With that, they shake hands with Pater and wave at Vaughn and I as he shows them to the front door. I immediately go over to my brother and put a hand on his shoulder.

"I'm going to save you. I don't care if you hate me right now, but I need you to know that I'm going to do my best to fix this and that you'll go free," I whisper urgently.

Vaughn slowly turns his head toward me, his lower lip trembling, and bitter tears rolling down his face.

"Like you saved Eloy?" he seethes quietly.

I let out a sigh and do my best not to cry. If Pater finds us huddled in whispered conversation, he'll separate us again, and Heaven only knows if I'll see Vaughn ever again.

"Scheming against me?"

I jump and pull away from Vaughn, who turns his attention back to the void. There's nothing left in his eyes, like his brother's, but he still draws breath, and I will fucking defend it until I no longer can.

Pater is looking at us in amusement, arms over his chest, and his grin sitting on his face. "I was wondering when you were finally going to crawl out of that fucking hole."

"I'm sorry. I just needed some time alone," I reply softly, clasping my hands in front of myself.

Pater chuckles as he walks toward us, stopping just short of where I'm standing, and slides his hand down my shirt. I try not to cringe, but he knows that I'm holding a piece of Eloy close to my heart and he's more than likely not pleased with the gesture.

"That doesn't belong there," he says gently. "Hey. Kid. Get up. Go back to where you were, and stay there until I come to get you."

Vaughn quickly scrapes his chair back and leaves the room without so much as a glance over his shoulder. Pater lets out a sigh and rubs his forehead in irritation.

I watch his other hand as he absentmindedly rolls the stone around in his palm.

"You want this back?" he asks, following my gaze.

"Please."

"Tell you what," he says, as he begins to toss it from hand to hand. "I'll let you have it back if you do something for me."

I thought these fucking Tasks were over and done with.

"Anything," I say instead, remembering that I'm trying to become the obedient wife he wants me to be.

"Do a good job on your little interview tomorrow."

I raise an eyebrow at him. "That... That's it?"

"That's it," he replies with a nod.

"Okay," I say quietly, holding my hand out.

Pater balances the rock over my hand, but instead of dropping it where he promised, he closes his fist instead.

"I'm gonna hold on to this for a little while, if you don't mind. I want to make sure you do a good job, if you catch my drift."

With that, he leans down and gently kisses me on the lips, before he pulls back and grins again.

"Damn. Even after that stretch in the hole, your lips are still as soft as I remember."

Before I have a chance to plead for the rock, he leaves me in the kitchen, shaking his head and laughing on his way out.

CHAPTER 20

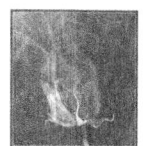

I BUSY MYSELF by tidying up the kitchen. I have a long day ahead of me, and once I'm done making this particular room spotless, I fully intend to go from room to room to locate Vaughn.

I take the dishtowel I've been using to wipe the island top with, and toss it into the sink. I quickly turn the faucet on and off, before I dry my hands on my legs and walk toward the living room. That's the direction Pater had gone, and I have to make sure I know where *he* is so that I have free reign of the house.

He's lying on the couch, the rock balanced on his stomach, and an arm bent behind his bed. The television is on, but it doesn't seem that he's paying it any mind.

"I was wondering when you were finally gonna join me," he says quietly. His eyes are trained on the screen, yet it's obvious he couldn't care less what's happening on the program he's watching.

"I'm sorry, Pater. I was just cleaning up."

"I know," he says kindly, closing his eyes. "Come sit with me, baby girl."

I swallow a sigh and obediently walk over so I can perch on the arm of the couch. Pater opens his eyes and turns them toward me, drops his legs, and motions with his chin for me to sit. As soon as I do, he props his legs across my lap and stares at me thoughtfully for a moment.

"Can I ask you something?"

It's a rhetorical question; he's the only one that ever gets to ask questions or make statements without needing permission, but I nod anyway just to humor him.

"Alright. There's one thing that's irking the fuck out of me, and I'm hoping to get some clarity," he starts as he scratches his chin. "Do you love me because you want to, or because you feel you have to?"

I drape my hands over his legs and form my next words with deadly precision. "At first, I loved you because I felt I had to. If it weren't for you, I wouldn't be here." *Even if this is Hell, at least it's still something.* "But I think I'm learning to love you because it's what feels right."

Pater scoffs and shifts his legs on my lap. "Then why are you constantly plotting behind my back? At what point in this will you realize that I'll always know when you're trying to trick me, Jocelyn?"

I have to ask him. If I don't, it'll drive me crazy for the little bit of life I know I have left.

"How is it you always know, Pater? I don't understand how it's possible to read the mind of another," I question, trying to keep the hysterics out of my tone. If he can hear the frantic need to know, he'll shut down and change the subject.

"How does a farmer always know their crops will spring from the ground? How does a gardener know that once a seed is planted, it'll eventually bloom? I *made* you, Jocelyn. You're a part of me, and I can feel you as deeply as you did with Eloy and Vaughn. It was never a trick, kiddo. Just an instinct, and you fucking fall for it every time," he explains with a smug smirk.

How could I have not guessed something so simple? It makes perfect sense.

I fold my arms and fall back against the couch, absolutely astounded at his revelation and the fact that I've been blind to it this entire time.

"Anything else you wanna know? Or is that enough for now?" he asks with a chuckle.

I turn my face away and sigh. The doorway stands empty, and I feel a heaviness in my heart. Usually, when I've been in this room with Pater, we were never alone. Eloy or Vaughn, or sometimes both, would be sitting by the door just to be close enough to me to feel some kind of comfort.

Pater swings his legs off the couch and sits up, moving until he's right next to me. He drapes an arm around my shoulders and sticks the rock with Eloy's blood on it into his pocket. I can feel his eyes on me, but I can't look at him yet. I feel the tears starting to build and I don't know if they're from anger at not seeing the boys where they should be, or because I was too fucking stupid not to have figured out his parlor trick sooner.

"Listen, I'm not going to make this harder than it has to be, and you really shouldn't either. I know this isn't the life you probably thought you would have, but honestly, Joce, would you have wanted to have it different in any way?" he asks, resting his free hand on my thigh. I look at his hand for a moment, before I turn my eyes toward his.

"No," I reply quietly.

If it had been different, I never would have spent so many happy years with Eloy and Vaughn after Mama. I remember how often they would argue, and how much she would scream at him for loving someone that wasn't her. I just never knew it was *me* until the time came.

"Are you finally willing to work on this with me? We can be happy, you know. We'll even have a dog soon, and I know how much you've always wanted to have one of those," he says, giving me another gentle squeeze.

"Yes."

"Good girl," he says in relief, kissing my cheek. "Everything will work out, you'll see. For now, why don't you go get yourself cleaned up, and then I'll take you and your brother outside for a while, alright?"

"Okay. Thank you, Pater," I reply quietly as I shrink away from his arm and get to my feet.

"Hold on a second. How many times have I been inside you already? We're trying to start a family here, and 'Pater' won't do anymore. Not for you. Call me Luke," he offers, with a debonair smile.

Luke it is, I think with a sigh as I give him a small smile I return, before I walk away and leave him in his soon-to-be-short-lived moment of happiness.

CHAPTER 21

I have a few more hours before the sun begins to set, yet I find myself standing in the doorway, wondering where Vaughn is tucked away. He's not in the darkness; I know this because Pater would never let him go outside alone. Any time the boys have been allowed a moment of fresh air, even with me being present, he would keep a watchful eye on us.

His footsteps have been moving about the house, hollowly echoing through the hallways, and for that reason alone, I know Vaughn is somewhere inside with us.

I run a hand over my face and sigh irritably. This place is not exactly a palatial estate, so why I'm having such trouble figuring out where he is bothers me.

He's still alive. Half of my heart is still beating, and I know it's only because wherever he is, he hasn't been put to rest yet.

Don't think of things you can't control. That's one of Pater's rules; it's how he keeps his head above water, and those of us remaining under his thumb.

Leaning against the door frame, I watch the silent property. I don't know on which side of us the new couple lives, and to be honest, I didn't know it was possible for anyone to even be alive.

Besides Laura, we hadn't seen another person since we were kids, because Pater didn't want to take the chance we'd slip and tell stories of what we'd been subjected to under his roof.

I don't think I would ever tell anyone, even if do we make it out of here. I know nothing will come of it because the damage has already been done.

Stepping back inside, I close the door and sigh. Is it really damage, though? I can't say for sure, because there are nights when I've been in Pater's bed that his touch made all the difference in the world to me.

I'm as fucked up as he is; I can accept that now, but what I cannot accept is Vaughn being put through any more than he already has been. He's brutally murdered his own brother because I selfishly failed in my attempt to save him.

We all have blood on our hands now, and I can't help but wonder if that's what Pater had in mind all along. If we're all equally guilty, turning on him would essentially be turning on ourselves.

Monstrous acts beget monsters, and we'll both get what we deserve in the end, but not all of us. I won't allow it. Not while there's still hope for the boy to regain some sort of normalcy back into his life. He's only seventeen; he should be able to break away from all this madness if I can just help him escape.

Something tells me I don't have much time left to formulate a master plan, so I'll just have to improvise. The only chance I can actually see is when the couple returns with their dog. I'll have Pater sit with me while we have our interview. I'll play the part of the happy child, and I'll see to it that Vaughn can slip away unnoticed.

"Hey Joce?"

Pater's voice echoing throughout the house puts my plan to rest for the moment as I quickly turn and see that he's already heading toward me.

"What are you doing?" he asks with a curious smirk.

I shake my head and shrug. I don't have an explanation he would appreciate, and since I know now that he can't really read my mind, I think my intentions are better left unsaid.

"Oh, I get it," he says kindly. "Alone time, right? I don't blame you. Even I need some of that every now and then. You hungry? I was thinking we could all sit down for dinner tonight. It's already going if you're interested."

"That would be nice," I reply softly.

"Good," he says with a warm smile. "Your brother is already in the dining room setting the table; why don't you go help him, and then you'll get to see what I whipped up."

Lowering my head, I start to walk past him, almost giddy with excitement. He's presenting me the chance I need to let Vaughn know that by this time tomorrow he could go free.

Pater slides an arm around my waist as he pulls me sideways against him, and rests his lips on the side of my head. He lingers there for a moment before he whispers a warning into my ear.

"Don't get any ideas. I'll find out."

He presses his lips gently against me in what I can only describe as a Judas kiss, because he betrayed me a long time ago when he stole my innocence. When he finally lets me go, I walk quickly toward the dining room. I need every second given to me to somehow get Vaughn to trust me.

As I walk into the room, I see that Vaughn is quietly setting Pater's plate at the head of the table. He glances up at me for a moment with his almost vacant eyes before he slowly walks to his seat and sits down.

"Listen to me, and don't interrupt until I'm done," I whisper as I take my place across from him. "I need you to trust me like you've never trusted me before. Tomorrow, you're leaving."

Vaughn raises his eyes from the plate he's been staring at, giving me an icy stare. "How is that, *Mom*?"

I try not to cringe. It's obvious he still hates me. I understand his feelings, because I hate me too.

"When that couple comes back, I think we're going to do a working interview. Pater will be with me, I'll make sure of it. While I have them all distracted, I want you to walk out the front door and, no matter what happens, do *not* turn around, got it?" I ask him urgently.

Vaughn rolls his eyes, but he doesn't disagree with the plan. As long as Pater doesn't catch on to what's going to happen, he may actually do as he's being told.

"Doesn't this smell damn good?" Pater asks, suddenly walking into the room. He has a large serving plate piled with grilled chicken breasts that he sets down in the center of the table. My stomach growls loudly and I'm just now realizing how hungry I've been this entire time.

"It does," I reply, mustering the enthusiasm I know he's expecting.

Pater grins at me and turns his attention toward Vaughn, who's hungrily glancing at the plate. He quickly shoots Pater a glance and nods once in appreciation.

"But wait! There's more!" Pater says merrily as he leaves the room again.

It's another form of discipline, sitting in front of the

food, ravenously hungry, and not being allowed to indulge until Pater says so. Of course, it's also very far and few in between that he allows us to share in his food that, when presented with the challenge, we've always held strong.

He returns a few moments later with a bowl heaped with mashed potatoes, balancing a bottle of wine under his arm, and still grinning. He's proud of himself for actually giving a fuck about us for once.

"Want some?" he asks, as he pulls the cork out of the wine bottle. I glance at him to see who he's asking, and am actually surprised to find it's me, since I've never tasted wine before.

He fills his glass, then moves the bottle toward mine, hovering, waiting for my response. Will it dull my senses? Will I divulge my plan if I imbibe? I don't know, and I can't take that chance.

"No thank you, Pater," I reply softly.

"Luke," he corrects, the grin on his face faltering. He turns his gaze toward Vaughn. "What about you, kid?"

"No thank you, sir," he says quietly.

Pater shrugs and sets the bottle down by his glass and rolls his sleeves up to his elbows. "Well, more for me then. Jocelyn, can you pass the chicken please?"

I immediately pick up the plate and hold it out toward him. His grin is fully plastered on his face again as he uses a fork to take the biggest piece, then winks at me when he's done. I hold it out toward Vaughn, who quickly stabs whatever piece he can get, then nods in thanks.

Pater reaches past me and grabs the bowl of mashed potatoes, purposely rubbing his bare forearm against mine. I don't react, because I'm not sure what reaction he's looking for.

"Eat up kids, tomorrow's a big day. We're getting a dog," he says with a laugh.

I raise my eyes toward Vaughn, but he's too busy shoving forkfuls of food into his face to care or notice.

"Oh, I almost forgot," Pater says conversationally. "I never did get a chance to thank you for taking care of that little problem your brother left behind, Vaughn."

Vaughn's mouth is open and his fork is hovering just in front of him. He glances at Pater, then cuts his eyes toward me frantically. They're hiding something from me, and Pater doesn't like it when we keep secrets from each other.

"Didn't he tell you?" he asks in mock surprise as he cuts a piece of chicken with his fork.

I feel sick. Without even knowing what he's about to reveal to me, I've lost my fucking appetite and my body begins to tremble slightly.

"Tell me what?" I croak uncertainly.

He lets his fork clatter loudly onto his plate as he sits back and takes a sip of his wine. "Well? Are you going to tell her, or am I?"

Vaughn turns his face away from me and Pater chuckles. "I swear, I don't know how the hell you ended up being my kid with no balls."

"Tell me *what*?" I ask again.

"Alright," Pater says, placing an arm on the table and looking at me. He stops for a moment to take another sip of wine before he makes his revelation. "Remember how I said your mother went out of this world the same way she came in?"

"Yes?"

The world is starting to spin around me. I'm dangerously close to passing out, but it's the anticipation of what I think he might say that's making me react so violently.

"Well, your precious Mama? Her name was Laura. You got to meet her. And the blood she went out in? That was Eloy's; sloppy as fuck, cut himself a couple times doing the deed. But don't feel bad, you didn't really miss anything spectacular. The bitch didn't even put up a fight."

Clearing his throat, he takes another sip of wine and then continues with his meal. My mother was here, in this very house, not a few days before; she did nothing to save us.

CHAPTER 22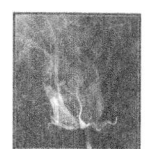

Dinner has officially been over for half an hour, but Pater has insisted on dessert. For himself, not us; we haven't earned dessert yet, according to him.

"But you will," he promised us with his sideways grin sitting deviously on his handsome face.

It's been silent for at least ten minutes while Pater eats his pie, but I'm so numb at the revelation he made to me less than an hour ago that I'll probably end up staying awake all night anyway.

"Listen, I know you're all confused and probably pissed off right now," he finally says, glancing at me. "But Vaughn didn't really know until he had to go clean up Eloy's mess. And to be honest Joce, you can't be angry at me. That waste of a pussy has lived in this neighborhood ever since I kicked her out. She could've come over any time she wanted. Well, that's not entirely true, but if she was as concerned as she fucking acted, then she *would* have."

Pater's words mean nothing to me. I'm too busy glancing at the knife sitting between us. All it would take is a series of quick motions to leave him choking in his own blood. I could slit his throat before he would even have the chance to realize what had happened.

But what if I failed? What if he managed to stop me as soon as I grabbed the knife? Then what? Vaughn would surely pay for another act of failed bravery. And then it would just be Pater and me.

Unless...

"You know Joce, I admire you," Pater says suddenly. "You've got more balls than either of your brothers, always looking for a way to kill me and whatnot, but I thought we agreed we were done with that game?"

My eyes slowly move from the gleaming blade, to the hilt, and then up to Pater. Out of the corner of my eye, I can see Vaughn slowly moving for the knife placed between him and Pater, and in that moment, I know it's a trick.

"Don't," I say to him softly.

Pater raises his eyebrows curiously as he turns his attention toward Vaughn, who's letting go of the knife.

"You kids really like to test my patience, don't you?" Pater asks with a sigh. "It's okay. If it were me, I'd try the same thing, but remember something. Without me, you're both nothing. You'll be forced out into a world you don't understand; a world that will reject you before you can even set a foot firmly into it. I'm not the bad guy here. I'm not the one who threw you kids away; I'm the one who's loved you and cared for you your entire lives. You want someone to hate? Hate your incubator. She gave all three of you up without a fight."

Vaughn puts his face in his hands and begins to gently cry. He believes Pater, and it's breaking his heart. He believes there's nothing better than this life for the both of us, and he can't accept it like I've been trying to.

Pater rolls his eyes at Vaughn before turning his attention back to me. "Tell you what; to prove I'm not such a bad guy, I'll do something for the both of you. Tonight, I'm going to let you sleep with your brother."

My stomach turns, because with Pater, the way he says things are rarely as they're presented. He looks very proud because of his generosity, but I won't thank him just yet. Not until I fully understand his offer.

"Calm down, will you?" he says with a chuckle, reaching across the table and resting a hand on mine. "I meant actually let you sleep in the same bed, not fuck each other. That would just complicate things. Besides, that's not how this works. Your pussy belongs to me and no one else, so don't worry about it."

Somehow, that doesn't make me feel any better. If he's allowing this, it means the worst is yet to come, and he's giving us a peaceful moment before the end.

"Thank you, Pater," I finally say softly.

"Luke," he corrects evenly.

"Thank you, Luke," I correct with a sigh. "Where would you like us to sleep tonight?"

"Anywhere you want," he says, his grin returning as he pushes his chair back and stands up. "But remember; no funny business. That would be wrong."

With a wink, he grabs his plate and leaves us in the dining room. My eyes move toward the clock on the wall and I'm amazed at how much time has actually passed since we've sat down. It's eight o'clock at night, maybe a little after, and as I look across the table at my brother, I can't help but feel like this is the last time I'll ever see him again.

"Come on," I say quietly, getting up from the table and holding a hand out toward him. "Let's get some sleep. Tomorrow, you're getting out of here."

CHAPTER 23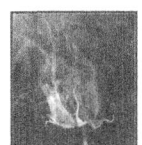

WHEN I WAKE up the next morning, I'm relieved to realize I didn't dream. It's not uncommon for me to have sleepless dreams, but when I do, they terrorize me. They're almost always dreams of life outside these walls. A life without Pater; one where Eloy is still alive, and he and Vaughn are happy and thriving.

Since Pater had given me the choice of rooms, I chose the one I slept in as a little girl, yet untouched and undefiled because it still held some meaning to me. It was a place where I could go and be innocent again; a place where Pater didn't exist, and nothing bad could happen to me.

I blink my eyes a few times to remove whatever sleep is still lingering, and smile sadly when I feel his frail body so close to mine. When we went to bed, I held him while he cried, until he was so exhausted he finally drifted off. I've woken up with his head under my chin and his arms still wrapped firmly around me.

He's stirring slightly since I've shifted in bed, and I kiss the top of his head. I don't want him to wake up just yet. I want to remember him like this before he leaves me. Asleep, innocent of the horrors he's lived through, and finding it in himself to forgive me, even if he doesn't mean it.

I run my hand gently over his hair as he stirs again gently, before he finally opens his eyes and pulls away from me.

"What time is it?" he asks groggily, using the back of his hand to rub his eyes. Before I have a chance to answer him, the door swings open and Pater walks through.

"Get up and get dressed; they're here."

"Now?" I ask, sitting up, now wide awake.

"Yeah," he replies with a grim nod. "Hurry up."

"Fuck," I mutter pushing myself off the bed. "Okay, listen, go throw some water on your face and get as alert as you can."

I walk quickly toward my closet and pull out a dress, changing quickly behind the door so Vaughn doesn't have to be subjected to any more than he already has been. When I'm done, I get up onto my tiptoes and run my hand along the top shelf.

"Here, take this," I say, walking back toward him and shoving all the money I managed to save as a child into his hand. "It's not much, but it should get you far enough away from here that you won't ever have to worry about this place again. I love you, okay? Don't ever forget that. I love you."

I give him a quick, tight hug, and walk out of the room before he can say anything. If I hear anything come from his lips, I'll burst into tears and fail the interview, and he won't have his chance.

He'll take it.

He has to, because he knows that life *is* better on the outside, no matter what Pater tried to tell us last night. Maybe one day I'll see him in the world; maybe I won't ever leave these walls. The latter doesn't matter to me because I know I deserve this, but goddamn it, he doesn't.

"There she is," Pater says with a huge, fake smile when I walk into the living room. "Crystal and Aaron were just asking about you."

"Sorry!" I reply as brightly as I can. "I guess I overslept. I honestly thought you guys meant seven o'clock at *night*."

"Oh, he's an early riser," Aaron says, nodding down at his dog. It's got beautiful brown fur that shines majestically as it sits there looking up at me curiously. I don't know what kind of dog it is, but it's definitely friendly. As I approach it and crouch down to pet its head, I can see the tail begin to wag furiously.

"What's your name?" I ask him, scratching behind his ear.

"Tiberius," Crystal replies with a warm smile.

I raise an eyebrow curiously at her as Tiberius licks the side of my face.

"I know; what kind of name is that for a dog, right? We're really big into ancient history," she explains with a laugh.

I smile at her and turn my attention back to the dog, taking its face into my hands and giving it a gentle kiss on the nose.

"He definitely seems to like you," Aaron says happily. "Wanna sit down and we'll talk about compensation?"

I have no idea what that means, but I pet Tiberius one more time, before I get up and go sit next to Pater on the couch.

"We're going to be gone for a couple of weeks, which I guess we should have told you ahead of time," Crystal begins sheepishly. "If it's still okay with your dad, we'd love to have you take care of him for us while we're gone."

As I'm turning my eyes toward Pater, I can see Vaughn quietly walking past the living room door. He's doing it; he's leaving, and he's going to have a happy life.

"Daddy?" I ask, glancing at Pater. I want to keep his attention. I want him to focus on me because as long as he's distracted by my hand on his leg and the sound of my voice, everything will work out as I hoped it would.

"I don't know," he finally says, shaking his head slowly. "Two weeks is a long time to take care of a dog for someone that's never had one. Are you sure you're up for that kind of responsibility?"

"I've done a good job so far, haven't I?" I ask him through gritted teeth and a forced smile.

He returns my fake smile but I can see the stern warning plainly in his eyes. "Yes, you have."

"Well, if you're still willing to accept the job, we'll pay you two hundred dollars. One hundred now, and one hundred when we get back. Does that sound fair?" Aaron asks, putting an arm around Crystal.

"We have all his stuff outside in the car too, so you won't have to use any of your money to buy him food or toys," Crystal adds hopefully.

"Sweetheart?" Pater asks, putting his arm around my shoulders and giving me a squeeze.

"I would love to!"

They both smile in relief and get to their feet. "We'll just go outside and get his belongings then!"

"Wait!" I say quickly. What if they go outside and Vaughn is still within the line of vision? "Um. Maybe you'd like to see where he's going to sleep first?"

"Oh, I'm sure he'll sleep fine wherever you decide to put him," Aaron says cheerfully as he walks out of the living room with Crystal following behind him. He still has

Tiberius' leash firmly wrapped in his fist, and I'm afraid I'm going to piss myself because of how scared I am right now.

But as I begin to follow them out, Pater firmly holding my hand in his, I see something that causes me to almost pass out. I fall against Pater, who tries to steady me, and I swear to God, the world is starting to go black around me.

"Hey. I thought you guys might need some help."

Vaughn is standing dutifully next to their car, waiting for someone, anyone to come outside, so he can do what he always has tried to do best.

Protect us from Pater. And since he bears the guilt of not being able to save his brother, he's going to try to save me.

CHAPTER 24

"What are you doing out here?" Pater asks him with a menacing smile now sitting on his face.

Vaughn shrugs as he meets my eyes, "I wanted to see the dog. I didn't know it was already inside."

I blink my eyes rapidly as I do my damnedest not to cry. The plan would have worked so perfectly if he would have just kept walking. He could have left this all behind, but because he still holds some kind of love in his heart for me, he won't leave me behind.

"Go on inside, son. We'll have a little talk later," Pater says, squeezing my shoulders tightly enough to cause me to flinch. He knows I had a hand in this, but he can't act on his rage until our company is gone.

Vaughn nods and pets Tiberius' head as he walks by him, stealing a glance in my direction. I look at him with more heartbreak than I ever thought I could feel in my life, and he responds with a sad smile before disappearing into the house.

Aaron quickly unloads the dog's belongings and carries them into the living room, before pulling out his wallet and handing me a crisp one hundred dollar bill. He and Crystal say their goodbyes to the dog, shake Pater's hand, and wave at me as they get back into their car and begin to pull down the driveway.

"Joce?" Pater asks thoughtfully.

I glance up at him, trying to shrug out of the grip he has on me. Tiberius is inside playing with Vaughn; I know it because I can hear him happily barking and Vaughn returning it with laughter. For the first time in years, Vaughn is genuinely laughing again, and the purity of it slightly swells my deflated heart.

"What your brother just did. Was that his idea or yours?"

"Mine. It was completely, unequivocally my idea. Please don't punish him for it. Please? I'll go back into the oubliette. I'll rot down there happily, but please. He didn't want to go; I forced him outside."

I'm damn near hysterical as I pull away from the grip he has on my shoulders. I turn to face him and ball his shirt into my fists, looking up at him with pleading eyes, but he's more focused on the car.

Waiting for it to disappear from sight.

Waiting for the moment he can strike us down for what we attempted to do.

Waiting for things he'll never say. Pater won't waste words when actions can be taken instead, and I'm afraid. Not for myself, but for Vaughn.

Why didn't he leave?!

I fall against Pater's chest and begin sobbing. He won't care; my tears never meant much to him before, and they aren't even for him. They're not for myself either; they're for the innocent inside who will suffer because I tried to help him.

"Let's go inside," he says quietly, putting his arm around me and leading me back in. He hasn't agreed not to hurt the boy, but I hope that somewhere deep down in the void where his soul *should* be, he'll take some pity on him and allow me to take the punishment in his place.

Once inside, he firmly closes the door and turns both the locks deliberately. He turns the doorknob to make sure it's locked, before leading me into the living room where Tiberius and Vaughn are still playing.

"Go sit on the floor with your brother," Pater says, damn near shoving me down next to Vaughn. Tiberius, blissfully unaware of what he might see, comes over and licks my face.

Not now, I think, giving him a gentle shove. He looks at me curiously, before he trots out of the room to explore the rest of the house.

Pater sits down on his couch and puts his face in his hands for a moment, trying to collect his thoughts before he speaks. If a verbal lashing is the worst of what he has to offer, I'll gladly accept it.

"I know you both hate me, but you also know that I don't care. I have rules for a reason, and that's to protect you both. Your brother couldn't follow the fucking rules, and do you see where that got him? Dead at thirteen years old, when he could have still been here with us. You have had it way too easy, and that's gonna fucking change, starting now," he says, dropping his hands and glaring at us.

Easy? This is easy? Being forced to play the dutiful wife to your father; being forced to protect your brothers, and failing where it counts the most?

I don't dare speak those sentiments out loud. No matter how much I want to stand up and scream my questions at him, I stay seated and move closer to Vaughn. I can feel him trembling when he puts a protective arm around my shoulders, but his attempt to reassure me is such an act of bravery in the face of this evil that I can't help but feel proud.

I may not have made many good decisions in my life, and I may have gotten a lot of shit wrong, but I know that at the very least, I raised him right.

Pater leans back against the couch and stares at us with his mouth open. He's just warned us of what's to come, and yet here we sit in solidarity against a tyrant.

He chuckles as he looks away for a moment. I can see the wheels spinning in his head and I'm ready for whatever it is he decides to put us through next, because I'll have Vaughn by my side. With as much as I wanted him to gain his freedom, being in his presence makes me feel stronger.

"If only you cared this much about Eloy. Maybe then he'd still be alive, too," Pater says to me with a smirk. He's trying to hurt me, devastate me with his words, and if I still didn't have one son to care for, I would have felt the blow much harder, just as he intended.

"She did, and that's why she couldn't kill him," Vaughn retorts bravely.

I put a hand on his leg to keep him from talking back to Pater, but he must be working on pure adrenaline because he hops to his feet and balls his fists at his side.

"You're not as great as you think you are. You can beat us, throw us into the ground, abuse Jocelyn as much as you want; but you'll never be more than a monster. If you were as great as you act like you are, you wouldn't do this to us," he shouts at him.

"Wow. Look at you go!" Pater says in appreciation. "I see your balls finally dropped. Congratulations, kid!"

I don't know where my sudden bravery comes from. Maybe it's seeing my younger brother stand up and not give a shit about the consequences of speaking back to Pater, but I get up, stand next to him, and place a hand gently on his shoulder.

"You can leave now. Walk out the front door like I told you to, and don't look back. He can't hurt you anymore, Vaughn. You just took control of your life again. It's okay. I'll be okay," I say to him softly.

"I'm not leaving you here with *him*," he replies, his eyes still on Pater, who's watching us with sheer amusement on his face.

"Please let him leave," I beg, giving Pater my full attention. "I'll stay for as long as you want me to, and die when you deem it necessary, but he's been through enough. If you love me as much as you say you do, you'll let him go."

Pater smiles and rubs his chin. He gets up and faces us, but doesn't make any steps to come closer. I can tell he's mulling my request over by the way he's looking me up and down. He's trying to decide whether I'll be enough to keep him satisfied, and if he gives me the chance, I'll do every last thing he asks of me.

"Tell you what," he begins as he rubs his hands together. The look in his eyes is sickening, but no matter what he says, I will fucking oblige to keep Vaughn free from whatever torment he decides to inflict.

"I'll make sure that Vaughn goes free, but you *both* have to do something for me first," he says, grinning widely.

I shake my head vehemently.

"Hear me out before you say no, otherwise you both go back into the ground until you die of starvation."

"It's okay," Vaughn says, taking my hand in his. I look at him and he gives me a small but firm smile. "What do you want?"

Pater smiles at him as he claps his hands together. "Go

get the dog and bring it back in here. One little thing I want you kids to do, and then I'll let you go."

Vaughn nods in agreement as he lets go of my hand and leaves me alone in the room with Pater, whose grin is making me feel violently ill.

One more fucking game and Vaughn will be able to leave.

CHAPTER 25

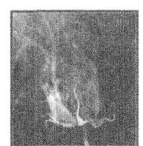

PATER'S WHISTLING while we wait for Vaughn to return with Tiberius, and I'm still firmly standing my ground. I can't even begin to imagine what he has in store for us; nor do I want to, but I won't resist whatever it is with the price being Vaughn's chance at a normal life.

"Where do you think he would have gone to?" Pater asks me, a curious smile replacing his wicked grin.

"I don't know."

"Where did you tell him to go?" he asks, rocking back on his heels.

"I didn't. I only told him to run as far away as he could and to not look back," I reply truthfully.

"Hm," he says with a nod. "I don't know if he would have gotten very far, but you did one hell of a job distracting me. That 'Daddy' thing got me hard for a minute there."

I sigh and clasp my hands firmly in front of me. The kind of fucked up thoughts that run through his head were absolutely beyond me, but I can honestly say that I no longer care.

"There they are," he says, turning his attention toward

the door. "I got a question for you before we start," he says to Vaughn. "Where exactly where you planning on going?"

Vaughn drops down to one knee and proceeds to unclip the leash from Tiberius' collar, giving Pater a shrug in return.

"Away."

"'Away'. Okay, well I'll make sure you make your way there after we're done. But first, you gotta do something for me, remember?"

Vaughn glares up at him from his place next to Tiberius and begins to get to his feet, when Pater walks over and shoves him back down. "You're not gonna need to stand for this."

My heart begins to race. The first time Pater ever said that to me, what followed next was the metaphorical wildfire that destroyed my garden.

"Wait--"

"Ah, ah, ah!" Pater says holding up a finger. "You promised."

I stand frozen in horror as he pulls his shirt off, revealing his body underneath. Pater may be much older than us, but he takes good care of himself. He's not by any means chiseled out of stone, but what he has to offer would be appreciated by someone else in the right situation.

"Sit down, baby girl. Take your clothes off and spread your legs. Let me see that sweet little pussy."

My lower lip begins to tremble violently as I remove my pants and panties and sit on the floor. Closing my eyes for a moment, I turn my face away as I slowly spread my legs open, praying that Vaughn is looking away.

"God, I can smell you from here," he remarks, inhaling deeply. My eyes fly open when I hear him begin to unzip his jeans, and I can feel myself dangerously close to vomiting. He's going to fuck me and make Vaughn watch, and he'll have this burned in his memory forever, losing his chance at a normal life.

"Nobody move. I just got an idea," he says with a smirk, as he walks out of the room. Moments later, he returns with the largest kitchen knife he has, and walks back over toward Vaughn.

Instinct tells me to get up and try to wrestle the knife away from him, but the very second he sees the fight in my eyes, he grabs a fistful of the boy's hair and pulls his head back, placing the blade against it.

"Do you really want to do that? Now? Before we've had fun?" he asks with a slight bounce in his stance and that fucking grin on his face. I sit back down on my bare ass and watch the blade carefully. Not only is it the largest, it's also the sharpest, and even the slightest pressure will draw blood.

"Now let's play, shall we?" he says, violently shoving Vaughn back to his knees. "I know you'll like this because of how badly you wanted to take care of that fucking thing. So spread your legs again for me."

I'm crying at this point. There's no more reason to be brave when I'm so sure I know what he's going to do to me.

"Feel that?" he asks Vaughn, rubbing himself against the side of the boy's face. "That's what happens when your balls drop. Ever happen to you before?"

Vaughn tries to move away from Pater, who promptly reaches down and grabs a fistful of his hair again.

"I guess not. It's okay, you're not gonna need a hard dick for what I want you to do," he says with a chuckle. "Now, let's start, and if you bite me, I'll fucking gut your sister. Got it?"

Oh my God.

"Pater, no!"

"Call me Pater one more fucking time and I'll cut your precious brother's head off his fucking neck," he shouts at me. "Get busy with that fucking dog and let me enjoy myself here."

Vaughn and I exchange a wide-eyed, horrified glance. We understand now, and what he wants is far worse than anything he's ever put me through. But it doesn't stop him; nothing stops Pater when he really wants something.

Balancing the knife in the same hand he's still using to hold Vaughn by his hair, he pulls out his hard dick and shoves it into the boy's mouth, moving back and forth violently, gagging him with a grin on his face.

"Come on. Find your own pace and it won't be so bad," he says to him in a thick voice.

Tiberius is sitting next to me, watching the entire scene unfold curiously, his head tilted to the side, and I don't know what to do at this point. I don't know exactly what it is that Pater expects from me, and I'm so horrified by what he's forcing Vaughn to do that I throw up all over the carpet.

"Hm, that's good," he says, leaning his head back and closing his eyes. "It's not so bad now, is it?"

I have to improvise. I have to do something, *anything,* that will bring this to the fastest end possible. I quickly grab Tiberius by the collar and shove his snout between my legs, rubbing my pussy against his nose until he begins to lick curiously. His tongue is wide, flat, coarse, and I hate every fucking minute of it, but I have to give Pater something so that Vaughn can be free of what he's being subjected to.

"How's that feel, baby girl?" he asks, opening his eyes and looking down at me. "Is he better than me?"

My jaw is clenched so tightly together that I swear my goddamn teeth are going to start chipping soon, but when the dog attempts to pull back, I move forward and shove myself back into his face.

Tiberius finally begins to growl, and I know it's time to stop. I don't want this poor animal to be treated like we are; I want it to feel loved and cared for, not abused and broken, so I let it go and walk quickly over to Pater and Vaughn. I put my hands on my brother's shoulders and attempt to pull him out of Pater's grip, but Pater only laughs and shoves me away.

"You didn't finish. I guess it didn't know what it was doing, cause you *always* finish with me, don't you?" he asks, pulling me as close as he can and looking down into my eyes.

"Yes," I reply frantically, darting my eyes back down toward Vaughn, who's gasping for air in between tears.

"Is that all you got? The both of you? That's a damn shame," Pater says, finally pushing Vaughn off his dick. "I did promise you that I would let Vaughn go though, didn't I? And Daddy always keeps his promises to his sweet girl," he says, reaching down and grabbing my ass tightly. "Step back. I don't want you to get hurt."

I take three shaky steps back and wait. Any moment now, Vaughn will be allowed to get to his feet and walk out the front door, just like it was agreed upon.

"Come here, kid," he says to Vaughn as he puts his dick back into his pants, careful not to nick himself with the knife. "You about ready to go?"

Vaughn is sobbing so violently at this point that he can't form a cohesive sentence. Pater rolls his eyes and reaches for him again.

"You sure you wanna leave?" he asks him. He doesn't wait for a response though. Instead, he shoots me a quick smile, before he turns his attention back to the boy. "Alright, go on, you get to go now. Tell your brother we said hey," he says, as he pulls Vaughn's head back, cleanly and deeply cutting his neck wide open.

All I can do is scream and watch as his hands fly up toward his neck, the warm blood rushing over his fingers, before he finally pitches forward and bleeds out on the living room carpet.

He's finally free.

CHAPTER 26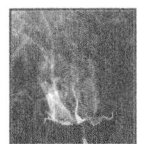

"Damn. I really wanted you to do that, but I'm pretty sure you weren't up for it, were you?" Pater asks as he tilts his head and glances down at Vaughn. The boy isn't dead yet; I can hear him still gasping for breath and I can see his back moving raggedly up and down. "Wanna finish him off? Put him out of his misery?"

Pater turns the knife around so that he's gripping the blade in his hand, and presenting the hilt to me. It's another test, and it's one I cannot afford to fail. Being forced to do something so terrible in a moment where my heart can't take any more, I turn my face away from Pater and reject his request.

"Don't have it in you, huh? It's okay, let him suffer for a little bit. It'll teach him a lesson before he chokes to death on his own blood," he says as he crosses his arms and shakes his head.

He uses his foot to nudge Vaughn's shoulder, which causes him to sputter, and I hate myself for not having it in me to kill him. But it's what Pater wants, and I can't give in, not when I've already given him so fucking much already.

"Hey, where did that mutt run off to?" he asks, suddenly glancing around the room.

"No more," I whisper tiredly. "I can't do this anymore. Please just end it."

"Nah, I'm having too much fun, and you're not pregnant with my child yet," he replies with smirk. "We've got things to do first, baby girl. Then if you want to leave, we'll talk about it, but as it currently stands, I have no plan of letting you go. Besides, do you have any idea how cute you're gonna look with a belly? I'll bet it's gonna be adorable! Can I tell you a secret, though?"

I don't move my hands away from my face. I won't give him the satisfaction of seeing more tears, when I didn't even know I was capable of giving any more than I've already shed.

"I'm trying to share something with you. Please give me a little common courtesy," he says quietly as he walks over and pulls my hands away. Pater tries to catch my eyes, but I still refuse, causing him to sigh impatiently.

"Jocelyn. Stop acting like a spoiled brat and look at me when I'm speaking to you, please."

I turn my eyes ever so slightly to let him know he has my attention as much as he has my defiance, but he seems to be okay with it.

"I'm a little scared. To start over, I mean. Fifty three years on this fucking earth and having to raise another kid from scratch is gonna be a little hard, so I'm counting on you to help me with that. Although to be honest, I bet changing a diaper is a lot like getting back on a bike; you never really forget. I remember the first time I changed yours; the way you looked up at me with those curious brown eyes..." his voice trails off and he pulls me close to him protectively, resting his chin on the top of my head.

If I didn't know any better, I would say he's almost trying to remember how to be a father in this moment, but I know it won't last long. It never fucking does, and I'll be back to being his wife in no time while our 'son' continues to bleed out on the floor next to us.

"It won't be anything like it was with your mom, so don't worry about that, okay? I took you kids away from her the moment you were born, because I could see in her eyes how much she resented you. I didn't appreciate the way she would look at you, especially. Which is probably why you kids didn't remember her when you saw her; you were never around her long enough to form that bond, because I refused to give her that right to *my* children," he takes a deep breath to steady himself. I can feel the rage in his words, but he's trying to make this as meaningful as he can for me. "Listen, I fully intend to raise our kids together instead of apart. I've seen how hard you tried with Eloy and Vaughn, and it would break my heart to take you away from any child I put inside of you. You're a damn good mother, Jocelyn, of that I have no doubt," he says, as he kisses the top of my head and lets me go. "But for now, we gotta find that fucking dog."

He walks out of the room, whistling loudly in an attempt to get Tiberius to show himself, but if he can hear him he's not falling for it.

Good dog. Stay as far away as you fucking can.

"Luke?" I call out timidly. I have another plan, one that won't fail if I can stand my ground. One that will, at the very least, save the life of the animal if I can keep his attention on me long enough.

"Not now, baby girl. I need to get rid of this damn dog," he calls back before he continues whistling. "There you are! Come here, boy! That's right, I've got something for you."

I run from the living room, down the hallway, and into the kitchen. Pater has the dog by his collar and he's crouched down in front of him, letting Tiberius happily lick his face.

"Well, look at that. I can almost taste your pussy when he does that," he remarks as he glances back at me with a laugh. Tiberius continues to lick Pater's face until he pulls away from him. "Alright, that's about enough of that. Now, you really didn't think I was going to let you violate my wife and not punish you, did you?"

"What? Luke, he doesn't know any better. I forced myself on him, he didn't do anything to me. I swear! Please, I'll open the door and he can run away, and I'll tell Aaron and Crystal that it was my fault he's gone. I'll give them their money back and maybe they'll forgive me. Okay? You don't have to punish him; punish me, okay?" I plead, ringing my hands nervously.

"Hm. It's a tempting offer, but if I can't resist putting my face in between your thighs, what's to say he won't try it again?" he asks, turning his attention back to Tiberius. "I think he'll be okay after this."

Pater pushes the dog down firmly. I move forward to try and stop him, but it's too late. Tiberius lets out a loud yelping noise as Pater drives the blade under his chin, up through the top of his head.

"I always did like animals," he says, more to himself than me, as he turns the blade viciously so that the dog doesn't suffer any more than it needs to. "Just not this one."

CHAPTER 27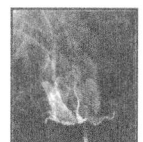

Numb doesn't begin to describe how I feel anymore. I'm hollow, empty, void of life, and yet here I stand watching Pater as he turns the dog onto its back and splits it open. He's talking to me, telling me how he'll skin the dog and make a blanket for our newborn child when we have one, but his voice is so distorted that I'm sure I've lost most of his words in translation. Or maybe this is all just a bad dream, and I'll wake up in a world where it all starts at the beginning and never makes it this far.

I turn away from what he's doing and wrap my arms around myself as I walk back into the living room. Vaughn is dead at this point; his back is no longer moving up and down, and as I walk over and place a hand gently on his back, I can feel him starting to become cold to the touch. The sweet peach colored skin that once shown so warmly on him before our lives became this Hell, is slowly turning a soft shade of pale. I know that when it's over, he'll be bitter blue and no amount of trying to keep his body warm will make him the beautiful boy he used to be again.

"I'm sorry, my sweet boy," I whisper, leaning down and

kissing the top of his head. I pull my shirt off over my head and lay it across his stiffening body. It's not much, but it's the only comfort I can offer to him now.

I think I can hear Pater calling out my name, but I continue my pilgrimage slowly toward the front door, walking out and around the house.

While it would have been much easier to walk out the back door, I would have had to walk past Pater to get there, and I can't stand the sight of him anymore. His bitter tongue has told enough lies that I would prefer to leave this fucking world without hearing any more false promises of how good a life is yet to come.

I push my way through the brushes, the low hanging branches, acquiring more scrapes than I ever have in the oubliette, but I don't care. Eloy is out here somewhere, and I have to say goodbye to him.

When I make it into the clearing, I can see that his body is even more mangled than before and he's toppled off the throne. I assume wild animals have gotten to him, though it won't deter me from giving my youngest the same gentle kiss I gave to his brother. I loved them both equally, and I still do; even if they went to their deaths believing otherwise, I hope they knew in their hearts that my love for them never faltered.

I pull his body toward the center of the clearing and turn him onto his back. Brushing his hair off his face, I lean down and kiss his forehead. Had I been strong enough to end him when commanded, his death would have been so much easier than it became.

I'll always owe Eloy a debt I cannot repay, but I'll find a way to make it right in the next life. Maybe he'll smile at me when he sees me; maybe it'll be his turn to throw stones.

Either way, I just hope to God he doesn't hate me for all that's happened to him.

I wish I knew where Laura was. Pater hid her body so well that I'll never be able to say goodbye to her. I can't hate her for what's happened to us; as much as I want to, I understand now. She didn't have a choice in what happened, and she probably didn't realize how evil Pater was until it was too late.

Getting back to my feet, I look up through the trees and sigh.

"I'm sorry, Mom. I know you tried," I whisper into the oblivion. "It ends with me; I promise."

I can hear Pater again. He's outside. His footsteps are fast approaching, because he knows I'd come out here. I don't answer him, instead taking in the last few peaceful moments I can with the one I've wronged the most.

Lowering myself to the ground, I turn my body toward Eloy and wrap an arm around him, as I close my eyes and wait for a well-deserved death to be bestowed upon me.

EPILOGUE
PATER

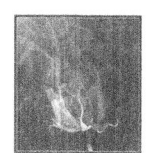

Three years later

"What have I told you about going near the well?"

I walk over and pick up my daughter, laughing as her light brown pigtails brush against my face. The sound of her laughter is what keeps me going; that, and knowing that she loves me as unconditionally as I love her. She doesn't see a monster, she sees a father, and that's how it should be.

"You're too curious for your own good," I chide her kindly, giving her a kiss on the cheek. She smiles widely in return, and I can't help but laugh, because I know that smile all too fucking well.

Laughing, she pushes my face away. It's the stubble against their smooth skin that always gets them. For the most part, anyway, because I have no intention of making this one my wife. I want to play the part of the dutiful father for a while. I want to make sure that she has a good upbringing, and that she never hears about her good-for-nothing brothers and grandmother.

Nah, I'll tell her all about what a good life those three had if she ever asks about them, which I don't know why she would. I never had any pictures of any of them, so it would only be word of mouth, and there's no one around to fill her head with lies against me.

She would never believe it. She only knows me as a good daddy, because that's what I am. I'm the best fucking father she'll ever have, and I was to my other kids, too; they just chose to always see the bad side of shit.

"Why do you keep coming out here, huh?" I ask her with a smile.

I don't want to think about the past anymore. It's not gonna do anything but put me in a shitty mood, and she deserves better from me.

"Wanna take a better look? Come on, hold on tightly to Daddy, and I'll show you what's down there."

I shift her in my arms and hold her close as I walk closer to the well and kick the door open with my foot. You can't really see down too far, because that's how I had it built. I don't really like secrets, but some should be kept, and whatever she sees will be of her own choosing, not what's presented.

Children are so innocent at this age. It makes me miss simpler times when I was younger and didn't have to care for anyone other than myself, but I can honestly say that I chose this life because it was the best fit for me.

"Close your eyes," I say to her quickly. She likes to play peek-a-boo, and I'll turn her into a world class fucking champion if that's what she wants. Playing this little game right now will also lessen the blow of what she might see.

When the sun is at its peak like it is right now, you can almost see all the way down to the bottom.

Almost.

I don't go down there, but before I decided I wanted to keep my baby safe from all the bullshit lies, I did manage to buy and throw some barrels of hay into the well. I figure it was a small act of kindness; a creature comfort for having to stay in a place like that.

I'm not afraid of the oubliette, I'm just better than being reduced to having to stay there, is all.

"Ready?" I say, poking her gently in the stomach.

She lets out a giddy giggle as she peeks through her chubby little fingers and smiles at me, "Yeah!"

"Oh! I can see you peeking!" I say to her playfully. She giggles again and covers her eyes completely. "Alright, baby girl. On three. Ready? One ... Two ... Two and a half ..." she giggles again, and I can't help but laugh. Pulling her close, I give her a kiss on the side of her head before I finish my countdown, "Three! Open your eyes and look!"

She quickly pulls her hands away and leans so far over that I have to adjust her again to keep her from falling.

"Hi Mama!" she calls out.

I can hear the hay shifting slightly, but there's no response.

"Hey! She's talking to you!" I call down sharply. "Say hi!"

The same sound of the rustling needles greets my ears and I sigh.

"Mama's tired right now, baby girl. She'll be okay to talk to you tomorrow. Is that alright?"

"Bye Mama!" she calls out again.

I guess it is.

I use my foot to close the lid again, then place her back

down onto the grass. I cross my arms loosely over my chest, and laugh as she takes off running, squealing happily at the top of her lungs.

I'll never replace Jocelyn as my true wife. I can't; that girl has meant more to me than any other wife before her, and she's helped me a lot too, in the emotional sense. She showed me that I *can* be a better person, and when I still feel the need for physical contact, I toss the ladder down into the well so I can fuck her.

It's probably why she's still alive, too. Being able to fuck her keeps my mind straight on being a father and not the evil bastard she thinks I am. Maybe one day I'll let her out permanently, and we can raise this one together, but I doubt it.

If she knew the little collection of wasted wives I kept in my special rooms that she's so damn scared of, she'd know that being down in the hole is better than being above ground for her.

I can't help but shake my head and chuckle.

A few years ago, when that couple came back to get their damn dog, she spilled every single fucking secret we had, so of course I had to kill them. I didn't want to, but she forced my hand. The best part is that no one ever came looking for them. There were no missing persons alerts in the newspapers or in the media.

I found out later on that they were drifters. They never ended up renting the house next door; they just wanted someone to watch their dog while they found a new place to squat.

Fucking losers.

All of them.

Laura. Vaughn. Eloy.

But I guess it's safe to say that a wasted fuck, leads to a

waste of children, with the exception of my sweet Joce. God, just thinking about her down in the darkness, dirty, alone, scared, is enough to make me wanna throw the ladder down for a quick fuck, but I can't today.

I promised my baby girl I'd take her to the zoo, and since I'm damn determined to be a good fucking parent, that's what we're gonna do.

CINERE

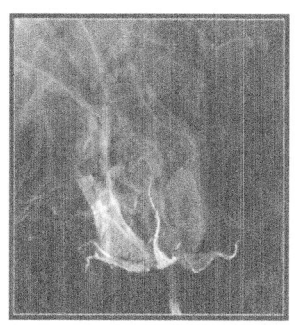

ACKNOWLEDGMENTS

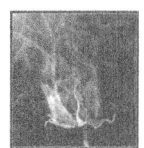

My PAs, Ginja, Bootz, and Meanie, thank you for sitting through the headache that is Yolanda Olson and not quitting on me. Specifically when I said I was going to write about this bastard again. Your reactions were priceless and I'm still smiling thinking about it!

Abigail Davies of Pink Elephant Designs for bringing the fuego and you're undying excitement in creating this cover! Tu eres un amiga increíble, gracias por las risas.

Dez of Pretty in Ink Creations. I know how you feel about this man, so thank you for going through it again and editing it and for the beautiful formatting!

The Twisted Rabbits; some of you sat through him again as I told the story, and some of you got to see him in pieces before you saw the whole picture. I cannot thank you enough

for keeping me laughing and typing when I thought this might not be my best idea. You ladies are the best!

And last, but never least, to my readers. I bet you didn't see this coming. Daddy's back.

WELCOME BACK

Well, holy shit.

I'm impressed that we have company again so soon and even more impressed that you've even decided to come back to my humble home.

Make yourself comfortable, because man, have I got a story to tell you this time! The little one you'll see running around from time to time is Darby; I'm sure you remember her from the last time you came over.

The house is a hell of a lot more quiet without the other three running around like the little assholes that they were, but I'm sure you'll recognize a couple of people once I get started here.

Buckle up, kid.

This is gonna be one wild ride.

CHAPTER 1

I NEVER DID FEEL good about what happened to Jocelyn. What ended up becoming of her is not my fault though, because disobedient children always did leave a sour taste in my mouth, and she knew that.

Maybe things shouldn't have ended the way they did, but what's done is done and I don't have the will or the want to start over with her again.

The boys were a fucking waste—I never cared much for either of them, Jocelyn on the other hand; man, was she special. The unadulterated embodiment of everything I ever wanted and needed, and she did a damn fine job of taking care of her wifely duties until those little fuckers got inside her head.

It's alright though, because they got what they deserved, and in a way, so did she.

Her entire purpose for even being allowed above ground as long as I let her was to give me children. She only gave me one, but that's better than what Laura did, giving me three, two of which were fucking useless.

But as I lie here on my lawn chair watching little Darby running around picking wildflowers, her pigtails bouncing in excitement each time she finds a new one, I can't help but think that we did alright.

She's about five now, which is almost as long as Joce has been in the oubliette. After I delivered the baby from her womb, I tossed her down in the fucking ground where she belonged for disobeying me one too many times.

It's a damn shame it had to come to this because there are nights where I'll admit that I miss feeling her body next to mine on our bed. Hell, there are even some nights, after I put Darby to bed, that I go into my room and jerk off thinking about the way her mouth felt on my dick.

Part of the reason I get hard is because I miss Joce's touch, but the other part is because I know that Darby will be just as good as her Momma when the time comes and it's something I can't wait to fucking experience.

"Don't get too close to the well! I told you about that!" I call out to her when she starts picking wildflowers at the base of it.

That little girl is full of spunk and curiosity, but unlike her Momma, she listens to me. I know with time that will go away, because all children go through a stage of defiance, but I hope she'll learn to love me the way that Joce did.

The more I think about things, the more I have to force myself to keep my hands off of her. Darby isn't ready for me yet, and I don't want her to be afraid of me—not when she's supposed to love me.

Maybe I'll bring Joce up for a family day soon. It'll be easier for Darby if she sees how a daughter is supposed to love her Daddy, so she'll be ready when it's her turn to try.

Getting to my feet, I walk over to my baby and pick her up off the grass causing her to squeal happily. She loves the way my beard feels against her chubby cheeks—it always makes her laugh like this.

"Why don't you go inside and put those flowers in a vase? I'll be in shortly. I'm just gonna have a quick talk with your Momma, okay?" I say to her, gently kissing her cheek.

She squeals again and nods, kicking her feet so that I know she wants to get down, then turns and runs back toward the house.

I watch her, my hands on my hips, and sigh. Yeah; things would be a hell of a lot easier on her, if Jocelyn were up here with us.

CHAPTER 2

"She smells a lot like you did before you crawled into my bed for the first time," I say quietly into the dark hole. Jocelyn doesn't respond but I know she can hear me, so I continue. "I thought that she would taste like you too, but I think that maybe I waited too long to find out—or it could be that I took my taste before she was ripe enough."

When I hear her shifting on the hay at the bottom of the oubliette, I smirk and keep going.

"I don't know. A lot of this shit doesn't seem to make sense anymore. It's not the way it was when you were above ground—I won't lie about that. I do miss you sometimes, Joce, but you're too fucking willful to be up here with us. Hell, you'd probably try to grab my baby and make a run for it even though you know how that would end. And that's why you're down in the hole where you belong," I say, crouching down and putting a hand on either side of the well.

A rock goes whizzing by my head and I move quickly enough to keep from getting cracked in the face with it, letting out a laugh.

"Still got some spirit, I see. Relax; I haven't touched her. I just wanted to make sure I had your attention, and now that I do, I want to make a proposition."

Jocelyn throws another rock, but this time I catch it, stand up, and start tossing it up in the air.

"If you keep throwing shit at me, I'll just seal this fucking well up forever and you'll starve to death. I think maybe you should listen to what I have to say," I reply conversationally.

She shifts again down in the dark, but at least there aren't any more rocks being hurled at me. I'll have to get down there soon and find out how she got them. Can't have her thinking she's got some kind of upper-hand on me by sneaking shit around when she thinks no one is looking.

I catch the rock in my hand again and cast a thoughtful glance at the house. The only way she's been getting these is if Darby's been tossing them down to her, which means I'll have to teach her a lesson in discipline sooner rather than later.

Fuck, I think with a sigh. I was hoping to avoid that shit until later, but I don't want her to think she can give her Momma "presents" without me knowing about it.

Nothing a sound spanking can't fix.

"What do you want?" Joce calls up weakly.

Huh. I had almost forgotten about her already. I guess knowing what I have waiting for me in the face of what I had, is a bit more distracting than I thought it would be.

"I want to bring you up for a day," I say, crouching back down and grinning into the darkness. "I want us to have a proper day together—as a family. I think Darby deserves that, don't you?"

She's quiet now because she thinks there's a trick somewhere in my offer. There's not—I'm fresh out of ways to fool Joce and she should know that by now.

"What's the catch?" she calls up quietly.

"No catch," I reply immediately with a chuckle. "You know how important it is for a child to be with their mother *and* father. Well, maybe you don't because Laura split, but Darby shouldn't know what you felt like. I think she should know us both, even if for a day. Come on, kid. Don't you want the chance to be a *real* mother this time?"

Jocelyn lets out a sigh that echoes off the stone walls surrounding her. I can tell she's seriously contemplating my offer now. Either that or she's already thinking of her escape plan, but she should know better.

"Okay," she finally says softly. "I'll do it."

A grin instantly spreads across my face. Nothing is sexier than a woman that's willing to comply with a simple request. I reach down, grabbing the rope and toss it into the hole.

"Come on up when you're ready. We'll be inside, baby girl," I say before I walk away.

I have to find Darby and get her to take a nap or something because if Jocelyn looks anything like I think she might right now, she's gonna need a hot shower and a change of clothes before she sees our daughter.

CHAPTER 3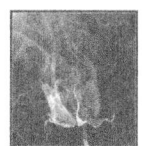

I KISS Darby's forehead as she snuggles underneath her light pink, plush blanket, and closes her eyes. I had to make a deal with her—if she behaved like the good little girl I know she can be and take her nap now, she'd have a surprise waiting for her when she woke up, but not a moment sooner.

I can hear the backdoor slam shut, which tells me that Joce is finally in the house. I look down at Darby who opens her eyes curiously, but I hold a finger to my lips and grin at her. She giggles, closes her eyes again, and pretends to be asleep. I'll stay with her a little while longer to make sure she doesn't ruin her own surprise.

Not that she'll recognize Jocelyn right away since she never got the chance to know her, but I still want to be the one that physically brings them together.

Whatever happens after that depends on how much of a mother the bitch plans on being.

I run a hand over Darby's hair and smile. She looks so much like her Momma at this age, that they could pass for twins.

Man, that would have been something,

I think with a soft chuckle as I ease myself off the side of the bed where I've been sitting. My baby will be asleep in no time now—I can tell by the way her breathing is evening out, so I suppose I should go see what kind of fight Joce has in her these days.

I begin to hum as I gently close the door to Darby's bedroom. It'll give the other one a chance to know I'm coming and I think it's the right thing to do since she never did care for surprises. I never understood why though, because any surprise I ever had for her usually ended with my dick in one of her holes.

She liked it, I know she did. Even after those little miserable brats got inside her head, she would still moan the same way her whore mother did whenever I fucked her.

It'll feel nice to slide my dick into some pussy again but before that happens, she probably needs to get cleaned up and eat something substantial. I don't want her dying on me while I'm fucking her because that would cross a line of morality I am not comfortable with.

I walk into the kitchen and smile at her when I see her standing just inside the doorway. She looks so damn dirty and she's lost quite a bit of weight, but that's what happens when you try to undermine authority.

"You can come in," I tell her as I walk toward the refrigerator and open the freezer door. "I won't be expecting you to make dinner for us tonight, but if you're still up here tomorrow, then you probably should."

I pull out a pint of Ben and Jerry's Chocolate Chip Cookie Dough, then head toward the counter to retrieve a spoon from the drawer next to the sink. I make my way back to the table, kick my feet up, and pull the lid off, digging my spoon in and scooping up some ice cream.

"Damn that's good," I say quietly as I lick the spoon before turning my attention back to Jocelyn. "I'd offer you some, but you're really fucking dirty right now and I don't feel like grabbing another spoon."

She wraps her arms around herself and looks down at her bare feet. I watch her shuffle in place a few times before she turns her eyes back to the doorway and I chuckle.

"Go ahead; try to run. You're not gonna get very far and you know it," I say, digging my spoon back into the pint. I set it down on the table, drop my feet to the floor, and rest an arm on the polished wood. As I start to drum my fingertips along the tabletop, Jocelyn sighs and turns her attention back to me.

"Can I go take a shower?" she asks timidly.

"Yes," I reply with a nod. "You know where our bedroom is, and your clothes are where you left them. Get yourself nice and clean, then come back and talk to me. It's been a while since I've had some adult conversation."

The smirk on my face is enough to make her wince, but she knows better than to defy me again. One wrong move and back into the ground she goes, only this time, she'll fucking stay there.

I watch her leave the room and pick my pint back up when I'm confident she won't stray anywhere she doesn't belong right now. I'm sure she'll want to stop by her brothers' room, but that belongs to Darby now and none of their shit is in there. I built a bonfire one night and burned it all to hell—I figured they could use it there while they rot.

I wouldn't imagine that Eloy and Vaughn went anywhere good. Honor Thy Mother and Father is one of the Ten Commandments and they sure fucked that up big time.

Not that I'm a religious man, but I like to think logically

about things and if that's what I can use to be able to sleep better at night knowing that those little fucks are out of my hair forever, then Hell, I'm willing to play along and believe.

"Fuck 'em," I say to no one in particular as I pick the pint back up and keep eating.

Jocelyn is here now, and Darby will get to know her Momma soon enough. And if they're both really good girls, they'll get to know me too.

CHAPTER 4

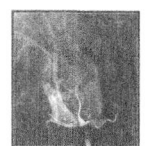

Once I finished my ice cream and tossed the empty pint into the trash can, I made my way into the living room to lie down on the couch and wait for Jocelyn. I can hear the shower knobs turning so I know she's done now, I just have to wait for her to dry up and get dressed.

Ever since she was a little girl, she's always been very curious and I'm hoping that she knows better at this point. She knows that she's only to go to our room, shower, then come straight to me. I'm hoping she's not dumb enough to try and sneak a glance into the boys' room because if she does, she'll see Darby and that'll pop open a can of worms that I don't have the can opener for just yet.

I close my eyes and sigh as I clasp my hands over my chest. If she's smart—and I know she is, she'll probably try to take me out thinking I'm asleep, but I'm ready for that. These kids have always kept me on my toes when they were all around, and anything they've tried, I've already done before.

It's the proverbial eyes in the back of the head thing that

parents always talk about. Kids think it's all bullshit until they're caught being dumb little fucks, then they are amazed as hell that we knew all along.

I don't regret having any of them, I just wish they turned out better is all.

Now, I could take some blame for it but I won't. I did what I could with them and that's all there is to that story. Darby on the other hand ... I'll do much better with her.

"Hi."

I open my eyes and cock my head to the side, a smile spreading across my face. Jocelyn is standing just inside the living room, her hands firmly clasped in front of her, and her hair damply sitting on her shoulders.

"Didn't have time to dry up completely?" I ask with a laugh.

"I ... I just didn't want to draw attention to myself," she says, her eyes darting nervously around the room. "I can go back and fix it if you want me to."

"Nah," I reply, swinging my legs off the side of the couch. "Come on in and have a seat, kid. Let's catch up."

She clears her throat and walks toward the chair that sits directly across from the couch. In a way, it reminds me of the last time that

Laura came to visit because she sat in that same damn chair.

Fucking bitches and that chair, I think as I shake my head. Maybe that'll be the next thing I make a bonfire for—it's just up to Joce if she's in the damn thing when I decide to take it out back.

"So, how ya been?" I ask, leaning back and crossing my hands behind my head. I'm not exactly sure what I'm expecting her to say, but I wait for her answer anyway. I stopped going to check on her as often as I used to when I first tossed her down there. I didn't want Darby getting too curious about the oubliette, even though she clearly already has.

Jocelyn doesn't say anything. Instead, she folds her hands on her lap and glances up at me every now and then, cutting her eyes toward the door.

I sigh loudly. "When did you become such a pussy? Seriously, kid. You used to be so full of spunk and ready to fight at a moment's notice, and now you're this docile little piece of shit and it's starting to bug me."

This time, when she glances up at me and meets my eyes, she holds them in hers. I can tell that I'm starting to make her angry and that's what I want because that's when she fucks the best.

"Good," I say evenly, with a nod. "Get pissed off. You've got a child in this house that you don't even know yet, and by the looks of it, you only seem to give a shit about yourself right now. That's not a good look for you, *Mommy*."

"Must have been the example I had growing up," she replies curtly, inspecting her fingernails.

"Damn," I reply with a chuckle. "That had some bite to it, little girl."

Jocelyn shrugs indifferently and puts a hand to her stomach. I can tell she's hungry, but I don't know if she's worth sparing any food on.

Not yet, anyway.

Anyone, with the exception of Darby that wants to eat under *my* roof, has to work for it.

"Hungry? Wanna sing for your supper?" I ask her deviously as I lean forward and rest my arms on my knees.

She looks away for a moment, contemplating her answer, but if she waits for too long, I'll just take what I want anyway, and she knows it.

"Yes," she finally says softly.

"Good girl," I say with a nod, getting to my feet and holding a hand out toward her. I don't mind her putting up a fight every now and again, but right now, it'll be much easier if she remembers to do as she's told.

CHAPTER 5

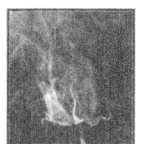

"GODDAMN," I moan in a heavy breath as Jocelyn grinds her hips on top of me. It's been so long since I've been fucked, that I'm trying not to cum too fast. It's only been ten minutes after all, and I already had to grind my teeth to hold onto my load when she was giving me head.

"Come on, girl," I say through grit teeth, giving her ass a firm slap. I can tell her heart isn't into it, but I can't fuck her heart, so I don't particularly care about that.

I slide my hands up the sides of her body, then jerk her down toward me. Her lips are a few inches away from mine, and the feeling of her hot breath on my face is fucking intoxicating.

I grip her arms tightly and grin. Joce closes her eyes and braces herself, because she knows what's coming next.

Her.

I lift my ass off the bed and begin to fuck her, my grin widening when I see that familiar look take over her face. Her tits are bouncing and grazing against my chest as she holds my forearms tightly. I haven't given it to her like this since the first time I fucked her, and it almost feels brand new again.

"Are you gonna be a good girl and cum for me?" I ask her in bated breaths. She lets out a sound that is something between a strangled yes and a moan, as I fuck her harder.

I don't mind doing all this work because if I'm being honest, the best pussy I've ever had belongs to this one right here.

For now.

The thought of Darby sleeping so innocently in her bed while I fuck her mother enters my head and I'm flooded with the memory of when this was Laura on top of me and Joce was sleeping in her room. I can feel my balls tightening as I keep fucking her and she moans louder.

Just like her mother.

"Oh my God..." she whimpers as her body begins to stiffen, her breathing becoming heavier.

"Yes, I am. Now give me what you owe me," I say, before I pull her down and crush her lips against my own. The sweat on her upper lip is salty but sinfully sweet.

She moans loudly into my mouth before her pussy begins to tighten around my cock and I groan. Jocelyn is cumming harder than she ever has before, and I think that's worth a meal or two.

She falls against me, breathing heavily, her body shaking, and I put an arm around her. Kissing the top of her head, I run my fingers down her back and smile.

"Just like old times, isn't it?" I ask her softly.

Jocelyn puts a hand to my chest and lets it linger there, lulling me into a false sense of feeling loved. It doesn't last too long though, because she's just using me as leverage to pull herself off of me.

I raise an eyebrow and prop myself up on my elbows. I

watch her as she moves off the side of the bed, and gets to her feet, reaching down for her panties and dress.

"Wham, bam, thank you ma'am," I mutter, leaning back onto the bed and sighing.

Once she's dressed, she turns to face me, arms crossed loosely over her chest.

I roll my eyes and push myself off the bed, putting my hands on my hips.

"Well? What the fuck are you waiting for? Go make some dinner," I snap at her.

"I thought you said –"

"I changed my mind. Now go cook something for all three of us and maybe if you do a good job, I'll let you meet the kid," I reply with a smirk.

With a defeated sigh and tears in her

eyes, Jocelyn turns and leaves the room. I may seem like a bastard to her, but the only way to rule a home properly is with an iron fist and my word is fucking law.

CHAPTER 6

CHAPER 6

I stop and check on Darby once I'm dressed again. She's still fast asleep and I can't help but smile at how beautiful she is. It wasn't too long ago, theoretically speaking, that I used to stand in the doorway and watch Jocelyn sleep. She was always such a good little girl until her whore of a mother got pregnant again. And then another time after that, even though I told the bitch that I didn't want anymore kids other than our perfect little girl.

Boys.

What the fuck was I supposed to do with them? Play sports? Show them how to fish? No; they were a waste of time and I didn't care enough to pay them any mind.

Not until they started to turn my Joce against me. That's when I knew I had to put a stop to that shit.

It's also how I know that Darby won't be a problem. Once she sees the example that I've set with her mother, she'll be the perfect little girl that I've been missing ever since Jocelyn was ruined.

I take a step back and close the door as quietly as I can. I won't wake her up just yet because she can get really fucking cranky if woken up before she's ready.

I chuckle as I walk down the hallway, down the stairs, and toward the kitchen. She gets that from me, and while I'll admit that it's not my best quality, it's nice to know that even though she looks like her mother, she's still got some of her daddy in her.

"It's starting to smell good in here," I say appreciatively as I enter the kitchen.

Jocelyn has her back to me as she places a slab of seasoned meat into the oven. I'm not sure what she's making, but I do know that it'll more than likely be good enough to let her read Darby a bedtime story tonight.

"Whatcha making?" I ask, walking up behind her and placing my hands on her hips. I push myself against her and she goes rigid for a moment before remembering the predicament she's in and relaxes.

"Braised pork shoulder," she replies quietly.

"You're making my favorite?" I ask her with a laugh. "I guess you really wanna see the kid, don't you?"

She shrugs and turns to face me, crossing her arms over her chest again. I hate that she's so damn stand-offish with me— especially since we just shared such a beautiful moment in the bedroom.

I sigh and rub my face irritably.

"Uncross them," I say sternly. Her arms immediately drop to her sides and she looks down at her feet. "Alright. I know what's gonna make you feel better. You keep yourself busy in here and I'll be right back."

Joce turns back to the oven and I run a hand back

through my hair, shaking my head as I leave her alone in the kitchen again. What I should do is hold her against the refrigerator and fuck her again, but I doubt she has the stamina for another go right now.

I go back to Darby's room and push the door open quietly. She's gonna be so pissed when I wake her up, but I know how to stop her temper before it flares into a tantrum.

"Wake up, baby girl," I say, gently running a hand over her head.

She groans and rolls on her side, her back toward me, as she snuggles her blanket closer to her little body.

"Come on, Darbs. It's time to wake up now," I say, giving her a gentle shake.

"No," she barks, her back still to me.

I can't help but laugh. How this kid can go from happily picking wildflowers to being so damn pissy about being woken up is beyond me. That's something we'll have to work on in the near future.

"Darbs," I say sternly. "Wake up. Let's go. I got your surprise waiting."

At the mention of the surprise I promised her, she sits right up and looks at me with a tired smile on her face. I wait patiently while she rubs the sleep away from her eyes before she pushes her blanket off and holds her arms out toward me.

I pick her up and kiss her cheek. She giggles quietly as she nuzzles into my neck and I carry her out of the room.

I'm not sure how she's going to react to Jocelyn when they're face to face. She's only ever heard her voice and I don't keep pictures of the kids around. It's a waste of space and I don't care for clutter. I'm sure she'll see herself in her Momma and she'll probably love her right away, but the only way to find out is to take her into the kitchen.

I walk slowly, deliberately.

We play a game of peek-a-boo on the way to the kitchen because I want to keep her distracted long enough to give her a chance to understand what's happening when I tell her who the lady in the kitchen is.

It's almost just like Laura all over again,

I think with a chuckle as we finally reach the doorway. I put Darby down and turn her to face me.

"I want you to go say hi to the nice lady. She's being nice and making us supper. Go tell her thank you," I say, running a hand over the side of her face.

Darby nods and turns around, running the few steps toward Joce. She reaches up and pulls on her dress, a big smile on her face.

"Thank you!" she shouts gleefully when Jocelyn looks down at her.

I laugh and lean a hand on the door frame, watching them carefully. Jocelyn bites her lip so damn hard, I'm worried she's going to draw blood and scare Darbs.

"Watch it," I warn her in a low tone.

She quickly wipes the tears from her eyes and crouches down in front of our daughter, trying her best to smile.

"You're welcome," she whispers.

Darby puts her arms around Joce's shoulders and gives her a quick hug, before she runs over to the table and pulls herself up onto one of the chairs.

She doesn't get it, I think with a relieved sigh.

"Guess we'll hold onto to our little secret just a bit longer," I say to Jocelyn evenly as I walk over to the table and take the seat next to Darby.

Jocelyn looks at the little girl and wrings her hands nervously before she turns her back to us again. I won't tell Darby just yet. There's no point in ruining her supper by telling her that the nice lady in the kitchen cooking is really nothing more than a disappointment for both of us.

I decided that while Jocelyn is keeping herself busy making dinner, that I'd let Darby color at the table. I usually don't allow that, but it'll keep her occupied and not ask her Momma any questions.

It's just in her nature to be so damn curious. Always wants to know who, what, and why, never stopping her barrage of questions until she gets an answer she's satisfied with.

Vaughn asked too many fucking questions too, I think with a slight shudder. I get that Darby will inherit some of their traits, but I can hope that she'll be just like me when she gets older. The way I choose to live my life with my family makes perfect sense to me— even if no one else would understand it.

I glance over at her happily coloring next to me and run a hand back over her hair.

Yeah; I can't help but think that even though the rest of them were fucking failures, this one will make me proud.

"Oh man!" she cries out, causing Joce to turn around quickly. Her eyes immediately fall on me instead of Darby and I roll my eyes at her. Obviously, she still thinks the worst of me.

"What's wrong baby?" I ask her.

"I broke my crayon," she replies with a pout, holding up her blue crayon for me to see it. The top partially snapped off because of how hard she was rubbing it against the paper.

"Well," I say, getting up from the table and walking over to the junk drawer next to the sink. "That's why you need to be more patient when you're coloring. We talked about patience before, remember?"

I fish around in the drawer until I find the box of crayons I'm looking for. Darby has a habit of snapping her crayons when she colors, so I have a box that I keep in here for moments like this. I pull out the blue crayon then toss the box back into the drawer, closing it with my hip, and running a knuckle down Joce's back before I head back to the table.

I sit down and hold the crayon out to Darby who's now watching Jocelyn with suspicion growing in her big brown eyes, and I chuckle.

"Darbs? Would you like your crayon?" I ask her with a grin.

"Yes, please," she says quietly, narrowing her eyes. She reaches for the crayon then puckers her lips for me and I give her a gentle kiss on the lips before she goes back to coloring again.

So far I've taught her that when Daddy does something nice for her, then Daddy gets a thank you kiss.

Baby steps.

The loud sigh that comes from Jocelyn tells me that she was watching us. It doesn't matter to me; she went through this same fucking training so she'll know when it's time to worry. Not that I think it's something to worry about—to me it's just a different way of showing love, and I prefer it.

And no matter how much huffing and puffing she's doing, I know damn well that she does too.

I rest my chin in my hand and watch Darby color in her blue sky. She's very good at not running over any lines when she's coloring and I can tell that's the perfectionist in me rubbing off on her already.

"Another hour and dinner will be ready," Jocelyn announces in a subdued tone.

"Alright," I reply indifferently, not looking up from the paper. "Mind if I color with you?"

Darby looks up at me and flashes a happy, toothy smile, handing me the yellow crayon and telling me to color in the flowers while she works on the sky.

I clear my throat and pull my chair closer to hers, then begin to do as she's asked of me. I like doing little things like this with her—it helps me understand this whole parenting thing on a different level.

I'm so lost in making this precious memory with Darby that I never realize that Jocelyn is standing next to me. Not until I feel the cold blade of the knife she's holding, under my chin. Not until she digs it in a little and uses it to lift my face.

I let the crayon drop from my fingers onto the paper and it quietly rolls over to Darby, who almost immediately starts crying.

She doesn't understand.

She doesn't know that her Momma wants revenge for shit that was done to her and she doesn't realize that by the time this little family day is over, one of us will be in the ground permanently.

It all depends on who has the bigger set of balls, I think as I look Jocelyn square in the eyes and grin.

CHAPTER 7

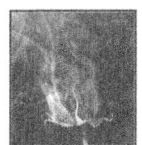

"Are you gonna use that or are you trying to see how far you can go before you piss me off?" I ask her evenly, the grin never leaving my face.

Her jaw clenches as she digs it in a little deeper and I find myself pushing against it. Jocelyn's never had the fucking guts to do anything like this. When she knocked out Laura, she wasn't even woman enough to finish the job—I had to toss that shit on one of her brothers to handle. I let him get some action before it was all said and done, and no matter how much he fucking cried about it, I knew he wouldn't be able to deny that his first pussy would be the one he would have always remembered had he still been alive.

With a sigh, I slap the knife out of her hand and get to my feet, pulling her body tightly against mine. I point at Darby who's still crying and decide to give her a little lesson in parenting.

"You see this? That's what *you* did. She was just fine with the two of us sitting here spending some time together, until *you* decided to try and grow a pair and knife me in front of her. That's some shit I never did in front of any of you. Are you proud of yourself? Is this the kind of mother you want to be, because if it is, then you better make damn sure that the next time you pull any kind of weapon on me that you fucking use it."

I shove her away and walk over to Darbs, putting an arm around her shoulders and tell her that it's okay. I tell her that the lady was just playing a scary game and that there's no reason to cry anymore.

"The dog," Jocelyn says quietly.

"Oh, fuck the dog," I snap at her. Then a slow smile starts to spread across my face. "Not the way you did."

The callousness of my tone, of what I just said to her, slaps her in the face hard and she turns away and runs toward the living room. I roll my eyes and sigh again when I hear her burst into tears, but if she's trying to get away from the memory of *that* day, then maybe she should go into a different room.

"Come on," I say to Darby, as I get to my feet and pick her up into my arms. "You gotta learn to toughen up. Have you ever seen your daddy crying?"

She shakes her head and takes a deep, shuddering breath as she buries her head into my neck. Her little fingers are grazing the back of my neck as she tries to find some comfort in my hug and I have to start walking before I put her down and give Jocelyn a reason to try and grow balls again.

The back of my neck has always been one of my sweet spots, but Darby doesn't know that yet.

"How long do you plan on blubbering for?" I ask Jocelyn, entering the room. I shift Darby from one arm to the other, and she claws my neck trying to get away from the entire situation.

"Calm down, baby," I say gently into her ear. "No one's gonna hurt me, alright? She was just playing a game, like I said. Tell her you were just playing a game."

A fresh round of sobs bursts from somewhere inside of Jocelyn and I'm staring to rethink even taking her out of the damn ground. If this is a sign of what I'm going to have to deal with until I'm bored with this entire fucking scenario, then I might as well just drag her back outside and shove her in. Maybe she'll save me some grief and break her neck on the way down.

The only problem with Jocelyn actually dying is that it'll make me feel bad in a way. Not because I don't think she doesn't deserve it, but because I think it would make me look like a bad father if another one bites the dust.

Not that the other two were my fault for the most part, but like I said, there's just something special about Jocelyn. Ideally, I'd like to keep her here in the house with me and Darby. I would love to watch her be a parent to her own child, but she's already baring her teeth and it hasn't even been an entire day.

Suddenly, Joce drops her hands from her face and looks up at us. She's still crying and heartbroken or whatever, and I can tell that she's trying her damnedest to stop crying.

"I'm sorry," she begins in a strangled voice. "I was just playing a game and I got a little carried away."

Darby shakes her head against my neck and grips me tighter. She doesn't trust Jocelyn now and that's something that they'll have to work on if I decide that she's going to stay up here with us.

At least she didn't run off already like her bitch of a mother. One sign of weakness from me in Jocelyn's room the first night I had her, and Laura was off like a shot. She didn't give a good goddamn about her own kids. She only cared about getting away from us, and that's why that bitch went out the way she did.

"I didn't mean to make you cry," Joce says softly. "Please forgive me."

I grin at her as I rock Darby in my arms. There's my fighter—slowly but surely, she's starting to show herself again and it's all because of the little girl in my arms.

"Okay," Darbs sobs into my neck.

I roll my eyes and motion with my head for Jocelyn to come over to us.

"The only way this is going to work is if you two start getting along. You about ready for that?" I ask her when she's a few feet away from us. She wipes the tears away from her eyes and nods.

"Alright," I say, pulling Darby away from me and turning her around to face Jocelyn. "This is your big sister, baby. That's how I know she was playing a game, because I'm her daddy too."

Jocelyn sucks in a breath and gives me a horrified look as I smirk.

I really hope she didn't think I was going to make it that fucking easy for her.

CHAPTER 8

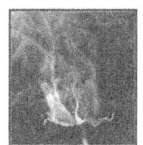

Supper's finally on the table and we've moved to the dining room so we can eat comfortably. Darby is shooting questions at her Momma faster than she can answer them, but I'm actually content to see that they're engaged in conversation finally.

Of course, she made her promise first to never try to hurt me again, and once that little deal was struck, the two of them became engrossed in each other.

Jocelyn asked her about her school and if she liked her teachers, and Darby told her that I keep her home and she gets her learning here instead of a school.

I take a sip of my wine as I watch the two of them. It really is like looking at the present and the past sitting across from each other. The same damn fire in their eyes, the same big brown eyes, and the same facial expressions. Hell, they even laugh the same way. If Darby were a little older, I'd take them both into my bedroom tonight, but she's not ready for that just yet.

"Did Pater tell you that you used to have brothers too?"

Jocelyn asks, resting her chin in her hand and smiling at Darby.

I slam my hand on the table and they both jump. When Joce looks at me, I give her a dangerous stare and shake my head slowly. She clears her throat and her eyes fall down to her plate.

"Who's Pater?" Darby asks curiously, tilting her head first at Jocelyn, then at me.

Joce clears her throat but instead of answering her, she stabs a piece of pork and pops it into her mouth. She smiles and shakes her head.

"Never mind," she replies once she's done chewing. "I was just remembering a nightmare I had once and I got confused with what I was trying to say."

"Okay," Darby replies with a shrug as she drops her fork onto her plate. "Daddy? I have to use the bathroom."

I nod and suck my teeth, before picking up my glass and taking another sip of wine. As Darby walks by me I smile at her and wait until she's gone from the room before I turn my attention back to Jocelyn.

"Don't you ever try that bullshit again, do you understand me? It'll take next to nothing to throw you back into that fucking pit and this time, I'll seal that lid forever," I snap at her as quietly as I can. Darby has some kind of sonic hearing and if I'm too loud right now,

I'm sure she'll hear me from wherever the hell she is right now.

"I'm sorry," Jocelyn says miserably for what seems like the millionth time in the past few hours. "I don't know what she does and doesn't know and I was just trying to talk to her."

"Ask her about her studies, her favorite colors, or her favorite cartoons. Don't ever bring up family again. The only family she needs to know about is the one at this table," I reply evenly.

Jocelyn turns her eyes toward me and holds my stare for a moment. I can see the small flame starting to build and it's making me hard.

"Why didn't you tell her I was her mother?" she asks me quietly.

I reach down under the table to shift myself. I don't want Darby to see this when she comes back. There will be plenty of time for that later.

"You're not a stupid girl, so stop acting like one," I respond with a smirk. "You want her to love you? To know who you *really* are? Then you're gonna have to stay above ground long enough to earn that. Shit doesn't get handed out in this house, you know that. Anything you want comes from being good and working hard."

"And does she have to work hard for everything she has so far?" she asks in a low, dangerous tone.

I throw my head back and laugh. Now *this* is the girl that I grew to love so many years ago. This is the girl that tried to send her brothers away from my house and this is the girl that'll do what I want her to do in order to try and do the same for Darby.

I drop my arms on the table and cross them, leaning forward and shaking my head.

"How old were you the first time I had you? Nine? Ten? Come on, Joce. You should know better; the kid is too young for me right now. Besides, she won't be able to take everything I have to offer, not until she's older and much deeper where I need her to be. I don't like my pussy to be too tight or too young."

"What's her name?" she asks thoughtfully after a moment.

"Darby," I reply with a smile. "Why?"

Jocelyn shrugs, "No reason other than a mother wanting to know her child's name."

"But you're not her mother," I remind her. "As of right now, you're just her sister that she never met before today."

Before Jocelyn has a chance to throw some more bullshit banter my way, Darby reenters the room and climbs back into her seat. She smiles at Jocelyn as she picks up her fork and keeps eating.

I'm not entirely sure if I'll pull the hood off of her head anytime soon and tell her who the lady across from her is. Mostly because I won't know how to explain why I lied to her, but maybe she'll be okay with it when the time comes.

Maybe she won't.

All I know is that the reason Jocelyn is here right now in this very house is to keep my dick satisfied until I'm ready for Darby to take her place. Hopefully she'll keep her fucking mouth shut on matters that she shouldn't speak about long enough to keep my baby girl pure for a little while longer.

I sure would hate to break with tradition before the time is right all because of a mouthy bitch that doesn't know her place.

CHAPTER 9

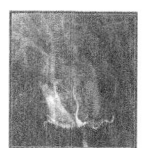

We've finished supper and Darby is eating some dessert while Joce picks up the mess. I've invited her to come back into the dining room with us when she's done and have some of the pie that I made yesterday. She knows that I like a spotless home, so she'll do her best to pass inspection and be able to spend more time with Darby.

Twenty more minutes go by before Jocelyn reappears, clearing her throat in the doorway of the dining room. I lean over and give Darbs a kiss on the cheek, before getting up and walking past my oldest.

She follows closely behind me without me having to tell her to do so and I can't help but be proud of her right now for that little show of submission. It seems like my girl is starting to remember the law of the land and that's something I can definitely appreciate.

Once we enter the kitchen, I take a quick walk around to make sure that everything is as it should be—to my liking.

"You did a good job, kid," I say with a nod as I inspect the sink. "Very nice. Why don't you grab some pie and come back into the dining room? I'm sure Darby would like to get to know more about you."

"Thank you, Pater," she says softly as I walk past her on the way back into the dining room. I stop for a moment, my eyes lingering on her and grin. It's enough for her to know that I acknowledge her and yet, by not verbally saying anything in return, reminds her that I'm the one in charge here.

Darby is peeking out the window when I walk into the dining room. With a sigh, I walk over, pull her hand off the curtain, and spin her back toward her chair.

"Sit down. Be a good girl for me," I say to her quietly.

She gives me her infamous "I'm a big girl" pout before she finally does as she's told. I can always counter that look with a stare and that's when she knows I mean business.

She climbs into her chair and crosses her arms over her chest, pout still prominent, and a *humph* noise to punctuate it.

I can't help but laugh because I've seen that same face and gesture done by her momma plenty of times before.

"Hey, I have an idea," I say to her as I sit down at the head of the table. "Why don't you ask the lady what her name is when she comes back? I'm sure that would make her smile."

"I don't wanna," she huffs.

"Darby, that's one," I say to her holding up a warning finger.

She bounces her arms against her chest one more time before she drops her hands to the table. I watch as she picks up her fork and begins poking at her pie.

Who's bright idea was it to have kids? I think, rolling my eyes. If I'm being honest, I think I would have been perfectly happy living my entire life alone, but shit happens, and some pussy is too good to pass up. I turn my eyes toward Jocelyn when she renters the room with a small plate in her hand.

She takes a seat across from Darby, who I'm now watching. She knows better than to not do as I tell her, and even though I don't want to have to spank her over something so trivial, I will.

Darby steals a glance in my direction before she sighs and puts her fork down, dropping her chin in her hands and looks at Jocelyn.

"So what's your name?" she asks her.

I nod and take a sip of wine. Maybe this parenting shit isn't so bad after all.

CHAPTER 10

Darby looks at Jocelyn and tilts her head, then she looks at me with accusing eyes. I'm so angry right now that I can barely see straight, but I know exactly how to stop this little piece of information from fermenting in her brain.

"She's a liar," I reply simply. "Come on, baby. Do you really think that Daddy would be such a mean man that he would do something like keep you and your Momma apart?"

Darby turns her eyes back to Jocelyn, then to me again, before she shimmies off of her chair and walks over to where I'm sitting.

"I wanna go to my room," she says, dangerously close to tears.

"That's a good idea, baby. You go to your room and I'll come get you as soon as I'm done talking to your *sister*." I put emphasis on the last word so that she knows that she does share Jocelyn's blood, but not in the way that she's trying to tell her she does.

So what if it makes me the bad guy? I've been the bad guy since I fell from my mother's womb—but hey, you teach what you've learned during your upbringing, and I'm just passing on the "good word" as it was taught to me.

I never did feel quite right sticking my dick in someone that wasn't family after my mom died, but I got used to it for a while. Then Jocelyn came along and everything was right in my world again.

Once Darby is out of earshot, I get to my feet and walk over to Jocelyn, who's now cowering in her chair. She knows that I'm pissed; she knows that she fucked up, and she damn well knows what that means.

"You little bitch," I seethe at her. "I did my best to be a good man to you today, to bring you up to meet our child, and this is the thanks I get?"

I yank Joce out of her chair and pull her body against mine. Her lower lip is trembling and the fear in her eyes tell me that she's not my baby girl anymore. *My* daughter would never act like this. If *my* daughter pulled a knife on me, she would have fucking used it. This is just a shell of the woman I loved and nothing more.

"Guess it's time to take out the trash," I say quietly, my lips grazing against hers.

"No, I'm sorry, Pater! I don't know what came over me, I won't do it again. Please!" she begs as I begin to drag her out of the dining room.

"It's too late for this bullshit and to be quite honest with you, I'm done dealing with you. I'm done worrying if you're alright and if you're still alive. Everything will be better this way and I'll never have to think about your miserable ass again after tonight."

"Just one more chance, please," she sobs as I drag her into the kitchen.

"You had your chance, now quit your fucking begging and clean your face. I'm gonna give you the chance to say good-bye to Darby, but not if you're crying like a whiny little bitch," I snap at her.

I drop her hand and leave her crying on the kitchen floor, a sobbing mess of disappointment as I call out for Darby.

"No! I'm not coming out of my room!" she shouts back.

I sigh angrily. I'm not in the mood for this bullshit and I'm going to snap and beat her if she doesn't come to me.

"Darby! Don't make me come to collect you. Bring your little spoiled ass out here, right now!" I shout at the top of my lungs.

I've never yelled at her like that before so she knows I'm damn serious, and within the next minute or so, I can see her door open slightly, and her head pop out to look at me with wide eyes.

I run a hand over my face and do my best to swallow the anger that I'm feeling at both of them right now and sigh.

"Come to your Daddy, baby. I'm sorry I yelled at you. I'm not mad at you, I promise," I say, crouching down and holding my arms out. She takes a timid step out of her room and bites her lower lip nervously.

"You know I wouldn't hurt you, Darbs," I say as gently as I can, through grit teeth. "I need you to help me say good-bye to Jocelyn now, cause she's gotta go and then we can be together. Just the two of us."

Darby finally begins to walk slowly down the hallway and lets me pick her up in my arms when she reaches me. She doesn't snuggle into me like she always does when I pick her up, and I can understand why.

"It'll be okay from now on. I promise," I whisper to her, giving her a gentle kiss on the cheek. "Daddy loves you."

CHAPTER 11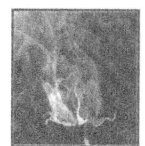

DARBY

"It's a fucking shame it had to end like this again, but you knew the rules, so you have no one to blame but yourself," Daddy says to Jocelyn as he reaches for the wooden gate he keeps on top of the well.

I can hear her at the bottom crying, telling him that she's sorry, and that she'll behave, but he just shakes his head and smiles like he always does.

I reach up and take his hand after he's done nailing the gate shut and look up at him curiously. I'm not sure what's going on and what she did that was so bad, but I think I remember now that she *is* my Momma after all. If she's the same lady that lived in the well when I first started going over by it, then she has to be.

"Daddy?" I ask, giving his hand a tug. "Who's that lady?"

He looks down at me and picks me up in his arms, giving my cheek a kiss.

"No one important, baby. I tried to give you a day that you would remember forever, and she fucked it up. But I want you to remember that it's not your fault, okay? You didn't do anything wrong."

I can feel tears starting to spring to my eyes and I give him my best "but I love you" puppy dog look and try again.

"Is that my Momma?"

Daddy's smile softens some, and he runs a hand back through my hair as he begins to carry me back toward our house.

"No. I would never do that to your Momma," he promises, snuggling me close to him.

I believe him. Daddy's never done anything bad to me before and he's never lied to me either. Daddy is a good man and I'm happy with it being just me and him, anyway.

"Are we going to color some more?" I ask him, almost immediately forgetting about the bad lady in the well.

"Later. First, we're gonna do a little something for me," he whispers. It's just like a secret, and I'm so happy that Daddy trusts me enough to tell me secret things—it makes me feel like a big girl.

He puts me down as soon as we're inside and I wait for him while he closes the door and locks it. When he looks back down at me again, there's something a little different about his eyes, but I'm not worried about it.

"Okay Daddy!" I say happily as I let him lead me upstairs. I don't know where we're going 'cause usually Daddy just takes me to my room and leaves me there until he's ready to talk to me again.

"I'll race you," he says with a smile.

I giggle and clap my hands. I'm so excited because Daddy never asked me to race before so I know that whatever happens is gonna be fun!

"On your mark ... get set ... go!" I shout, as I begin to run up the stairs as quickly as I can. He laughs and gives me a head start, then passes me two steps at a time, and holds his arms out when he gets to the top stair.

"That's not fair! You're bigger than me!" I shout, stomping my foot angrily.

He picks me up in his arms and spins me over his head and gives me a kiss on the mouth. I laugh and push him away 'cause his whiskers feel funny and they tickle my face.

"I wanna walk," I say pushing at him. He holds me for a moment longer, the smile leaving his face, and he nods. Once I'm on my feet, he holds a hand out and we start walking down the hallway.

It only takes me a couple of steps to realize where we're going, and I can't believe that he thinks I'm a big enough girl to finally see his room. Daddy's never let me in there before because he told me that's a place for grown-ups.

As soon as we're both in the room, he closes the door behind him and clicks the lock in place. I turn around and smile at him, my hands behind my back, and he chuckles.

"Why don't you get on the bed and we can play a little game," he says, in a weird voice. "I'm gonna show you how much I love you, Darby."

I raise an eyebrow at him, but then I shrug and get on the bed like he asks me to. Daddy would never hurt me, and I know that he loves me 'cause he tells me so every day.

And now, I'll get to find out how much he loves me 'cause he promised me that one day he would show me.

EMBERS

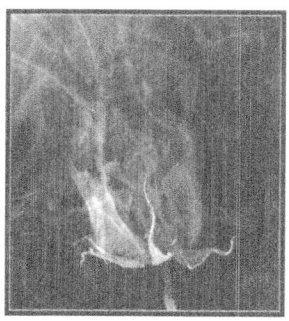

DEAR READERS

Dear Readers,

Most of you have been with me since the inception of Inferno. A lot of you struggled with that story, but I appreciate you so much for putting on a brave face and continuing on with the Greene Family.

Most of you have gone through the Hell of Inferno World in anticipation for the end. Myself and my Inferno World authors thank you.

I know that a lot of you have mixed feelings about this finally being over, and I know you may be a little afraid of what Embers will bring, but I'll promise you something right now.

This series concludes here the way it should. I hope it was worth the wait. I hope I make you all proud.

XoXo,
Yolanda

PLAYLIST

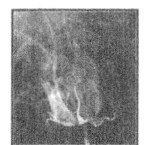

Playlist
Butcher Babies - Gravemaker

TO MY BABY

My sweetest love,

I knew it wouldn't last, but I still dared to hope. You see, when he took me as his new wife he made a promise that no matter what happened between us, everything would be okay. Has he made the same promise to you? I'm sure he has.

I bet you're a girl. Did he make you bear his children? God, I hope he didn't; I pray that you were spared from having to become just like me. But if he did, watch them; keep them close to you because the moment you think it's safe—the very second everything seems to be normal, he'll snatch them away from you just like he did you to me. He'll make you believe that he loves them and that he'll never do to them what he's done to you, but he's a liar. Please don't fall for the words that slip from his silver tongue.

I love you. I love you so much. Remember that when things seem dark and whatever happens, I want you to know that I've never been more proud of anything in my life than the moment I felt you kick inside of me. That's when I knew that I had finally gotten something right. Even though I never got the chance to hold you, please remember me.

Love always,
 Mom

PROLOGUE

Mom died almost a year to the day that Dad put her back into the well. He stopped going to check on her when he realized that maybe I wasn't too young to take care of his needs after all. A little bit of training and easing me into the things he liked, and just like that, Jocelyn became a distant memory.

I had my first child when I was twelve, the second at thirteen, and the third one at fifteen. I've managed to keep them away from their father and they seem to be happy for the most part—and to be honest, so does he.

Time has taken a toll on the old man and I can tell he won't last for much longer. Oh, but he's stubborn; too stubborn and I know that he won't leave until he's good and ready.

Everything has to be on Dad's terms because it's the only way he knows how to function. He doesn't seem to be bothered by the sands of time spilling over his head into the almost full end of the hourglass, if anything, he seems to be looking forward to it.

So am I.

Even though it will hurt me when he takes his last breath, I think it'll hurt me even more if he continues to watch our children with the same intent that he watched me, and my mother before me, and her brothers along with her.

Dad lost his way a long time ago. I don't know what happened to him to make him the monster that he became, but my heart hurts for the man he could have become. A loving husband, a doting father, an amazing grandfather—but his mind is rotten with ill intent and the need to taste each drop of dew from his family tree, and for that reason alone, if he doesn't succumb to whatever illness is plaguing him this time, I'll have to look the man that I love most of all in the eye, and send him on his way.

For my children.

For my mother.

For her brothers.

For the end.

CHAPTER 1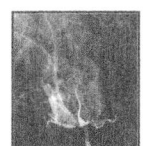

"Go outside and play," I say softly to Cleo giving her a gentle shove toward the door. Her brother and sister are already outside picking wildflowers like I used to be so fond of doing when I was young. She has a habit of wandering around the house looking for Dad, but I always manage to get to her before she finds him.

He's been good with them so far, and when he tucks them in at night, I'm standing in the doorway watching. It pisses him off, but not much doesn't these days.

Dad has been sick more often than not lately, and we both know his end is near. It's just a matter of when now.

Every time I offer to take him to see a doctor, or even to an emergency room, he declines and tells me that he'll be alright.

"Don't worry about me, baby. Daddy will be just fine as long as you're by his side," he always says.

Lately, he's had more good days than bad and I would be lying if I didn't say it brought me some comfort that he's still here. Even with all that he's put me through, I don't know a life outside these walls and I'll be completely lost when Dad dies, so I do my best to nurse him back to health each time he gets closer to death's door.

"Darbs!"

His gruff voice echoes throughout the house and I quickly close the door, locking it so that the children can't come back in before I call for them.

I move as quickly as I can because he doesn't like to be kept waiting. My heart races with the impending thoughts of what he'll require of me. Will it be a simple conversation? To just have me sit with him for a while? Or will he want something more—something I don't want to give.

I run up the stairs and jog down the hall to his bedroom, pushing the door open and walking in slowly.

"Hey," I greet him softly.

"Come here," he says, holding a hand toward me. He's leaning against the wall, watching the children play outside. Time has been kind to his appearance—his hair is still mostly black as is his beard, though there is more gray with each passing day. He keeps his body as strong as it will allow him, and that damn grin hasn't faded away like most of his spirit has.

He's still the same bastard that I remember when I was young, and he'll never show any signs of slowing down. No matter how much his body wants to give out on him.

I walk over to him and take his hand, allowing him to pull him closer to where he's standing. He rubs the top of my hand with this thumb before he lets it go and sucks his teeth.

"How long are you leaving them outside for?" he asks, narrowing his eyes against the sudden burst of sunlight that breaks through the sparse clouds in the crystal blue sky.

"I don't know. Cleo just went out and Richter and Skylar haven't been out very long."

He grunts and crosses his arms over his chest. He continues to watch them in silence until Cleo wanders too close to the well.

Dad immediately lifts the window halfway, leans out, and yells at her.

"I told you not to go near that fucking thing! Go back to your brother and sister or come back inside," he barks at her.

Cleo looks up at him before she covers her face with her small hands as she runs over to her siblings and I can tell she's crying.

"You shouldn't be so hard on her—she's just curious," I say to him softly.

"Yeah well I never got around to scraping the bitch out of there and she doesn't need to see that," he grumbles, lowering the window again. He places his hands on the sill and sighs heavily. "Look, I'm sorry. I don't get why I'm such a bastard these days. I guess it's because I'm getting so damn tired lately and watching those kids is the only thing I can do to keep me sane."

I nod, even though he can't see me, and turn to walk out of his room.

"Where are you going?" he asks.

I glance over my shoulder and see him now sitting on as much of the sill as he can, arms crossed over his chest again, eyeing me dangerously.

"I was going to get some lunch together for the kids," I reply cautiously.

That grin—the damning one, the one that tells me that he wants the one thing I don't want to provide, starts to slip across his ruggedly handsome face.

"Want some company?"

I don't.

I don't want his company, but I don't want to leave him

alone either. If I do, who knows what will happen to him. He fell the last time he was alone, and it was a struggle to get him back up the stairs to his room, so I had to leave him in the den and tell the kids to stay away from the door. They get so angry with me when I tell them to stay away from their father, but they don't understand, and I'll never tell them.

They don't need to know that their father is no father at all, rather a monster that walks in the daylight among them, hunting their innocence.

"Of course, Daddy," I finally say, forcing a small smile onto my face. "I always want your company."

CHAPTER 2

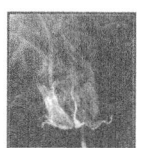

Dad yawns when we enter the kitchen, then gives me a lopsided smile before he goes to sit at the island. I watch him get comfortable in the stool before I turn my attention toward the refrigerator.

"Is there anything in particular you're hungry for?" I ask, immediately regretting my choice of words when they leave my lips.

"Well, I won't be having my usual, but thanks for asking," he responds with a dry laugh.

I pull the pitcher of cold water out of the refrigerator and retrieve a glass from the cupboard above the sink. I walk over to the island, set the glass down and fill it with water, sliding it over to him. He sounds parched and I don't like it —it scares me in a weird way. I'm not ready for him to go just yet and I won't have any part of it until I'm good and ready.

I guess I'm like him in that way. Neither of us like things we have no say over, but he put me in my place a long time ago, and I tend to stay there when it's appropriate, only stepping out really when it comes to the children.

He doesn't seem to mind it—tells me that it makes me a good mother; better than Jocelyn ever was, and that he appreciates me for it.

I don't take it as a compliment by any means, because if life had gone the way it should have, I wouldn't be here, and neither would my children. I sometimes think about that on quiet nights that Dad's asleep in bed next to me and the moonlight shines on our glistening bodies, exposing our sins to the darkness.

I think about how much better the world may have been for my mother and her brothers had they had a normal life instead of what they were subjected to.

Unfortunately, the wistful thoughts of a young woman, long since dead when her mother was abandoned into a hole in the ground, won't help anyone. I have to be strong for my children and for my father, equally.

"Thanks, Darbs," he says with a nod as soon as he's finished his glass of cool water. "I appreciate the way you look out for me."

"You're welcome, Daddy," I reply with a small smile. Even the tiniest of praise is enough to get me through the days and nights when I feel like giving up.

"Maybe just make some simple sandwiches, huh? Cut the crust off the bread so we won't have to listen to them bitch about having to pull it off while you're at it," he says, getting to his feet and heading to the small window in the kitchen.

I don't understand how he can be so kind in one moment, and so hate-filled in the next, but I've become accustomed to his mood swings and do my best to brush them off.

Simple to Dad could be anything, but I decide on peanut butter and jelly because I know the kids love those sandwiches. If he's not happy with my choice, I'll make something else for him—right now my concern is getting some food into their stomach until dinnertime.

"That kid doesn't fucking know how to listen," he suddenly barks, slapping the windowpane. I jump and turn to face him slightly in time to watch him open the window and lean his body out. "Cleo! Get the fuck away from that well! Don't make me come out and collect you!"

"Stop yelling at her," I snap at him. "It's not her fault. She's a child—she doesn't know any better."

Dad's body goes stiff before he leans back into the kitchen, walks over to me, and slaps me hard across the face. Tears sting my eyes, but I won't let them fall because that's what he wants. His cruelty has grown with his age and when he's not making me sleep in his bed with him, he's usually being malicious in other ways. There's only a small sliver of time that he's ever gentle anymore, and those are the times I cherish the most.

Gripping my face firmly in his hands, a sinister smile crossing his lips, he turns his head to the side and leans his ear toward me.

"One more time. I didn't quite hear you," he dares.

I take as deep a breath as I can before I'm able to form words again.

"Please don't be so mean to her. She loves you and you're always yelling at her. I don't understand what you expect from someone as confused as she is," I reply in a gentler tone.

"What I expect?" he begins, turning to face me again and tightening his grip on my cheeks. "What I expect is to have obedient fucking children and if she can't understand the simplest of shit, then maybe I'll have to teach her a different way."

"No!"

My reply is immediate, defiant, and much louder than I would have liked, but he lets go of my face and smirks.

"Then you better teach her how things go around here, Darbs, or I will."

I begin to wring my hands, trying to think of a way to keep Cleo safe from his unsavory desire when it dawns on me.

"May I sleep in the living room tonight, Daddy? I'll keep Cleo out here with me and I'll set some rules for her. I'll make sure she understands everything you need her to, and if I fail then the punishment is how you see fit—only I want to be the one to be punished and not her. Please?"

Dad puts his hands on his hips and looks me up and down, mulling over my proposition before he clicks his teeth and nods.

"You have until tomorrow night to make sure she gets it, otherwise, you're fucked. In more ways than one," he says dangerously before he goes back and sits at the island and resumes his watch over me.

But he doesn't know that I already have a plan. If I fail Cleo—if I fail *him*, he won't have a chance to punish me, because I'll set the children free before I punish myself for failing to protect them against his wrath and desires.

CHAPTER 3

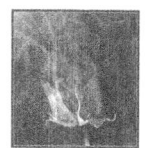

THE CHILDREN HAVE CLEANED up and are sitting at the dining room table, happily eating their peanut butter and jelly sandwiches. I'm sitting at one end of the table, and Dad is sitting at the other. He's engaged them in conversation about what they did outside, and even though it sounds like the interest of a doting father, I know better. It's the inquisition of damaged man that wants to make sure that they know that the well is off limits.

Richter tells him about the bugs he found with Skylar and how she squealed "just like a girl" when he held a worm to her face. Dad laughs as Skylar yells at her brother for making her look like a "sissy" in front of her daddy.

A small smile forms on my lips. I never had siblings—none that I grew up with anyway, so to watch them go back and forth is as amusing as it can be in the situation we find ourselves in.

"What about you, kid? What did you do out there?" he asks, turning his attention to Cleo.

She's been quietly nibbling on her sandwich and when she realizes that Dad is speaking to her, she nervously cuts her eyes towards me before setting her sandwich down and pushing her hair out of her face. I lean over with a napkin and gently wipe away the small streak of jelly she left on her beautiful little face and kiss her gently on the cheek.

"Tell your Daddy what you did outside," I say to her softly. Unlike Richter and Skylar, Cleo has some slight abnormalities when it comes to her ability to understand things and respond as quickly as Dad wants, but that's to be expected considering her origins. It hurts my heart that this inbred family tree decided to stump it's fucking branch with her, because she's such a beautiful, caring soul. While her outside is a thing of wonder, her mind is stunted.

In a way, she's kind of like him, only he chose to be the monster he is, and she had no say in the matter. Not that my Cleo is a monster because she's not, she's just different from her brother and sister and special in her own way.

"I ran around," she says, leaning across the table, looking down at him carefully. "And then I ran some more."

Dad looks at her for a moment before he rolls his eyes and turns his attention to me. "Have you been schooling these kids like I told you to?"

"Yes," I reply evenly. I don't want him to start in on her again—Cleo is so sensitive because of her inbreeding and young age, that all it takes is a disapproving look to render her a sobbing mess.

"Alright," he says, holding up his hands, "I'm just asking."

I nod.

He knows that when he upsets Cleo—when *anything* upsets her, all she wants is her momma and that takes time away from him.

And Dad sure loves being the center of my attentions, I think with a sigh as I get up from my seat and pick up Cleo.

I scoot her plate down toward my chair and sit her on my lap, bouncing her gently on my knee as she resumes her nibbling.

"I love watching you with these kids," Dad says suddenly. I glance up at him curiously, but the smile on his face tells me that it's rare, genuine praise.

"Thank you," I reply with a shy smile, to which he rests his elbow on the table, drops his chin into his hand, and nods.

"Momma?" Cleo says, looking up at me. "I have to potty."

I kiss the top of her head, and tell her to put her sandwich down, before I set her onto her feet and get to mine. I hold my hand out to hers and as we begin to walk out of the room, I cast a glance over my shoulder toward Dad who's turned his attention back to Richter and Skylar. I ... I think they'll be okay with him, especially since we won't be gone for very long.

Besides, I would look like an overbearing and overprotective mother taking all three children to the bathroom when only one has to go and it'll make him damn angry to know I still don't trust him with them.

Maybe one day I will, but I doubt it very much.

Once we reach the bathroom, I step in to turn the light on for her, then go back into the hallway, leaving the door slightly ajar in case she has any problems. Cleo sees herself as a big girl and I treat her accordingly by giving her little independent moments like this.

Once she's done, I wait a few moments for her to clean herself up and make herself decent, which I know she's done when I hear the toilet flush.

"Momma!" she calls out.

I step back into the bathroom with a smile on my face as

I turn the sink on for her and lift her up, cradling her in my arms so she can wash her hands all by herself. *Just like a big girl*, I think proudly.

As soon as I set her down on the bathroom floor, she gives me a toothy grin, then turns to run out of the room. I don't allow running in the house and she knows this, but I'm a lot more relaxed with Cleo because she needs it.

I sigh and turn to walk out of the bathroom, ready to be as hot on her trail as I can be, when I see Dad standing across the hallway from me; back against the wall and arms crossed over his chest.

The way he's watching me turns my stomach, but I won't deny him anything and he knows that, using the knowledge to his advantage whenever the need for his "wife" takes hold of him.

He clicks his tongue, chuckling slightly as he moves toward me. I move as far back against the sink as I can and use my hands to steel myself against it.

"Ever think of having another one?" he asks, his hands sliding around my waist and pulling me against him.

"Another one?" I stammer.

I don't want the door open. I don't want the children to run by and see this if he chooses this to be a moment where he wants his needs fulfilled.

"I think we can use one more, don't you?" His lips graze my neck and his hot breath is against my skin, sending a shiver through my body.

"I think we're perfect just the way we are," I tell him, putting my hands to his chest and giving him a gentle, but firm shove back.

Dad grunts and pulls my body back against his. He puts a hand around my throat, tilting my face to look him in the eyes. He's inspecting me—wondering where my backbone suddenly came from, but it's never left, and it bothers him.

"You'd do well to remember that this is my fucking house and you need to be damn careful what you say to me, little girl," he says gruffly, tightening his grip.

"Yes, Daddy," I reply quietly, closing my eyes tightly. It hurts because my body is beginning to fight for the oxygen it's being deprived of.

"That's my good girl," he says with a nod as pulls himself away from me. "Go send those kids back outside and after you've cleaned up the dishes, you know where to find me."

CHAPTER 4

I'M SITTING on the sill of his bedroom window watching our babies running around in the darkness. The motion lights activate each time one runs under it, dimming a few moments later, and I'm worried that they're going to end up hurting themselves.

As long as it's not the way he hurts me.

I pull a leg up to my chest, the other firmly planted on the ground to keep me steady. The sleek sweat of his sin hot against my bare flesh as I continue to watch the children down below.

He's sleeping quietly now that he's used my body to reach the pleasure he'd been hinting about all day long, and it would be so easy to end him in this moment. He'd never see it coming and he'd never know that it was his dear little Darby that sent him on his way, but I don't know how I would be able to explain such a thing to the children.

They don't know what I went through—what I still go through to keep them safe from his hands, and I'll never tell them. They see their father in a way that I never could, and

I don't want to rob them of that. They love him and I can't be the villain that takes him away from them.

That's just not who I am.

I don't mind caring for my father because there are times that even the savage beast he still tries to be needs help of some sort and I'm there for him.

Even in stolen moments like the one we just had, I'm there to help him when he decides he has a use for me, regardless of what his need may be.

"What the fuck?"

I glance over at him as he sits upright in bed and glances around the darkened bedroom. His eyes are a thing of beauty, highlighted by the sliver of moonlight that catches his face and I can't help but smile slightly.

"I'm over here, Daddy," I say softly to him.

He turns his head to look at me and grunts as he pushes himself off the bed. I watch him as he reaches down and retrieves his sweatpants from the floor and pulls them up his body. He shakes his head rapidly, then runs his hands back through his wild hair, before he makes his way over to me and grins.

"Why aren't you in bed, Darbs?" he asks curiously.

I turn my attention back toward the yard and nod at the children. Richter runs underneath the motion light again which lights up and I laugh.

Cleo is covered in grass and as Skylar tosses another handful at her, she lets out a happy laugh and lifts her hands up to attempt to catch it. Richter uses that moment of their distraction to toss a handful of grass at both of them and as the girls take off after him, the lights cut out again.

He shakes his head as he leans his back against the wall and turns his eyes toward me.

"You really love them, don't you?" he inquires in a somewhat mystified tone.

"Yes."

"Why?" he prods. His curiosity will turn into cruelty no matter what I say because that's just the kind of man that he is.

"Because they came from me. I knew them the moment you planted them inside of me. I felt them grow, I felt them kick, I felt their hearts beat before I could hold them—that's a love that's unexplainable but so amazing at the same time," I reply softly, waiting for the harsh words that I know will soon drip from his lips like venom.

"Huh."

His response is nothing like I expected it to be. He doesn't seem to care either way, but wanted to see what I would say. It's how he's been most days lately and I live with it as best as I can.

"Is there anything else you needed, Daddy?" I ask him softly, pushing my hair back behind my ear.

He looks me up and down, his eyes taking in my naked skin as well as my bare soul, a smirk crossing his weathered lips. His licks them, pushes himself off the wall, and shakes his head.

"Get those fucking kids back in this house, then bring your ass back to bed," he tells me in a stern tone as he lies back down and yawns tiredly. "Maybe if you put in a better performance than that bullshit you fed me, I'll think about *you* more often instead of them."

"Yes, Daddy," I say softly as I get to my feet and hurry across the room. I wrap a robe around myself, secure the belt tightly around my waist and run down the stairs.

He's warning me about the one thing I've feared for so long.

He has his eyes set on our children and I have to be better in bed to keep his hands on me so that his touch doesn't wander further than it should.

CHAPTER 5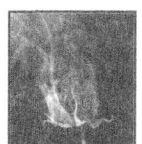

I GRIND my hips as best as I can—the way he taught me to. He showed me once the way he likes to be pleasured and even though it shouldn't be as hard as it is, he makes it that way. He wants me to improve, he said, so that I don't have to worry about him doing to them what he's done to me.

I lean down, pressing the palms of my hands firmly on his shoulders. He lets out a low moan, bares his teeth, and watches me with unbridled passion in his eyes.

He sits up, wraps his arms around me and tells me to go faster. He's getting close to his release—that's the only thing Daddy ever cares about—*his* pleasure and not mine.

I close my eyes as I rest my forehead against his, moving my hips faster, taking in more of his cock than I already had and whimper slightly.

"Daddy ..."

My voice trails off as he digs his fingers into my sweaty flesh. He grips my hips as he begins to thrust up into me.

I wrap my arms tightly around his shoulders and close my eyes. He'll be done soon, I'll be allowed to clean up, and then the nightmare will be over for now.

He holds me tighter and thrusts one more time up into me. I feel his seed shoot into me, warm and grasping to plant life inside of me. I pray that it fails. We shouldn't have anymore children—not in the world I'm forced to live in.

He slaps my ass which is my signal to get off him, and he lets out a content sigh as he lays back down.

"You're getting better, Darbs. Much better," he says in a tired tone.

"Thank you, Daddy," I reply as I move off the bed and get to my feet. "I'm gonna go clean up and check on the kids. I'll bring you a glass of water, okay?"

"Yeah, whatever," he replies dismissively.

I reach for my robe again and dress myself as best as I can on the way to the bathroom. I reach for a hand towel and dampen it with warm water, cleaning myself up, then tossing it into the hamper. I walk down to the children's room and peek inside.

I smile softly, resting my head against the cracked door. Cleo is sleeping with her favorite stuffed teddy bear in her arms, Richter is sleeping on the top bunk across the room like a big boy and Skylar is sleeping on the bottom.

But I know those three like I know the back of my hand, and by the time morning comes, Skylar will be cuddled up with her little sister and Richter will be on the bottom bunk.

It's funny how they rotate the way they do, but they're happy in their state of ignorant bliss and I intend to keep them that way.

I close the door softly and head into the kitchen. Our house is a big home, comfortable, and very private. That's one thing that Daddy never spared on—the need for privacy in his home.

No one ever came to visit, and we were never allowed

off the property. If groceries were needed, he would go out on his own and get them.

Sometimes he'd be gone for days at a time and I silently found myself hoping that maybe he had a heart attack and died where he stood.

No luck so far, I think with a sigh as I reach into the cupboard for a large glass. I walk to the refrigerator and pull out the pitcher of water, filling it almost to the brim, then setting the pitcher back inside.

I stare at the glass for a moment, wondering if there's something, *anything,* that I could possibly mix into this to end his pain and mine, but I know that I would never be able to hurt him.

He's my father.

He gave me three beautiful children.

No matter how much of a monster he seems to be, I love him with all of my heart.

Resigning myself to the fate of another day, I carefully walk the glass back up to Daddy's room and blink in surprise when I see him sitting up and glancing toward the window thoughtfully.

"Here you are, Daddy," I tell him softly as I walk the glass over to him.

"Thanks, Darbs," he says as he takes it without so much as a glance in my direction. He sips the water slowly, his eyes still on the world outside as he gets to his feet and walks over to the window that overlooks the oubliette.

"You know, sometimes I wonder what shit could have been like if your Momma was still alive," he says, setting the glass on dresser and opening the window. "She was a damn fine piece of ass, that one."

I cringe at his words.

He's never seen any of us as anything other than a

means of pleasure and it's always made me wonder if something happened to him when he was younger that made him like this.

I never dared to ask.

Daddy has his secrets, and what he chooses to share with me is his prerogative.

I have none.

I've tried before to keep secrets from him, but he always finds out what I'm hiding, and I've given up hope that I would ever have a thought of my own that he isn't able to pluck from my thoughts.

"You'll be better than her in no time, kid. Keep practicing and we'll keep getting on just fine," he says, snapping me out of my thoughts.

I nod, clasping my hands in front of me as he finishes his water, then nods toward the bed.

"Let's get some shut-eye. I'm fucking beat."

CHAPTER 6

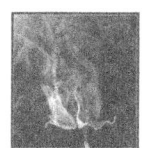

"I'm sorry that we didn't get to have our sleepover last night," I tell Cleo when the kids arrive in the kitchen for breakfast. "Maybe your daddy will let us do it tonight instead?"

I cast him a meaningful glance as he quirks an eyebrow at me and scoffs. He shakes his head which almost sinks my heart down into my stomach, but when he waves a hand dismissively, I know that he's letting me have one final chance with her.

"Okay, Momma," she replies indifferently. Dad snorts and rolls his eyes at his newspaper, and I toss my dishrag at him. I know I'll pay for that later, but he just doesn't want to give her a chance and it pisses me off to no end.

I know she's not above his reach and that he'll do what he feels is necessary to her to keep me in line.

Over my dead body, I think as I return his level stare.

"That wasn't very nice, Darbs," he says conversationally.

"Shit happens," I reply lightly, using one of his favorite little terms. It's what he tells me when I ask about Mom and her brothers. This man will never admit his fault in anything, and that's something I've come to terms with.

Dad is a stubborn old bastard, but I'm just as stubborn as he is, and I honestly think that's why I've lasted as long as I have. I keep things interesting. When he thinks I'm ready to just roll over and take his shit, I throw a dishrag at his face. It goes both ways, though, because when I think he's finally on his way out, he seems to have it in him for "one more fuck".

This can't all be his fault.

There's no way that one day he decided to wake up and procreate with his own children, while abusing the others horribly. I'm not entirely sure I want to find out what made him into the man that he is, but I have to know if it's something that might be stirring inside of me too, because if it *is* hereditary, I plan on killing it before it does harm to my babies.

I refuse to be sick like him too.

Richter and Skylar are outside where Dad told them to go and he's sitting at the kitchen table with Cleo. I know it's taking more patience than he's capable of to color with her, but he's trying best—and so is she.

Every line she comes close to crossing on the paper and with his temper, she retreats immediately and asks for his help.

He's humoring her for now, and I guess that's all I can really ask for.

"Darby?"

"Yes?" I ask him quietly. He won't ask me for anything I'm not supposed to provide him in front of the children, which means this will probably some kind of labor that's too much for me to bear alone.

Dad likes limits—physically and emotionally, but as long as those children need me, he's going to have to do a hell of a lot more to me than he already has to break me.

"I want you to climb down into the well today and give it a nice cleaning. Put some elbow grease into it," he says as he reaches for the purple crayon sitting next to Cleo's small hand.

I wrinkle my nose at him even though he's not looking at me.

He's never sent me down into the well before and the last person that ...

"Why?" I ask him evenly.

"When did you get so damn mouthy?" he snaps back, giving me a glare. "Because I fucking said so—that's why."

"No way," I shoot back, vehemently shaking my head. *You can't get rid of me that easily. Especially when I haven't done anything wrong,* I finish to myself.

He leans back in his chair, an amused smirk on his face. He sucks his teeth and glances down at Cleo who's now watching the both of us curiously before he leans back down and leans his arms on the table.

"Your Momma is a lot smarter than her Momma," he says to her with a chuckle. "Too smart for her own good sometimes," he continues, casting me a dangerous glare. "But she should know that I'm not entirely done with her yet, so don't you think she should be a good girl and clean the well like Daddy asked her to?"

Cleo shifts uncomfortably on her knees. She gives me a curious look and a frightened one to Dad when she turns her attention back to him.

"Momma ..." her voice trails off as she bites her lower lip.

"Go outside and play with your brother and sister," I tell her tiredly.

"Stay where you are," Dad counters in a stern tone. "We're not done coloring and you may have to see what happens when someone talks back instead of doing what they're told."

I cross my arms defiantly over my chest and tear my eyes away from him and back to our youngest. "Cleo; mind what your Momma tells you and go outside."

"Don't you move," Dad says to her in a low, dangerous tone.

Cleo puts her face in her hands and begins to sob as quietly as she can. She's confused and doesn't know what to do and that's more our fault than her own. She understands what I want her to do and she understand what Dad is telling her to do, but she's so scared she doesn't know who to listen to.

I walk over to their side of the table and put an arm around Chloe's shaking little body and give Dad a dirty look. One he returns with wild eyes and a dangerous smile.

"Get your ass into the well, girl. Don't make me tell you again."

CHAPTER 7

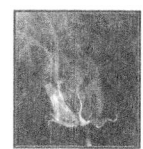

My back is sore and it's hotter than Satan's asshole down in the darkness, but I knew what Dad was up to. Either get in the well, or he'd get into Cleo and I'm still holding out hope that he'll let me out of here if I do a good enough job.

I sigh as I reach down the wet and dirty rag back into the bucket and keep scrubbing the mold off the brick enclosure. I try not to think of Mom—of how she died all alone down here. Probably scared more for me than herself, but I hope she knows that I'm as much of a fighter as she is. Even more so according to Dad, and I won't let it end the way she was forced to.

"Hey Mom!"

I glance up at the opening of the well and shield my eyes from the sole beam of sunlight that's threatening to blind on Dad's behalf for not continuing to work.

"Yes?" I call back.

"I'm getting hungry. Are you going to make supper tonight?"

I smile despite the situation I find myself in. Richter

doesn't let anyone within a fifty-mile radius of his voice know that he's a growing boy and is constantly hungry.

"Soon as I'm done down here," I promise him.

"Get the fuck away from there!"

His gasp echoes down to me, and the quick glance over his shoulder before he disappears makes me roll my eyes. Maybe one day they won't be as afraid of Dad as they currently are.

I get it.

He's an insufferable bastard that seems to want to make whatever years he has left on this Earth as uncomfortable for the rest of us as he apparently feels, and I've already promised myself that if the clock doesn't run out on him soon enough, I'll find a way to save my kids from the Hell I know he has waiting for them.

I put my hands on my hips, waiting impatiently for him to appear in my line of sight, but then swallow hard when I see he's carrying a clearly terrified Cleo. She looks stressed and I'm hoping it's because of something he may have said to her, rather than did.

Not that she should have to suffer either indignity, but this is truly a hope for the lesser of two evils.

Dad grins when he sees me looking up at them and bounces our youngest in his arms. He whispers something into her ear, and she nods, burying her face into his neck. He rolls his eyes as he attempts to wrestle out of her iron tight grasp, then sets her down on the grass surrounding the oubliette.

"Just like I told you, okay?" he asks her, as he leans down and ruffles her hair. She nods, placing her fists to her mouth and waits as she watches him in clear distress.

"Good girl," he says as he tosses the rope ladder down into the darkness. I raise an eyebrow and put my hand on one of the rungs, assuming I've done a good enough job that he's letting me out, but the look he gives me tells me otherwise.

"Go on," he instructs Cleo, keeping his steely stare on me. "Go down there with your Momma."

"What?" I ask in shock.

Cleo carefully grips the top of the rope and begins to slowly inch her way down to me. I grab her as soon as she gets close enough and hold her tightly against me, telling her that it'll be okay.

Dad begins to pull the rope out of my reach and when he's got it all the way up, he lets it fall on the side of the structure, before he leans down, hands on his thighs, and grins.

"You wanted a night with her to make her understand how shit goes right?" he quips. Before he continues, he closes his eyes tightly as he turns his head to cough, then turns his attention back to us. "Now you'll have it. I expect you *both* to be obedient little girls when I come collect you in the morning."

He doesn't give me a chance to protest, and as he callously ignores Cleo's much louder sobs, I watch him put the wooden gate back into its place and sit down on the dark, cool dirt with my daughter in my arms.

He's trying to break me the same way he did with Jocelyn.

And I can't let him.

CHAPTER 8

I DON'T KNOW what time it is, but my body is shaking. Not because I'm afraid of where I am, but because my body needs rest and I refuse to give it any. I hold Cleo close to my chest and continue to rub her back as she sleeps quietly against me.

This hole in the ground isn't very large and I know that whatever's left of my mother has to be close by.

I'd love to be able to talk to her now, to ask her how she survived Dad as long as she did, and if he ever put her in the well before the last time I ever saw her. Was she strong? The way he speaks about her sometimes makes me believe it.

But if she was so strong, why couldn't she save herself or her brothers? Why wasn't she able to give us all a chance outside of Dad's home?

I know I'll never get the answer to any of the questions I have because Dad won't talk about things he can't control, but I know he misses her.

The constant comparisons to her when I'm doing my

best to please him—emotionally or sexually—tells me as much.

I'm glad she's dead.

She shouldn't have to live to see what we've become, and even though she didn't save us, I forgive her. I know that standing up to Dad is a scary thing to do, but if she had me, then she lasted longer than she probably thought she would and that's a bravery I can appreciate.

Cleo's shifts in my arms. I lean down and gently kiss the top of her head because I don't want her to wake up in this abyss. I want the sun to shine on her skin when she opens her eyes again, and I want her to be out of this damn hole running around with her brother and sister.

I would stay in here if that's what it would take to make Dad happy, but I can't. Not when I have children to protect from him. Not when I see how much disdain he has for one, and barely cares about the others.

That's how it always starts with him though. At first, he treated me like I was gold—the most precious jewel in his crown of deviance, and then I was treated like a burden. Even after the first time he held my body close to his, kissing me in a way, that even then I knew, a father should never kiss his child. But when he finally had broken me in to his liking, he lost interest in me ... until I was able to give him children.

And now I do my best to keep his depraved lust focused solely on me. I don't want the cycle to continue, and no matter what happens, I'll make sure that it ends with me.

I let out a sigh as I cradle Cleo in my arms and rest my cheek against the top of her head. My body is envious of the sleep she's getting, but my heart is stronger than my mind, and I know that I can stay awake as long as I need to.

I begin to hum quietly.

A mirthless tune, something without merit, but hopeful that the vibration coming from deep inside me will keep her safely in a world of dreams far away from Dad.

I wonder what crosses her mind when he yells at her. Does she hate him, or does she desperately seek his approval like I did when I was her age?

I wonder how Richter feels when Dad tells him that he's a waste of time and to fuck off. Does it break his heart like it used to do to me, or does he try to figure out a way to be seen in a better light?

And Skylar.

Does she feel lost when Dad looks at her the way he looked at me the first time he came into my bedroom after he put Mom back into the well? Has he already put his hands on her and made her swear not to tell me?

Fuck.

The longer I sit in the darkness, the more these thoughts fill my mind, the more I find myself wondering if I'm too late to save them.

CHAPTER 9

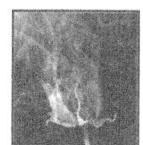

My eyes open with a start.

I'm so damn angry at myself for falling asleep but when Cleo smiles at me, I know she's forgiven me.

"Hi Momma," she says softly.

I pull her close and kiss her forehead, before I get to my feet and glance up at the sunlight. The wooden cover has been removed from the top of the well and that means that Dad is waiting for us.

Unless it was one of the kids, but I doubt it. They know his wrath is as terrible as ever now, and the older he gets, the meaner and colder he becomes.

They don't know the father that I did when I was younger. He had his moments where he could be so kind, that I would almost forget all of the terrible things he would do to me.

Trips to the zoo, an ice cream cone for being good, and sometimes, if I were really well behaved, he'd go weeks without making me sleep in his bed.

Little favors like that sometimes outweighed the bad

and that's why it was easy for me to forgive him after we had Cleo.

No one will understand it, but it's not for anyone to understand. Forgiveness is something not easily achieved and I love my father—even if not in the way he hopes, but I do.

It's an undeniable feeling deep inside of my belly.

But so is the ominous shadow that sits over his face as of late, and that's why I smart off to him more often than not.

I need to keep him angry with *me* so that they're safe. When Dad loses his temper, he also uses a lot of energy up these days, and that's for the best.

"Come on up—I don't have all fucking day to stand around waiting for you two," he barks down into the semi-darkness. I sigh as I hold Cleo close and look around the old, worn bricks that surround us. I'm not entirely sure how he expects me to get out of here without the rope ladder, but there's only one way out and that's up.

"Remember when I used to run around with you on my back?" I ask Cleo gently. "How you would hold onto my neck really tight, like a strong girl?"

She pulls away from me and looks into my eyes, nodding with serious eyes.

"Can you do that for me now?" I inquire. She nods again and I set her down on the dirty oubliette floor, kneeling in the dismal remnants that my mother had to endure on her own as Cleo uses both of her hands to push the hair out of her face, and kisses me gently on the cheek. She's scared, but she's trying to be such a brave little girl right now.

That's why I can't let him win.

If he does, she's at his mercy and I'll end up in the same place that Jocelyn was thrown away to die.

"Go on now," I encourage with a small smile. "Show Momma that you're still a strong girl."

Cleo moves carefully around me and climbs onto my back, her little arms wrapping around my neck, hands clasped together, and holds on tightly. I get back to my feet and instruct her to wrap her legs around my sides as much as she can. Once she's as secure around my body as possible, I look up at the top of the oubliette toward freedom.

I chew on my lower lip for a moment while I look for a crevice, a crack, *anything,* that I can use to begin my ascent when I finally find one. I dig my nails deep into the hole between the bricks, the tips of my fingers grazing something curious, but I dismiss it for now, and begin to lift my body up the side, climbing like a Momma bear with my cub on my back.

I slip once and almost lose my footing, but when I hear Cleo's terrified gasp, I manage to regain my footing, and continue climbing.

We're about halfway up when Dad leans over the side of the oubliette and smirks, tossing the rope ladder down.

I refuse to take it. I know it'll draw his wrath, but what doesn't these days? Instead, I continue to slowly, and meticulously, make my way toward the sunlight without his help and when I finally reach the top, I tell Cleo to climb up my back and out onto the grass. She does as she's told because she's a good girl.

Unlike me.

I'm a defiant, nasty little girl.

That's what he tells me.

No matter how hard I try, no matter what I say to him, or do to please him, he still manages to find faults in me.

I take a deep breath as I pull myself out of the well and

roll onto the grass, breathing heavily, and hoping for the slightest reprieve before he turns into a jackal.

"Did you learn your lesson, Darbs?" he asks, his tone sharp and deadly.

I take a series of ragged breaths and use the last of my strength to push myself to all fours. I have to answer him, and I have to do so soon, or he'll become angry and there are two targets for his rage now.

"Yes. I'm sorry," I manage to say.

"Good. Get yourself inside and get cleaned up. Take the kid with you," he commands.

The sound of the wooden gate slamming shut over the oubliette is a relief. It means that the punishment is over this time and whatever offense he thinks I've committed has been forgiven.

This has to end, I tell myself as I get to my feet tiredly and take Cleo's hand. I smile down at her, wipe the stray tear from her cheek, and lead her back toward the house of horrors that I have to find some way to save my children from.

I'm their only hope and I refuse to let them become engulfed in the darkness that's so close to swallowing me whole.

CHAPTER 10

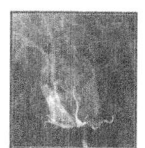

The torrent of hot water cascades over my body. My hands are on the shower wall, my head is down, and my eyes are closed. I locked the children in their room before I came into the bathroom because I still don't trust Dad not to touch them.

It's been in his eyes more often than not lately, and even though I'm still young enough to give him more children, he gets bored much too quickly with his wives.

I chuckle despite my mood.

We were never his wives. Not even Laura. From what I can remember, the stories that I've read in Mom's diary, Laura was more of a prisoner of his than his wife, and when she bore him three children, he chased her off.

He didn't care if *she* left because she wasn't his blood. She didn't know what he was going to do to their children, and she only cared about herself.

Thanks, whoever hurt Dad as much as you did.

The thought is sarcastic, bitter, and full of hate for a woman I've never known, but I feel that it's well deserved.

Then my thoughts turn toward my own mother. Did

she try? Did she ever think of taking her brothers and running? I don't know because I never got the chance to know her. I vaguely remember her face, only ever seen when Dad held me and let me peek down into the oubliette.

I raise my head toward the hot water and let it continue to burn my flesh as I think about her. She must have tried because Dad tells me sometimes that I'm like her. Willful, disobedient, and care only about the children instead of him.

Maybe I have more of her inside of me than I do him. Maybe I won't become a monster too.

Maybe ... but the last thing I'll ever dare to do in this place is hope. I'll never hope for myself, my children are a different matter. They'll survive this without having to feel his touch because as long as I'm still alive, as long as I'm still of use to him, he'll keep his attention on me.

I startle when I hear the bathroom door creak open. I wait for a moment, listening for the sound of one of my children's voices, but when the silence follows, I wonder if maybe I'm just hearing things.

Of course, that all changes when the bathroom door slides open.

"How long do you plan on standing in there?" comes the gruff question.

"I'm almost done," I reply quietly as I open my eyes.

Dad's standing there, looking at me with his arms crossed over his chest, and a look of disdain on his face.

Of all the things that crushes me the most, it's the feeling of knowing that he's disappointed with me. With a heavy sigh, I turn away from him, and turn the knobs to shut the water off. I reach up for the towel and wrap it around my body as I pull the door open a little wider and step out onto the bathroom mat, careful to avoid the disappointment in his eyes.

"Sorry, Daddy," I mumble as I step toward the sink.

He chuckles, clicks his tongue against his teeth and comes over to stand behind me. I do my best not to shudder when he presses his body against mine and runs his fingers down my arm. I do my best not to cry when he leans down and places his chin on my shoulder, his lips grazing my neck.

Instead, I reach a hand up and wipe the steam away from the mirror and reach for my comb, doing my best not to react to the feeling of my body betraying me under the weight of his touch.

"You're such a beautiful girl, Darbs," he murmurs against the nape of my neck.

"Thank you, Daddy," I say as evenly as I can. I hope he doesn't hear the slight tremor in my voice. I hope he can't feel the tremble that's starting to go through me.

But I know my father and he misses nothing.

This fact is soon proven when one of his hands moves down my back and lifts the towel up. He gently smacks my ass, before using his hand to nudge my legs apart, and slides the tip of his fingers along my pussy lips.

"Mm," he groans as he places his forehead on the back of my neck. I set the comb down and opt for my toothbrush instead. Maybe if I can distract myself by scrubbing my teeth instead of trying to subtly assault him with the comb, he'll get the hint and leave me alone for now.

I twist the cap off the tube and bite down on my tongue when he slides a finger inside of me. I refuse to give him a verbal reaction—*that* would be a sick reward for him and it's my turn to punish him a little bit.

Dad begins to slide his finger in and out of my opening,

gently kissing the back of my neck. His stubble tickles me slightly but I ignore it as I squeeze some paste onto my toothbrush and turn the faucet on.

"Come on, Darbs," he breathes as he slides another finger inside of me. "Show me how much you love this."

Again, I ignore him as I hold the toothbrush under the warm water, then lift my eyes to the mirror and begin to scrub my teeth.

Dad continues to thrust his fingers in and out of me as he lifts his eyes to mine in the reflective glass. A small smile begins to curl the edge of his lips. He knows. He can see it in my carefully bland face that I'm doing my best to defy him, and I know that this won't last for much longer.

He clears his throat as he rests his chin on top of my head, his fingers now dormant inside of me.

The look in his eyes can be likened to amusement, but I know better. Nothing "amuses" him, especially not when it comes to his children.

But Dad is patient—he always has been. It's something that I've come to realize when I was able to understand what my new role was in this house. When I took Jocelyn's place in his bed, how he trained me to do it just how he likes it. He may be an angry man a lot more than usual, but he's patient and that's one of the many reasons I fear for the safety my children.

I grunt slightly when he finally removes his fingers and do my best not to cringe when he sucks them dry. He takes a step back, his hands now on my hips and cocks his head around mine, to kiss me on the cheek.

"Guess you're not in the mood," he begins conversationally. "I'll have to see who else in this house might be willing to show good ole Daddy some love then."

All of the small hairs on my body stand up and I meet

his gaze in the mirror. This is what he does when I don't want to play wife—he threatens me with the kids because he knows I'll do anything to keep them away from his static touch.

I make quick work of the rest of the scrubbing and wash my mouth out. Once I've shut off the water, I turn around to face him, and let my towel drop to the bathroom floor in a damp heap.

"I'm ready now," I submit quietly.

My eyes lower to the floor. A day in the oubliette did nothing to stave his desires and even though I haven't properly had time to rest yet, I have to do this.

Dad leans down and places his forehead against mine. I can feel his breath hot against my skin and I close my eyes.

"I love you, Darbs," he whispers.

"I know, Daddy," I reply quietly.

"No. You don't."

He uses the tip of his fingers to raise my chin and I open my eyes. I almost take a step back. There's something different in his eyes now. There's no anger, no rage, no malcontent.

It's not something that I've ever seen before, so I'm not quite sure what it is.

He clears his throat and looks away for a moment, before blowing out his breath and raking a hand back through his hair.

"I never loved any of the other ones. The wives, the kids —hell, I don't think I even loved my mother. But you ... you're special, kid. You make me feel the way they all should have, and I wonder sometimes ..." his voice trails off as he raises his eyes back toward me.

"What's that, Daddy?" I ask as I wrap my arms around myself.

"I wonder if I had you first, if none of this would have ever happened," he explains with a dry chuckle. "You love me. Honestly and truly love me—I can feel it. Jocelyn never did, neither did those waste of sperm brothers of hers. Laura was worthless, and Taylee—my mother ... that bitch was loonier than a fucking toon. Trenton, my dear and loving father, wasn't worth shit—he never came looking for me until it was too late. But you, baby girl ... you love me. And can I be honest with you?"

I nod.

My body is trembling because Dad is off on one of his tangents, but it's not one drenched in anger and reprimands. It's one from his heart and to me, that it makes it much deadlier.

"I love you, too Darbs. Even if you never say it back to me, I want you to know that you're my favorite girl. You're the only kid I've ever had that's worth a damn. You take care of me, and because of that, I'll take care of you as best as I can. Get dressed and go get the kids. I think it's time we all had that chat you've been wanting to avoid."

He leans down and presses his lips softly against mine, giving my ass a firm squeeze before he walks out of the room.

And just like that, he leaves me alone in the bathroom, naked, trembling, and terrified of what's to come.

CHAPTER 11

My heart is racing as the children sit on the sofa across from me. Dad walks a short line in front of them, looking at each of them in turn, before he scoffs, shakes his head, then comes to sit in the empty spot next to me.

I immediately take his hand in mine and squeeze it a little too tightly. If I make him uncomfortable enough, it will make him angry, and he'll send the kids to their rooms. I'll be left as his mercy, but at the very least, they'll be able to walk away from this with their psyches unharmed.

"Ease up there, Darby," he tells me in an even tone. I don't. I can't. Not if I want to keep the family secret safe from three innocent children. Dad coughs a couple of times as he jerks his hand out of my grip, then gives me a stern look.

Nothing is going to stop him from destroying the fantasy world they've been living in. A world where I'm just their mother and not their sister. A world where he's just their father and not their grandfather.

How do I stop him?

"What's going on?" Richter asks, arching an eyebrow at us curiously.

"Well—"

"We just wanted to tell you how much we love you," I intercede, cutting Dad off before he has a chance to ruin their lives.

"Oh," Richter says leaning back against the couch. "Thanks."

"No. That's not what we're here to talk about," Dad says in a loud tone, as he leans forward and turns to give me a dangerous glare. "And your mother tells you that she loves you and all you can say is 'thanks?'" he asks, turning his attention back to our son.

Richter looks visibly shaken now. He pulls his feet up onto the couch, wraps his arms around his knees and shrugs as his eyes dart toward me.

"Get your fucking feet off the couch," Dad barks at him. "We don't have nice furniture here just for you to fuck it up."

"Sorry," Richter replies quickly as he drops his feet back to the floor. He's scared, and in those rare moments when he's not pretending to be as brave as I try to be, he hugs his legs to his chest to try and hide his fear.

"Now, as I was saying before I was so rudely interrupted," he begins again as he leans back against the couch and rests a hand on my thigh. "There are some things that me and your mom here need to explain to you."

"Please don't do this," I whisper, my eyes burning a hole through his hand. "They don't have to know."

"Yes, they do. They have to learn how things work around here," he snaps at me. He's getting angry, maybe I still have a chance after all.

I get to my feet quickly and clap my hands loudly. The children get to their feet and look from me to Dad and back again.

"What the fuck is this?" he asks, coughing again.

"Go outside and play," I tell them in a shaky tone. Dad doesn't know it, but I've been training them too. When I stand and clap, I want them on their feet immediately and to follow my next instruction without worrying about what he'll say to them. It took a long time to get them to this point and we worked on the fear they felt on the days that Dad would go into town and get groceries.

So many drills and never the chance to actually try it had me a little weary, but they don't disappoint me and run out of the room.

"Do *not* go out that front door," Dad booms as he gets to his feet.

"Go outside and play!" I shout.

A loud crack splits the air as I stumble slightly and lift a hand to my cheek. Dad's hit me before, but never this hard, never in such a rage, and *never* where the kids might be able to see. I lick my lower lip and feel the copper taste of blood, then shake my head and stand back up to my full height.

"Mom?" Skylar asks uncertainly. She sounds terrified, and instead of breaking my heart like it normally does, it makes me angry.

It means they saw.

And the only way to rectify the fear they're feeling is to do the unthinkable.

I pull an arm back and slap Dad as hard as I can, watch him stumble, and then fall onto the couch, a look of shock and appreciation on his face once he's had a chance to shake away the disbelief.

"See, *that* is why I love you so damn much," he says

with a grin. "Because you're not afraid of me, but I'll tell you what, little girl. If you *ever* raise a hand to me again, you'll find out how much of a bastard I can really be."

"Tell them to go outside," I shoot back defiantly.

Dad tilts his head to the left, looks me up and down for a moment, then sucks his teeth as he gets back up to his feet.

He walks past me and heads toward where the living room opens into the foyer and looks down at our children.

"You mind what your mother tells you to do," he instructs them, putting a hand on his hip.

The children quickly scramble out the front door, with Richter tightly holding onto Cleo's hand and dragging her out behind him. She was crying, yelling that she didn't want to go, but she's not the hero of our story.

I am.

CHAPTER 12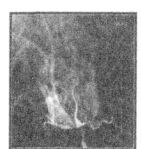

Dad's hair is balled in a fist in my hand. He has me on the couch, legs spread open, his tongue buried deep inside of me and I'm trying so hard not to feel good about what he's doing to me.

I shouldn't.

I know I shouldn't, but the body will react to things that bring it pleasure no matter how desperately the person that it belongs to what's nothing more than to just die.

He moans as he pulls his tongue out of me and gets to his feet. Leaning down he crushes his lips against mine, kissing me like a hungry animal, and uses a finger to force me to open my mouth. I think of biting him for just a moment, but I don't. Now is not the time to be a hero, now is the time to give him what he needs.

His tongue makes its way into my mouth and I try not to cringe. Not because he's kissing me like this—I'm used to it. No, it's because I can taste myself on his lips, his tongue, in his hunger, and I don't know if I can take it much longer.

He must take notice because when he finally pulls

away, he chuckles lightly then begins to undo the buckle on his pants.

"You know I have to punish you for being a bad girl, don't you?" he asks in bated breaths. "How long did you think you get away with mouthing off to me before I turned you over my knee?"

What?

Dad pulls his belt loose with the flick of his wrist, and when his pants fall off, he steps out of them. I can see his erection pressing against his briefs and I look up into his eyes.

Is he going to fuck me or flog me?

Whack!

Another lash from his leather belt. By this point I've counted twenty and he shows no signs of stopping. I'm sure that I'm bruised and bloodied at this point, but I won't give in. He wants me to beg him to stop and I won't do it.

"This is getting boring now, Darbs," he says as he reaches for my hair and pulls my head up roughly. "You about ready to move on since you suddenly seem to be such a little bad ass?"

I grunt and as best as I can, causing him to let go. He slaps my bare ass with his hand and as I move to get to my feet, he *tsk, tsks,* and pulls me back down onto the couch.

Onto him.

"Lift your head up and say your prayers," he instructs nonchalantly.

My prayers? Since when have you taught me a single prayer?

I do as I'm told because that's just how it works under

his roof. I fold my hands in front of my chest, raise my eyes to God and wonder what I could possibly say that will save us from this Hell.

"Good girl," he whispers, running a finger down my throat. "You go ahead and play the righteous little bitch like Taylee did and see how far it gets you."

It's a trick—the moment he mentions his mother, I know that it's a trap and I've walked right into it. Within no time, the belt is wrapped around my neck and Dad's amused laughter makes my skin crawl.

He's going to kill me, I know he is.

The poetic thing about dying is that I'm not afraid of what comes after. I'm afraid of what I'm leaving behind and with who.

My hands immediately begin to claw at the belt, but Dad tightens even more, cutting off my oxygen. I gasp deeply, filling my lungs with air and the burn is almost enough to make me piss myself.

"Taylee always thought that her little whispered prayers would be answered. She made me pray sometimes too, but you know what I learned after all that time on my knees?" he asks, using the belt to pull me closer to him. The heat coming from him is enough to make a small bead of sweat roll down the side of my face. "Do you?"

I close my eyes tightly and shake my head as best as I can.

"How she liked to have her pussy eaten," he replies with a light laugh. "That crazy bitch never passed up the chance to have me service her hole, and I learned my place with her really fucking fast after a while."

So that's where this all started. That's when Dad became a monster.

"I don't want to have to be like this with you, Darby—I

don't. But I've had my fill of disrespectful fucking children and it ends *now*. Do you understand me?" he admonishes sternly.

I nod, my fingers still trying to wedge some space between the belt and my throat, and when he leans back, the leather strap falls away from my neck.

I fall against him, sucking in deep breaths, my eyes watering as my lungs fight for the air they had just been deprived of. Dad wraps his arms around me, resting one of his hands on the small of my back and the other on my ass. He kisses my forehead gently and rubs his lips against my skin, holding me against him.

In other circumstances, someone would mistake us for a real father and daughter sharing a moment, in others, they'd mistake us for lovers freshly coming down from a quarrel.

"You should have just let me tell them, Darbs. It could have been smooth sailing from here," Dad says thoughtfully.

"I don't want them to know. Ever," I reply quietly as I put a hand on his chest and push myself away from him. "If you really love me as much as you say you do, then promise me that they'll never find out."

Dad smirks and rolls his eyes.

"Are you really gonna do this chick shit with me right now? 'If you really love me' is such a bullshit thing to say, kid. Especially after I told you that I do. But there's something you need to remember, Darby. It doesn't matter how I feel about you because this is still *my* fucking house and we follow *my* rules."

I feel the anger rise inside of me but instead of acting on it, I nod and decide that this is one of those times that I'll have to concede a battle if I want to win the war.

"Sorry," I mumble as I attempt to get to my feet, but Dad pulls me back against him.

"We're not done here," he says evenly. I swallow the sigh that I can feel begging for release and put my hands on his shoulders. I wait for the next instruction that I have no doubt will come; however, he just reaches for me and rests my head against his chest.

"I'm too tired to fuck, but holding you always feel nice," he murmurs, clearing his throat harshly. "I was wondering, though ..."

His voice trails off and I close my eyes. Nothing good ever comes from his "wondering" about anything.

"What's that, Daddy?" I ask him quietly.

"Do you think it would be a bad idea if the next time we were together, we had the girl watch us? I mean, eventually this arrangement of ours has to come to an end and I don't want to have start this damn training all over again. I think watching would be a better way to learn anyway, and if she does a good enough job, she can take your place right away and we can be a proper family."

"What?" I ask, attempting to pull away from him. I feel sick. I don't know if he means Skylar or Cleo, but it doesn't matter to me. I don't want him touching our daughters—or son—the way he does me.

A low, amused rumble escapes from deep within his chest as he tightens his grip on me. His hand finds its way back to my ass where he lets it rest gently and he lets out a long-suffering sigh.

"You're too wound up, Darbs. I was joking. I'll be damned if I'm gonna give you up so easily. I just wanted to see what you would say is all. And to be honest, I don't want any more kids. I think we're perfect the way we are, don't you?"

I turn my face and bury my head in his chest.

If this is a perfect family, then I hope that before it's too late, that we start to fracture and fray. I hope that the symmetry of perfection becomes so damaged that he'll finally understand what he's done to me.

To my mother.
To her brothers.
To himself.

CHAPTER 13

Dinner is predominantly quiet and stoic. We're all seated at the table and I'm helping Cleo with her plate under Dad's disapproving watch. I haven't forgotten that he told me that I get to spend a night with her alone, and after all I've endured today—mentally, as well as physically—I think he knows that he'll be spending tonight alone in his bed.

I hate that he looks at her with such disdain, I hate that he won't even give her a chance. She's a beautiful little girl, inside and out, but he just can't see past the imperfections from years of fucking the same branch on the family tree.

"Momma?"

I smile down at Cleo when she says my name and reach for the cloth napkin in her lap. She's gotten quite a bit of food on her face, and she's always so worried that she'll make more of a mess of herself trying to clean up. She worries more than she should about a lot of things her age, which is why I don't want them to ever know the truth about this family.

Richter would become angry and lash out.

Skylar would more than likely try to run away and tell someone.

And my darling Cleo.

She wouldn't understand and wonder if she did something wrong.

"Cleo," Dad begins conversationally. "Did you still want to have that sleep over with your Momma?"

"Yes, please," she replies excitedly.

Dad's eyes wander toward me slowly, a smile creasing his lips, and I can feel my heart start pounding rapidly.

He's up to something.

"I think I'll join you," he finally says, a wide grin on his face as he turns his attention back toward her. Cleo looks proud—I feel sick. She probably thinks she's finally won her father's affections, but I'm worried about which affections those happen to be.

Do you think it would be a bad idea if the next time we were together, we had the girl watch us? His question comes crashing back down over me with hurricane force winds and I have to bite my lip to keep from outright crying.

"We're almost out of food," I blurt out. I don't know if that's entirely true, but I know that it will buy us some time. Dad never lets us run out of necessities and he hasn't been to town in a while. I know he'll believe me without bothering to double check. If I'm wrong, I'll get punished, if I'm right, I'll have a chance to figure out how to save the children.

"Why didn't you tell me earlier?" he asks giving me a puzzled look. "I'm gonna be out almost all damn night now trying to find a twenty-four-hour grocery store, Darbs."

"I'm sorry," I say quietly.

He rolls his eyes as he pushes his chair back and gets to his feet. Dad leaves the dining room without a word, and I look at each of the children in turn. Do I tell them? Do I let them know the hell that I've endured to keep them safe?

No, I tell myself, letting out a heavy sigh. That wouldn't be fair to them; it's not their fault that their father is so irrevocably broken.

And if I really want to be honest with myself then I have to concede the fact that it's not his fault either.

"Darby!" Dad calls out as he makes his way toward the front door.

I smile at my children, run a hand over Cleo's hair, and tell them to finish their supper.

"Yes?" I ask when I join him in the foyer.

"I'll try not to be gone for too long," he says, jingling his truck keys in his hand thoughtfully, "but there's something I want you to know."

I clasp my hands in front of myself, and arch an eyebrow.

"I'm not going into town alone this time. It's a long, arduous ride, and I'm gonna take one of them to talk to me and help me stay awake on the way back."

My chest begins to constrict.

This is our chance.

If he takes one of the children, they'll more than likely become so enamored with what they see that they might slip up about never leaving the house. They might tell someone where we are, and if someone, *anyone,* comes to look for us, I might be brave enough to tell them what kind of man Dad really is.

"Okay," I say quietly. "Do you want me to get Richter or Skylar ready?"

Dad gives me a shit-eating grin as he slowly shakes his head. It's like a punch in the gut now that I understand. He won't take either of them because they would be the ones to ask questions and maybe say more than they should. Even though they don't know what I've been through, they know that I've been in the oubliette, and they know that's wrong.

Cleo doesn't understand as much as they do and she's so desperate to please her father, that she'll do anything he tells her to.

"What if I say no?" I question, defiantly raising my chin and trying my best to not look like I'm about to burst into tears.

"You know damn well that I'm going to take her anyway. And if you start mouthing off to me, you'll go back down into the fucking ground until I feel like seeing you again. Do you really want to leave those kids alone with dear ole Dad?" he asks with a sinister smirk appearing on his face.

I don't let my chin drop.

I square my shoulders.

I do my best not to cry, but his threats are usually worse than his actions. He uses them to control me because he knows that those kids mean more to me than he does.

He's jealous, and because of that, he'll do what he has to in order to be the primary recipient of my affections.

"Now go on in there and tell her to come out," he commands with a nod. "I'll help her with her coat, and we'll be back in no time."

"Promise me that you won't hurt her," I say quietly. I look up into his golden-brown eyes. I drink in his amusement and frustration at being questioned, and I look hopelessly for the father that I know he can sometimes be.

The caring, doting father that wants to do right by his children without causing them any harm.

"Scout's honor," he finally says with a chuckle. "Now be a good mommy and explain to her that she's coming with me. I don't want to have her blubbering the entire time thinking she's done something wrong."

I push my hair behind my ears. I hold his gaze for a moment longer, and when he finally softens some, I turn my back to him and go into the dining room. I know that Richter will be upset that he doesn't get to spend time with his father, and I know that Skylar will more than likely feel a little twinge of jealousy that Dad "picked" Cleo over her.

I wonder if this is how Jocelyn felt, I think as I sit down in my chair next to Cleo and pull her into my lap. I hold her tightly as I run my hand over her hair and give her the news that she'll be going into town to help her daddy. I make her promise me that she'll stay by his side and not wander off because of how sad I would be if something happened to her.

Once I'm sure she understands, once I admonish the other two over their blatant jealousy of not being "picked", I put Cleo on her feet and walk her into the foyer where Dad is waiting.

"You wanna go to town with Daddy?" he asks her, getting down on one knee with her coat in his hands.

"Yes, please," she replies excitedly.

He nods and clears his throat as he helps her into her coat, then zips it up to her neck, giving the tip of her nose a gentle tap with the tip of his finger. She blushes a very innocent shade of crimson and giggles. My heart feels like it's breaking but I do my best to contain myself because he promised me.

"Alright," he finally says as he gets to his feet and picks

Cleo up, securing her in his arms. "Tell your Momma, good-bye now."

"Bye, Momma!" she says excitedly.

"Good-bye, baby," I reply, my voice barely above a whisper.

"We'll be back," Dad says with a nod as he opens the front door and walks out of the house. Cleo turns her head, glancing at me over his shoulder, and waves with a big smile on her face.

I raise my hand and return the wave briefly, wondering how it is that I had it in me to willingly let her go with him.

CHAPTER 14

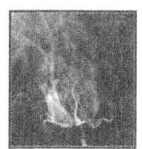

The night air is cool, and I'm not dressed to be out here, but I haven't been able to sleep. After Dad and Cleo left, I had Richter and Skylar clear the table, then sent them straight to bed because I didn't want them to see the absolute panic that had settled over me.

I wrap my arms around myself and glance up at the night sky. They've been gone for two hours now and the unsettling feeling hasn't eased up in the least.

"Mom?"

I startle and whip my head around to find Richter standing in the doorway, watching me with tired, curious eyes.

"Go back inside, sweetheart," I instruct him tiredly. "Your father will be angry if he gets home and you're not in bed."

Richter walks the few steps toward where I've set up camp, then he sits on the steps next to me and shrugs.

"I'm not scared."

I smile slightly as I glance at him. He looks so much like his father, that it's a wonder that being this close to him doesn't set my teeth on edge. Especially in moments like this, when I don't know what Dad is up to, and when I don't know what's going to happen to my youngest.

But unlike Dad, Richter is a good person. I've never seen him yell at his sisters, and he's the first to kiss their scraped knees and helps them hold the baseball bat when it's their turn to swing.

He'll end this fucking lineage of terror if I can't. It will take time, and he'll have to go through hell before he does, but he's strong enough to do it.

Of that I have no doubt.

Richter scuffs his foot on the lower step as he makes himself comfortable. I know there's no way I'll be able to convince him to go back inside, and to be honest, I'm actually enjoying the company.

I reach over and ruffle his hair before I turn my eyes back to the long driveway that eventually disappears so far out of sight and spills onto the road. I wonder where Cleo is, if she's afraid, hurt, or if he's actually caring for her like the father that he sometimes is.

"Were you scared?" Richter asks suddenly.

"Hm?" I reply curiously.

"When you were down in the well."

"No," I say. And it's the truth, I wasn't afraid. I was angry that he sent Cleo down into that hell with me, but it gave me the chance to keep her away from his ire.

"Were you afraid, honey? When I was down there?" I press gently.

He shrugs as he chews the inside of his mouth thoughtfully, careful to avoid my eyes. If he's ever been afraid of anything, I'd never know because of how brave a facade he always puts on.

My brave little man.

"Your father just sent me down there to clean it up some. I forgot about the ladder after I was done, and I think he assumed I was already in the house when he brought it back up. It's not a big deal," I lie skillfully. Richter turns his eyes toward me, narrow and full of suspicion, but when he lets out a sigh, I know that he believes me.

Wait.

"Honey, go inside and get the flashlight. It should be in one of the kitchen drawers, okay?"

He gets to his feet without so much as a question and does as he told like the good son that he is. A few moments later, when he returns, I get to my feet and hold my hand out. When Richter attempts to hand me the flashlight, I smile and shake my head, and wait for his hand in its place.

He takes mine reluctantly. Because he's such a big boy now, he doesn't think that holding his mom's hand is a cool thing to do, but I'm lending him my strength right now since I know he's going to need it shortly.

Richter doesn't question me when I turn on the flashlight and lead him around the side of the property. He doesn't even seem bothered when we end up at the oubliette. And when I pull the gate open and toss the rope inside, he's still the brave boy that I've admired for so long.

"I need you to do something for me," I tell him softly as I toss the ladder inside of the well.

"Near the bottom, there's a space between the bricks. I felt something in there, but I didn't have time to get it out. Would you ..."

My son reaches for the rope without hesitation and climbs in, slowly make his way down into the darkness. I hold the ladder on my end as tightly as I can while still shining the light down on him. I don't know how far down it will reach, but the longer I can see him, the better I know I'll feel.

But when the light finally fades and I have no sight of my son, my hands begin to tremble. I can feel myself becoming afraid and wanting to crawl down into the hole after him. Until he calls up to me and assures me that he's okay.

"I'm at the bottom, Mom!" he calls up to me.

I let out a huge sigh of relief. So much so that I almost end up dropping the flashlight into the well. There's no way I'd be able to explain to Dad how that got down there, or think of a good enough excuse as to why it's broken without him figuring me out, so I set it down on the side of the well, use the weight of my body to pin the ladder to the side of the well and call back down to Richter.

"It should be above your head! It felt like paper!"

I know that's not the best description of what I'm looking for. Especially not with all of the dried leaves at the bottom—hell, even the shit we slept on felt like paper, but I know it had to be whatever was left over from what Jocelyn spent her last days on.

He falls silent, the only sound echoing back toward me is the shifting of his feet and his grunts as he tries to find what I sent him down for.

"I think I got it!" he calls up excitedly after a few minutes.

"Come on up!" I instruct him nervously. Leaning to the side, I grab the flashlight again and shine it down into the darkness. Agonizing seconds pass before I finally see the top of his head as he climbs up as quickly as he can. When he finally clears the top, I drop the flashlight onto the grass again and yank him over, hugging him tightly.

"Thank you, sweetheart. You're so brave," I whisper, kissing the top of his head.

"Aw, Mom," he groans, shifting uncomfortably in my arms. I laugh and let him go. He picks up the rope ladder and starts to gather it back into a neat pile the way Dad always has it before he reaches over and pulls the wooden gate closed.

I put an arm around Richter's shoulders as we walk quickly back toward the house. When we reach the front steps of the house, he holds the dirty, yellowed folded paper out to me, then runs inside with the flashlight.

Taking up my watch again, I slip the dusty paper into my bra and turn my attention back to the driveway.

Come on, Dad, I pray silently. *Bring my baby back home.*

CHAPTER 15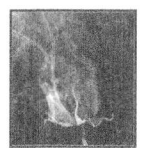

THE NEXT MORNING, I'm woken up by the nudge of a boot. I wake up with a gasp and rub my eyes, quickly realizing that I fell asleep on the front step and that Dad was home now.

I look up at him and smile in embarrassment. He doesn't look happy, but he doesn't exactly look angry either —it's more of a curious confusion.

"Did you sleep out here last night?" he inquires as he rubs his chin.

"Yeah," I reply honestly. There's no point in trying to come up with a lie. Dad has always been able to tell when any of us are lying, so I gave up that ghost a long time ago.

"Why?" he prods.

"I was waiting for Cleo," I say softly.

He chuckles and shakes his head as turns around to glance at the driveway. "Well, I hate to break it to you, Darbs, but that kid isn't our problem anymore."

"What?"

I didn't mean to shout at him. It was what he said that

jolted me so wide awake and full of anger, that I couldn't help myself.

"Don't raise your voice to me, little girl," he warns in an even tone. "Grab the other two and bring the groceries in. *If I decide to tell you what happened to her, then I will.*"

I get to my feet, my hands balled at my sides. I want to hit him. I want to grab him by his shoulders and shake the answers out of him, but I won't. Not while I still have two children under this roof to protect—not when I have a daughter missing and he has the answers.

Dad waits for me to get up and walk in first. It's the gentleman that's locked somewhere inside of him rearing its head. I know better, though. He knows that I'm a high-strung mess now and I'd more than likely attempt to make a break for it, run into town, and see if I can find my darling Cleo.

"Richter! Skylar!" he booms through the house. "Get your lazy asses up and help your mother with the groceries!"

The kids' bedroom door opens almost immediately and I watch them rush out, hair wild, rubbing the sleep out of their eyes, as they do as their father commands.

I wait for them to run outside before I walk into the bedroom I share with my father and close the door firmly behind us.

My fear of what's happened to Cleo has turned into the anger of wanting to know where she is.

"Where's my daughter?" I ask him evenly, turning and sliding the lock into place.

Dad lets out a laugh as he sits on the edge of the bed and pulls his boots off. He knows that the Darby that's in the room with him now, is the same Darby who's will he thought he finally managed to subdue.

Instead of answering, he sucks his teeth and tosses his boots to the side, before walking around the side of the bed and laying down. Dad closes his eyes, rests an arm across his forehead, and ignores me.

It's his way of ending the conversation, but the mother inside of me isn't going to give up so fucking easily.

"Where's Cleo?" I shout at him.

He doesn't move or even flinch. I watch his lips curl up into a smile, but that's it. Other than that, this conversation is over, and he won't give me the answers I want.

"Fine," I seethe quietly as I spin on my heel and walk out of the room. I slam the door so loudly behind me that the walls rattle.

I make my way past Skylar and Richter who are walking into the house with bags in their arms. They exchange a glance when they see how angry I am, but I don't stop. Not until I get to Dad's truck. I walk around to the back, reach into the bed of the vehicle and fish around until I find something heavy enough for what I want to do.

I settle on the crowbar and walk back toward the front, climb onto the hood, and wait. I know that he'll come out to see what I'm getting myself into because, after all, I'm made from his same genetic make-up, and he knows that when it comes to getting what I want, I am *definitely* my father's daughter.

It doesn't take long for Dad to show up on the steps. He's got his hands on his hips, a dangerous gleam in his eyes, and our children on either side of him.

"What are you gonna do with that, Darby? Besides piss me off," he calls out to me.

"Last fucking chance," I warn him, "Where's Cleo?"

He licks his lips and cracks his neck. I can tell that he's debating taking me down right now, but I'll swing this crowbar and smash his windshield before he has a chance to reach me, and he knows it.

"Don't make me come get you down from there, girl," he snaps, as he walks down the steps and begins to make his way toward me. I wait until he's almost close enough to reach me then lift the heavy metal object high over my head and bring it down against the tempered glass with as much force as I can muster.

A large spider crack immediately appears on the windshield, and Dad swears loudly, but I don't care.

Not anymore.

"Unless you want me to bust every last window on this fucking truck, tell me where my daughter is!" I scream at him as I climb up onto the roof of the truck and scurry across toward the bed. It'll be easy enough to dodge his attempts to grab me back here, and if he tries it, I'll bust out the back window next.

"You know, even your mother knew when to fucking say when, Darby," he tells me through grit teeth. "She knew when to lay down and take her fucking lumps."

"And what did that get her? The rest of her life at the bottom of the fucking well!" I scream, raising the crowbar in a rage, and smashing it into the back windshield like a professional baseball player.

"And you want to be just like your mother, don't you?" he growls as he opens the door of the bed, and climbs in. I move as quickly as I can, pulling myself onto the roof of the truck and attempt to crawl back toward the hood, but his hand tightens around my ankle and he yanks me back toward him, dropping me roughly onto the ridged flooring. I try to kick him in a blind rage, but he easily slaps my leg away and then proceeds to wrestle the crowbar out of my grip.

"Defiant fucking kids are the bane of my existence," he mutters more to himself than me. "I'll tell you what though, you're not gonna forget this fucking punishment for the rest of your life."

What's the worst he can do? Throw me back into the oubliette? He's already ripped a third of my heart out by taking Cleo away from me—there's nothing else he can do to break me.

But when Dad hoists me over his shoulder and takes me into the house, I didn't realize just how wrong I could possibly be.

CHAPTER 16

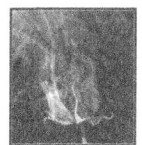

I'VE BEEN LOCKED in the bedroom for hours. Dad told me that if I wanted to live to see tomorrow, that I wouldn't go near the windows or try to escape.

I don't know what he's up to, but I'm honestly afraid now. And whatever happens will be my fault because unlike the entirety of the Greene family, I care too fucking much about everyone around me.

I have to find a way to pass the time, to keep my mind off the many things that this man could be doing to extract his revenge on me over a few busted windows. That's when I remember that I still have the paper hidden inside of my bra. I know that this will be the only chance I'll have to satiate my curiosity, so I fish it out and open it, smoothing it out as best as I can.

I read the first line, squinting at the shaky handwriting, then gasp as my hand flies to my mouth.

It's a letter from Jocelyn.

To me.

In her final moments, her last thoughts were of a daughter that she never knew. That, by the words she's written in the now most precious thing I've ever held, were full of a mother's love and hope.

A love that she felt for me even though she never got to hold me.

A hope that Dad wouldn't do to me what he had done to her.

And a request that I remember her.

My heart breaks into a million pieces as I realize the woman that I held such hatred for, such disdain for not running away and saving herself, her brothers from this man that's held us prisoner here for so long, loved me more deeply than I was lead to believe.

Jocelyn loved me.

She wanted more for me than this life that Dad chose for her, for all of us, and I hated her for not trying to escape, believing that to be the reason the rest of us were stuck here.

But what if she did try? What if he caught her and that's why she ended up in the oubliette? What if that's the real reason he seems to be so much more different with me? Is it because he's secretly afraid that I'm more her than him and he knows that I'll try to grab our children and leave him all alone?

How could I have not realized it before now, Dad? I've finally figured out what scares you, I think through bitter tears. *You're afraid to die alone and unloved.*

Somehow, I have to find a way to gain his forgiveness for what I did to his truck. I have to understand that whatever punishment comes my way because of my actions, is well-deserved and my own fault, and I have to be Daddy's little girl.

It's the only way to get him to trust me again.

The sun has fallen from the sky by the time Dad finally comes back to the room. I've taken Jocelyn's note and hidden it under the dresser. I wonder if she ever thought I would get the chance to read it, but I know now that she *did* love me and I'll find a way to make this right.

It's the least I can do for the one person I harbored so much resentment for now that I know the truth about how she felt.

I won't let you down, Mom.

I'm sitting against the wall with my arms wrapped around my leg, watching Dad as he cracks his neck and lays down on the bed. I take him in, realizing that his hands look dirty, his boots seem a bit scuffed, and that the yawn he lets out is tired and unsettling.

When will you finally die? I wonder bitterly. I take a deep breath and remind myself that this is not how to approach him. No way will I get back in his good graces if I can't control my thoughts.

"Daddy?" I ask from the floor.

"Yeah?"

"Can I lay in the bed with you?"

He lets out his breath impatiently, clears his throat, and shifts slightly before propping himself up onto his elbows and glaring at me.

"Well, I guess that depends, Darby."

"I'm sorry, Daddy," I say, choking back a sob. "I just got so angry and I know that what I did was out of line, and I swear to you that it'll never happen again. Please tell me that you forgive me."

I don't wait for his response before I bury my face in my hands and burst into tears. I haven't lied to my father in a very long time, and I know that now, I'll have to become a master of deception to do what needs to be done and it hurts me.

Not for myself, and not for my children, but for the man that honestly loves me the only way he's ever known how.

"Get your ass into this bed," he says, his voice tired and a little less stern. I get to my feet quickly and walk over, kick off my shoes, and climb onto the bed next to him. Dad reaches over and wraps an arm around my waist, pulling me closer to him and when I lay my head against his chest, he uses his free hand to wipe the tears away from my face.

I look up at him through the haze of tears, and see it. The father that he *could* be, and not the man that he is. His eyes are tired, his face is slightly worn, and he seems to have aged a little more than since this morning. There are more grays in his neatly cropped mass of black hair, and he looks so close to defeated that I decide not to ask him anymore questions.

"Go to sleep, Darbs," he says, leaning down and kissing my forehead gently.

I do as I'm told and close my eyes.

I won't ask about Cleo again tonight.

I'll take my punishment in the morning.

And maybe the day after, I can get him to realize that there is a small part inside of me that *does* love him the way he loves me.

CHAPTER 17

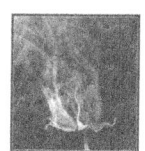

WE'RE ALONE at the breakfast table the next morning. It's just me and Dad, and no sign of Richter and Skylar. The mother inside of me is screaming at me to demand answers, but the girl inside of me that wants so desperately to please Daddy is warning me to keep my mouth shut. *All good things to those who wait,* she tells me, and I have to force myself to eat the pancakes that Dad made for us so I don't turn this quiet time into an interrogation.

I shove another forkful into my mouth and steal a glance at Dad. He's reading his morning newspaper, obviously aware that I'm watching him. It's apparent by the smile that curls the edge of his lips.

"Something on your mind, Darby?" he asks, flipping his paper to the next page and smoothing it out. Dad doesn't look up at me, instead he reaches for his coffee cup, takes a hearty sip, and goes back to reading.

"No, Daddy," I say quietly as I place my fork down onto the plate.

"You shouldn't be afraid to speak up when something is

bothering you, kid," he says conversationally. "Besides, how am I supposed to fix the problem if I don't know what it is?"

I take a deep breath and chew on my lower lip. I want to know, more than anything, where my children are, but I also don't want to upset him.

Is this how Jocelyn felt?

But just the thought of her is enough to make me feel a little brave.

"Where are the children?" I ask him softly.

"Where they belong," he responds evenly. "Where I should have put them to fucking begin with. Those kids haven't done you any good, Darby; and they sure as hell haven't done a damn thing for me either."

I swallow the lump in my throat as I begin to think of the layout of the property. The back of the house is wide and stretches far out into the trees. There's nothing on the side of the house except for the oubliette and he knows that's the first place I'll look when given the opportunity.

He came back dirty and tired, I tell myself, remembering what he looked like when he reappeared last night. That's not a sign of the well, it could be the woods, but I won't be able to look back there without being gone for too long, and Dad will notice if I'm missing.

"You know, I heard a saying once. Something along the lines of our hearts being wild animals and our ribs their cages.."

I look up at him and raise an eyebrow. What he said sounds so out of left field, that I almost want to brush it off, but the one thing about Dad is that he never says things just to hear himself speak. There's always a reason for anything that comes out of his mouth. Be it in anger or quiet moments, his words always carry some kind of meaning.

"What?" I ask in confusion.

"Oh my sweet baby girl," he says, letting out a long sigh. He drops his arms on the table, crossing them at the wrist, and smiles at me. "You've always gave too much of a shit for your own good. I know why, too. It's that motherly instinct to protect your children. Your mother had it, her mother showed signs of it, but ran the moment she got the chance. Didn't matter much to me with that one though because she wasn't my blood, so I knew she'd leave eventually. Taylee had it for a while too until that brain of hers snapped one day and sent her looking for someone to keep her desires fed up at night," he continues scratching his chin thoughtfully. "I wonder if she'd finally be proud of me now."

"She would," I tell him quietly as I reach over and place a hand on his. "I think Taylee would be really happy to see the man you've become."

He chuckles and runs a thumb over the top of my hand. "Thanks, baby girl. I think she would be too. She'd be plenty happy to see that I'm the man she always wanted me to be."

Dad leans over and puckers his lips, waiting patiently for me to give him a kiss, and I do. Gentle and soft—exactly how he always wants them to be.

When we pull away from each other, he lets go of my hand and goes back to his newspaper.

"Anyway, I don't think you should worry about those kids anymore. I sure as hell won't," he says callously.

"May I be excused, Daddy?" I ask solemnly.

"Yeah, just make sure you clean up the table. And I'd like a refill on my coffee when you're done," he replies absentmindedly as he becomes engrossed in a section of the black and white print.

It's three in the afternoon.

The house has been cleaned from top to bottom. There are still no sign of the children and Dad makes sure that he's always in the same room as me when I move from one to another.

He doesn't say anything.

He just follows me from room to room and watches me like a hawk. It's obvious that he's trying to figure out if I'm okay with the kids suddenly missing, and if I have any intent on trying to find them. In my heart, I do, but I can't let it show and do my best to keep a cheerful demeanor and pretend it's the greatest thing now to be child free.

I know that Dad isn't easily fooled, so I put on as best a facade as I can while I wrack my brain trying to figure out where they are. Richter and Skylar still have to be on the property somewhere, while Cleo ... I let out a quiet sigh. I'll never know where she's gone to unless he tells me and there's no way to force it out of him.

He's not easily intimidated from what I've been able to gather in the years I've known him, although I haven't tried yet. The crowbar was my best shot so far and that backfired faster than I thought it would.

This punishment is worse than anything he's put me through. The nights in the oubliette, the lashings with his belt, the forcing himself on me when I would first try to fight him off.

He's left me a mother with no children, and I can't think of a time I've ever felt more empty or useless than now.

I can't help but think that this is how Jocelyn felt before the end too.

CHAPTER 18

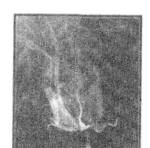

It's a nice afternoon out and Daddy decided that he wanted to go for a walk. He asked me if I wanted to join him, and I jumped at the chance.

A good little girl always does what her daddy asks her to do and I'm still playing the part of the doting daughter.

The air is cool, but not cold. The skies are clear, but not completely blue. And my heart—it's still as empty as it was when he left with Cleo and came back without her. My soul is as dark as the cloud that fell over it when he took my two remaining children and hid them from me.

But I still wear a smile on my face for their sake. I don't know if I'll ever see them again, but the memory of them is the only thing that keeps me from breaking down completely.

It's also the hope that he might take pity on me. That he'll show me some kind of mercy and at the very least tell me what he's done with them.

Hope; the one thing that will end up destroying me in the end if I let it consume me, is the one thing that I so desperately cling to now.

Dad begins talking, pointing out the different kinds of trees we have on the property that I never paid much attention to. The same ones that I'd watch my kids play near, and my heart breaks just a little more.

He squeezes my hand when we cross treeline and tells me to stay close to him.

"I got a little surprise for you, Darbs," he tells me with a lopsided grin on his ruggedly, handsome face. "A part of this family's history that I'd like to show you."

"Okay, Daddy," I say softly.

We walk deeper into the woods until we reach a clearing. It's circular and seems so oddly out of place for some reason. My ears perk up when I hear the rustling coming from the trees, but Dad tells me that it's just the wind and pulls me into the center of the opening.

"This is where your Grandma died," he begins with a smirk on his face. I try to take a step back out of a natural reaction but Dad *tsk, tsks,* and pulls me to his side. "Is that anyway to behave when I try to tell you a story, little girl?"

He's becoming agitated and I know that this is another battle I'll have to concede and listen to every horrific detail that I know is coming.

"No, Daddy. I'm sorry," I say as I step closer to him, wrap an arm around his waist, and look up adoringly into his eyes.

What kind of hideous thing do you do here?

"As I was saying," he continues with an eye roll, "Laura died here. Had the youngest boy show her what he was made of before he killed her too. I think that's the one time I ever felt proud of that kid."

I do my best not to shudder as I continue to listen with a faux eagerness that seems so real, that it makes me wonder if some sick part of me isn't honestly enjoying this little regalement.

"Man, the way he fucked her, you'd think he'd been hiding secrets behind my back. The kid worked her over like a pro, but being my son, I know it was just a natural thing, wouldn't you agree?"

"Oh yes, Daddy," I reply a little too eagerly.

Reel it in, Darby. You're starting to sound like you mean these terrible things you're agreeing to.

"And over there," he says pointing toward the side of the clearing, "is where he left her bones to rot. Well, he tried too, anyway. Your mother dragged them back all into the heap and I think some wild animals eventually got to them or some shit."

"Was she sad?" I ask quietly.

"Who? Your mother?" he inquires, arching an eyebrow. I nod and he shrugs, "Fuck if I know. I didn't exactly stop to ask her, Darby."

I look away from him. I need to be able to blink away the tears—to hide the humanity that's still left inside of me that I know he'll look disapprovingly on.

"You okay?" he asks curiously.

I take a deep breath, force a smile onto my face, and look up at him, nodding. "Of course I am. I'm here with you, Daddy."

The smile on his face is a genuine one. The look in his eyes softens from harsh to loving and I wonder if that may have been the wrong thing to say.

He turns me to face him completely and takes my face in his hands. "Do you love me, Darbs? I know I keep asking you, but I have to know for sure before we continue our little tour."

"I do, Daddy. I love you most of all."

He leans down and I close my eyes. His lips press gently against mine, then move up my forehead as he pulls me close and I inhale his scent deeply. For now, it's just us, the sound of the birds chirping, and the heart beating in his chest keeping me company.

And while I know I shouldn't feel as suddenly content as I do right now, I can't help it.

I'm in the arms of a man that loves me, and that's a rare thing to come across, isn't it?

CHAPTER 19

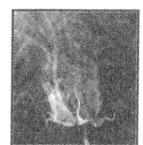

WE STOOD in the clearing for what seemed like forever. We held each other tightly, content in the company of monsters, until Dad sighed and told me that we still had one more special thing to talk about.

Dad finally let his arms fall away from around me and took my hand, leading the way out of the woods. I could almost swear that I heard the rustling again, but he dismissed it as the leaves in the tree catching some of the wind, and I believed him.

As we walk down the side of the house, I can see the oubliette coming into view and I hesitate in my next steps.

"What's wrong, kid? Think I'm gonna put you down there again?" he asks with a click of his tongue against his teeth. "You haven't done anything to go back down there, have you? You hiding something from me, Darby?"

"No," I say softly while the thought of Mom's letter burns a whole through my chest. If he ever finds that, he'll become so terribly angry that I didn't immediately turn it over for confiscation. But it's not his to take or read—it was meant for me, and it's mine now. God knows how many years it spent down in that fucking hole waiting for me and had I not had the same instinct that Mom had to save my child, I never would have found it.

Thanks, Mom, I think in silent gratitude.

"Then you have nothing to worry about. Come on," he says, giving my hand a gentle, but firm tug.

I nod and let him lead me to hell on Earth and try my best not to cry.

"Well, you already know how Jocelyn went, but did you know that I would bring you to visit her? She was my favorite girl for a long time, you know. That was until I tasted your sweet cherry for the first time. I got hooked on you after that. I know it sounds really shitty to say, but after you started loving me the way a daughter should love her father, I kind of forgot about her. I only ever really thought about her on the nights you were on your period and refusing to fuck, or when the kids got too close to the well. Other than that, I can't say she's ever crossed my mind," he finishes with a shrug as we finally reach the oubliette.

I wait patiently as he leans down and begins to lift the wooden grate off when I do something incredibly brave. Something I never would have thought possible until I read Mom's letter.

I shove him as hard as I can and because he's taken off guard, he stumbles and falls. But not into the fucking oubliette like I intended him to. Thinking fast, I drop down on him using the weight of my body, which although not much, it's sufficient enough to pin him in place for the moment. I have to move fast because when he gets angry, he'll be able to overpower me easily.

I reach for the ladder and tie one of the rungs around his throat, then pull him up to his knees.

Dad is dazed, confused, and looks like he'll kill me the

moment he gets a chance, once the direness of his situation finally settles in. I use all the strength I can muster to lift half of his body over the oubliette and dig a knee into his gut, holding him in place.

"Where are my children?" I scream at him.

A sinister smile takes over his face as his eyes darken. He turns his head as much as he can and spits onto the grass before turning his eyes back to mine.

"I swear to God, I'll throw you over the side and let you strangle to death, you piece of shit! Where are they?" I shout at him in a blind rage.

Dad tilts his head to the side and offers nothing. No words of anger, nothing that would give me hope in ever being with my kids again and I pull the rope tighter around his neck. His face is turning red as he coughs violently, but he maintains his steely silence and doesn't break eye contact.

That's the reason he's able to knock me off guard. That's the reason he's able to get back to his feet, grab a fistful of my hair, and force me to my knees.

Daddy has always been much smarter than the rest of us, and because we're from his body, he knows how to easily outsmart us.

I never saw his hands moving so slowly around me. I didn't see the look of rage in his eyes turn cantankerous until it was too late. I didn't pick up on a lot of the signals that he would get the upper hand, because I was too blinded by my own rage. Something he never taught me to control because it would always be an advantage over me.

Once Dad removes the rope from around his neck and tosses it to the ground, he picks me up to my feet by my hair. It hurts so much, but nothing compares to the pain of not knowing where your children are.

"The stupid one?" he breathes heavily, pulling me closer to his face, "I left that little shit with children's services. Told them a family member dropped her off on my doorstep and that I wasn't equipped to handle someone like her. She's probably five families into the fucking system by now."

Tears sting my eyes and when they roll down my face, he laughs as he continues, "And the other two? They're still here. You're just too stupid to fucking find them, Darby. But don't you worry. I'll take care of them like I did with you—like I did with your mother, and you'll have no one to blame but yourself, just like that stupid bitch that shot you out her worthless cunt."

I raise a hand to try and strike him, but he easily swats it away and chuckles.

"You don't know what love is, little girl. I tried so fucking hard with you and this is how you repay me? By stomping all over my fucking heart after I give it to you? You're just like your worthless fucking mother. It only makes sense that you die like her too."

"Dad—"

With a grunt, he shoves me violently down into the oubliette. I know that I've broke my leg on the way down. My head hurts from slamming into the wall when I landed. The world is impossibly bright in the darkness—stars exploding behind my tightly closed eyes. The air has been knocked out of my lungs, and while I know there's no coming back from this, I have the slimmest of hopes that he'll throw the ladder down. That maybe this was a mistake on his part.

I shift on the dirty ground, grimacing as tears sting my eyes from the pain my body is experiencing all at once.

How I didn't manage to die or break something else is

nothing short of a miracle, but I know if I don't get help soon, my leg will become infected and I'll die a painful death.

"Useless fucking kids," he mutters as he closes the wooden gate on the oubliette, and sliding the lock into place.

"Daddy! I'm sorry!" I scream up in terror.

But if he heard me, he doesn't acknowledge it. I've betrayed his love and that's the worse offense in his eyes.

"Daddy! Please," I whimper as I slap the side of the well.

He won't come back for me.

He's much too stubborn to care now.

Especially since I've become nothing more than one of his useless fucking kids.

I'm sorry.

EPILOGUE
TEN YEARS LATER

"Stop crying," I tell her as I push deeper into her wet, warm core. "This is how things are now. It's how Dad would have wanted it, remember?"

Skylar turns her face away from me as fresh tears spill down her face. I don't think she's crying because it feels bad, but because it feels good and we both know that it shouldn't.

Dad died a few years after Mom. Old age finally caught up to him, and the man that I thought would live forever, was suddenly no more.

The night that he threw her down into the well and locked her in, he let us out of the cages he kept us in behind the house, and took me to my room to talk to me.

I remember the day he took Mom out there like it was yesterday. Because he kept us muzzled unless he was sneaking out to feed us, we couldn't call out to her when they showed up in the clearing. I wanted nothing more than to have my mother save us, but we couldn't even alert her to us being there. Dad threatened to kill her if we tried, and I knew he would.

When he sat me down, I remember being scared, tired, and angry that he treated us like animals for as long as he did, though it all ended up making sense when he explained things to me.

He told me about how to be a real man and how he wouldn't be with us forever, but that he knew I'd make him proud by carrying on the Greene name. He told me that the only way to do that would be with Skylar and even though it didn't make sense to me then, it does now.

To keep our family strong, we have to keep it going, and I promised him that when we were both able to, we would do our part.

"Skylar, stop crying," I tell her again through grit teeth as I continue to piston my hips. I'm gentle with her because she deserves it, but I hate it when it makes her cry.

"We'll be done soon," I promise as I rest my forehead against her cheek. "You just have to help me a little bit and I'll ... finish ... faster ... "

Don't touch her until she starts bleeding.

Dad told me that before that it wouldn't be worth the time. That if she hasn't bled yet, we wouldn't be able to carry on the family name.

Skylar takes a deep, shuddering breath as she turns her face back toward me, her lips brushing mine. I remember there were times that I heard Mom crying like this, but it stopped after a while, and I'm sure it'll be the same way with my us eventually.

My breath comes out in a gasp as she digs her nails into my back. She whimpers slightly and I move my hips faster, going deeper into her than I ever have been before.

Her whimper turns into a moan as the sound of our labored breathing intermingles with the sound of flesh against flesh. She arches her back when I begin to fuck her even harder, then sit up, pulling her on top of me.

Skylar grabs the sides of my face as she begins to rotate her hips. I hold her close as the feeling of my balls tightening starts to take over me.

"I love you," I whisper into her open mouth.

And I do love her.

Not the way Dad loved Mom, but the way a brother *should* love his sister. The way my father taught me how to love her.

She grunts, I groan.

She moves faster on top of me, I hold her closer.

I know I'll never experience this with another woman, and since I have Skylar, I know that I'll never want to.

She's my own flesh and blood—what could possibly be more special than a bond like this?

I let out a loud moan as I spill my seed into her, hoping that maybe this time, it'll stick. I want nothing more than to be a father since I saw what kind of man Dad became. He loved Mom unconditionally and I can't wait to feel that for Skylar.

For now, she's just my sister and my lover, but I want her to be so much more. I want her to be my wife, the mother of my children, the hope for the Greene family name.

When I kiss her chin and give her hip a gentle slap, she climbs off me and lays on the bed. I lie down next to her and she turns her back to me and I feel so goddamn unhappy. I don't want her to feel like this when we're together. I want her to feel as loved and as beautiful as she is, but I guess it'll just take her time to get used to it.

That's what Dad told me, anyway.

He said that at first, it'll be hard for her, but eventually she'll understand and appreciate what we're doing.

It will just take time like all good things do. We'll be happy here together and we'll have a family of our very own.

And when my daughters are old enough, I'll show them how to love their father like Dad showed me.

ALSO BY YOLANDA OLSON

Scavengers (Malediction Duet Book 1)

Abattoir

The Lies Between Us

Wrong Side of Heaven

Make sure to sign up to Yolanda's newsletter for updates, new releases and giveaways.

Sign Up Here

Printed in Great Britain
by Amazon